HEART OF THE HOME

HEART OF THE HOME

Gwen Kirkwood

severn House

This first world edition published 2010
in Great Britain and in 2011 in the USA by
SEVERN HOUSE PUBLISHERS LTD of
9–15 High Street, Sutton, Surrey, England, SM1 1DF.
Trade paperback edition first published
in Great Britain and the USA 2011 by
SEVERN HOUSE PUBLISHERS LTD.

British Library Cataloguing in Publication Data

Kirkwood, Gwen.
   Heart of the home.
   1. Farmers–Scotland–Fiction. 2. Scotland–Social
   conditions–20th century–Fiction. 3. Domestic fiction.
   I. Title
   823.9'14–dc22

ISBN-13: 978-0-7278-6963-0   (cased)
ISBN-13: 978-1-84751-292-5   (trade paper)

Except where actual historical events and characters are being
described for the storyline of this novel, all situations in this
publication are fictitious and any resemblance to living persons
is purely coincidental.

All Severn House titles are printed on acid-free paper.

Severn House Publishers support The Forest Stewardship Council [FSC],
the leading international forest certification organisation. All our titles that
are printed on Greenpeace-approved FSC-certified paper carry the FSC logo.

Acknowledgements

I would like to thank Val Butler for her invaluable advice and support relating to diabetes and working farmers in the 1960s.

One

Avril's dark eyes lit up when she saw her parents arrive in readiness for the graduation ceremony.

'I wondered if you'd make it,' she said, hugging them both in her delight.

'We wouldn't miss it for anything,' her father assured her. 'We're both so proud of you, aren't we, Ruth?' He felt a glow of love and pride which could not have been greater if Avril had been his own flesh and blood. He owed her more than she would ever know. As a little girl she had welcomed him into the tiny circle of her family, consisting then only of her and her mother. Her warmth and trust, her ready acceptance of him, had done a great deal to help him break down the barriers of Ruth's fear and mistrust and eventually win her love. The past eleven years had been the happiest any couple could have dreamed of. His eyes clouded momentarily. Ruth saw and understood. She hurried into speech.

'You know we're proud of you, darling, and everyone sends congratulations, especially Grandpa Gray. He is the one who first awakened your interest in microbiology so he takes a special interest.'

'I remember,' Avril said, smiling, 'but Grandma Gray taught me how to ride a pony and that seemed the most wonderful thing in the world when I was eleven.'

Lindsay grinned. 'It seems my parents have a lot to answer for.' Avril knew they were far more proud of her achievements than she was herself. They had given her every support throughout school and university, so for their sakes she was pleased to have gained a first-class master's degree in science.

Her father had a demanding position as a senior surgeon in a large hospital just south of the Scottish Border so she had wondered whether he would be able to get here today. She should have known he would. Her parents did everything together if they could. Her mouth curved in a happy smile.

Lindsay Gray, or Lint, as he had been known to his friends

since he was a medical student, had adopted Avril when he and her mother married. She had been eleven and the memories of that wonderful summer would always remain with her. She could not have wished for a kinder or more loving father. He and her mother had filled her life, and the lives of her nine-year-old half brothers, with love and laughter, warmth and security. Avril had never lacked love from her mother and she had always had the necessities of life but she had no idea who her natural father was. It was the only topic she felt unable to discuss with her mother. If the subject was broached, however tentatively, it was firmly set aside. It had never mattered when she was younger but her interest had been awakened with the study of heredity, genes and DNA.

She had enjoyed the challenges and camaraderie of university life, and she was looking forward to returning in September to work for her PhD in bacteriology, but for now she was eager to be home, to see her twin brothers again, as well as friends and neighbours, especially Mr and Mrs Scott, who farmed at Sylvanside, and Dean, their nephew, whose parents had a beef and sheep farm further up the glen.

Avril remembered how delighted she been after her parents' wedding to have a daddy of her own. He had brought them to live in the rambling farmhouse just north of the Scottish Border. It had been called Eskriggholm Farm then but Bill and Molly Scott had bought the land, along with their own farm, when the estate was selling off outlying properties to settle death duties. Her parents had bought the house and buildings and the two small paddocks which remained. They had renamed it Riverview because it overlooked the River Esk and the land on the other side of the English Border. They had enjoyed planning and working together to modernize the house. Avril turned her gold signet ring round her finger. Her father had bought it for her when he had changed her name, and her mother's, to Gray. Although her adoption had never been a secret few people thought of Avril as Mr Gray's adopted daughter. She had been thrilled to be part of a real family and to have a daddy who cherished her and her mother as though they were the most precious things in his life. As an adult she knew the love her parents shared had deepened and strengthened with the years. They still exchanged tender glances and small secret smiles; it warmed Avril's heart to see them together and still in love. They spread an aura of happiness embracing those around them, especially herself and Callum and Craig.

'I'm ready for home as soon as we can get away,' she said. 'Who is looking after the boys today?'

'Molly Scott offered to collect them from school and give them tea,' Ruth answered. 'They love spending their time at Sylvanside, helping to look after the animals, but they're terribly excited about you coming home for the whole summer.'

Lindsay had negotiated his way through the traffic and they were on the open road, heading south for the Border and home.

'You're very quiet, Dad,' Avril remarked.

'Speechless is the word,' he teased, smiling as he met her eyes in the rear view mirror. 'You've done tremendously well, Avril.' Lindsay's words were sincere but they did not explain his air of preoccupation.

He had noticed Ruth's energy flagging as she sank into the seat beside him. Since her operation in the spring she had never regained her former vitality and he knew it would not be long before Avril realized this. He and Ruth had agreed not to tell her the results of the biopsies, or about the radiotherapy which had followed, until she had finished her studies. He was used to illness and death with his work but he could barely face his own fears, even less burden Avril with the truth.

'You realize my father takes all the credit for you specializing in bacteriology, Avril?' he said hoping to distract her attention from Ruth's lethargy.

'He was certainly enthusiastic, I remember.' Avril smiled reminiscently. 'He made invisible bugs sound more fascinating than fairy stories and he explained things so that I could understand. He even allowed me to read his precious book called *The Microbe Hunters.*'

'Dean Scott has been down several times to ask how you've done in your finals. I think he's looking forward to you coming home as much as the boys,' Ruth said, making an effort to join in the conversation, though all she wanted to do was close her eyes and sleep. She really would have to make more effort to cut down on the medication which Doctor Anderson had prescribed.

'That's nice of him, especially considering his mother grudged him the opportunity to go to university, even though he was the most outstanding pupil of his year at school. I was grateful for his help, and Dad's, during my first year there.'

'You would have managed anyway, wouldn't she Lint?'

'Yes, but it was a big upheaval in your young life at the time, Avril. First there was the wedding and you acquired a father,' he smiled and met her eyes again in the mirror.

'That was the best thing that happened to us, wasn't it, Mum?'

'It was indeed,' Ruth answered fervently, with a loving glance at Lint.

'Mmm, it certainly suited me,' he said. 'But it must have been an ordeal for you moving to a new area, changing to a bigger school and not knowing anybody. We've always been grateful to Dean for keeping an eye on you, especially that first morning when he found you waiting alone for the school bus.'

'He was always a pleasant boy,' Ruth agreed, 'and he's grown into a fine young man. No one would believe he had such a miserable, moaning mother.'

'She certainly objected plenty when Dean insisted he was going to spend his pre-college year at Bengairney,' Avril said ruefully. 'She didn't like the idea of him working for Uncle Steven.'

'I suspect she still holds us responsible for introducing Dean to Megan and Steven,' Lint reflected. 'I thought it was a good idea when he said he wanted to broaden his horizons and learn more about dairy farming, like his Uncle Bill. Working on a progressive dairy farm like Bengairney, or the Turners at Martinwold, was a great opportunity. His Uncle Bill agreed. It must have been difficult for Dean to stand up to his mother over that decision so I'm glad his father supported him too. I'll bet that infuriated Grizel Scott. Dean has proved himself though so she should be proud.'

'She'd never admit it,' Avril said. 'She never congratulated him when he did so well at agricultural college.' She had felt hurt on Dean's behalf over that.

'Never mind, Steven and Megan told him they were proud to have had him as their student. They're hoping Samuel will do the same course when he leaves school next year,' Lint said.

'I can't believe wee Samuel is at that stage,' Avril said.

'He's no longer wee.' Lint chuckled. 'He's shot up like a weed recently. He's as tall as I am now.'

'I can't believe that.'

Samuel had been a toddler when she and her mother had first moved up to Scotland from the Lake District. They had rented an apartment from Hannah Caraford and she had introduced them to her son, Steven, and his wife, Megan. Having no cousins or family of her own she had loved Samuel from the start. When his sister, Tania, was born she had loved them both. Their Granny Caraford had become Granny to her too and a strong bond of affection had grown between them all.

'I feel a bit out of touch. Does Dean still go over to Bengairney to visit?' Avril asked.

'He goes occasionally,' Lint said. 'Steven thinks Dean's abilities are wasted at Northsyke but I reckon he returned home for his father's sake. He doesn't get any credit from his mother for his hard work according to his Uncle Bill and they are neighbours as well as relations so he'll know.'

'Molly reckons her sister-in-law would never have got away with ruling the roost the way she does if Dean's father hadn't developed diabetes. I understand he was pretty bad by the time he was diagnosed,' Ruth said. Her eyes were closed and Lint had thought she was asleep.

'Sydney's diabetes would be a lot better if he had a better diet,' Lint said grimly. 'Dr Anderson says he has explained several times but neither Grizel, nor her daughter, realize how important it is. He says Mrs Scott thinks her husband should give himself an extra shot of insulin if she wants to make one of her suet puddings swimming in syrup.'

'Doris did badly at school, according to her Aunt Molly,' Ruth said drowsily, 'Apparently she was jealous of Dean's success, but Molly says it's her own fault for not paying attention. She probably doesn't listen to Dr Anderson either.'

'Jealousy is a corrosive emotion,' Lint mused. 'Bill Scott reckons Dean could make Northsyke more productive if his parents would give him some scope.' He had been making conversation in the hope of distracting Avril's attention from Ruth but out of the corner of his eye he saw she was sleeping now. Silence fell as the miles sped by.

Avril was content to relax. She found her thoughts returning to the journey the three of them had made together from Grandma

Gray's in Gloucestershire to what was to become their new home on the Scottish Border. It had seemed an interminable journey when she was eleven, but what happy years they had been. A reminiscent smile lifted the corners of her mouth as she remembered their arrival at Eskriggholm, the large sandstone farmhouse which they had all grown to love.

The exterior of the house, and the traditional stone-built farm buildings, had been well maintained by the estate but the interior was badly neglected. She realized now that her father had tried hard to make it more welcoming for their arrival but she had been too miserable to care about the house, she reflected ruefully. She had spent a glorious summer learning to ride and accompanying Grandma Gray on Chezzie, the pony who had stolen her heart from the moment she had seen him at the stables. She had gone to the stables every day, learned to ride and look after the ponies, spending all her spare time with them. Early on the morning they were leaving she had gone to say goodbye to Chezzie only to find his stable empty. She had been heartbroken to think he had been sold to strangers.

Even Bimbo couldn't console her. He was the collie pup Grandma Gray had allowed her to bring with her to her new home. She had cuddled him for comfort all the way back. Her eyes softened, knowing her faithful old dog would be waiting for her on the doorstep when they arrived home. His name had gradually been shortened to Bo. More than anything else though Avril knew she would never forget the overwhelming joy she had felt when she discovered Chezzie waiting for her in one of the stables. She couldn't believe her new daddy had persuaded the owners of the stables to sell him. He had bought Chezzie specially for her and had him transported all the way from Gloucestershire as a surprise. Even now she was grown up he still enjoyed giving her and her young brothers surprises, she thought affectionately.

Her parents had worked together to modernize and transform the house into a home. She would always love its happy atmosphere and the space and comfort, not to mention the lovely views of the river in the bottom of the glen with the woods and fields of Cumberland on the far side. To the north the house was sheltered by the hill which led to the top of Northsyke land. She had not known Dean then or that his family were the tenants. Avril recalled the first time she had ridden Chezzie around his new paddock. It had not been long before they had both wanted to explore the surrounding countryside.

'You must ask permission before you ride on any private roads or land,' her father had insisted. So she and Chezzie had ridden along the narrow public road below their house until they came to a more interesting looking track. Avril smiled to herself as she remembered. They had cantered along and eventually arrived at a farmyard with buildings all round a square and a low white house along one side. She had dismounted and shyly knocked at the door. Mrs Molly Scott had answered it with floury hands and a streak of flour across one rosy cheek. Avril knew at once she had interrupted her baking and she apologized for her intrusion.

'Bless me lassie, ye're not interrupting me at all. I'm pleased to see ye and such nice manners as ye have too. So your father is Mr Gray, the surgeon, is he, and you've come to live at Eskriggholm?'

'Yes, that's right. We arrived three days ago.'

'And what . . . ? Ah there's Bill!' She waved to a man who was striding across the yard with a sack on his back. 'Come and meet our new neighbour,' she called.

'I'll finish giving the calves their cake and then I'll be in for ma ten o'clock. You can tether your pony to the iron ring next to the water trough, lassie, then he can have a drink if he feels like it,' he said with a grin.

'Yes, you tether your pony, my lamb, and come in for some coffee. Walk right through to the kitchen. I'll go and put some milk on to heat.'

Mrs Scott had seated Avril at the kitchen table with a plate of newly baked scones, butter and home-made strawberry jam.

'So what's your name then, lassie?' Mr Scott asked as he washed his hands at the kitchen sink.

'Avril. I'm Avril Gray.' She glowed with pride as she said it. She was so pleased to have a daddy of her own. She held out her hand to show off her gold ring. 'These are my initials. Daddy bought it specially for me.'

'That's lovely, and Avril is a pretty name.'

'Mummy chose it because I was born in April.'

'So what age are ye, lassie? And which school will ye be attending?' Bill Scott asked.

'I was eleven in April. I shall be going to Langholm Academy.' Her young brow creased with anxiety. 'Daddy says he will go with me to see the Rector and ask if we can look round the school.'

'You'll get on fine, I'm sure,' Mrs Scott said comfortably. 'The school bus goes right past the end of your drive. Our nephew Dean gets the bus further along the road. He lives on the neighbouring farm. Over there. See on the other side of the glen?' She pointed through the kitchen window.

'Yes, I can see the farmyard, halfway up the hill.'

'This place is Sylvanside. Theirs is called Northsyke. It's bigger than ours even though we've bought the land that belonged to Eskriggholm. Did ye ken it used to be a wee farm?'

'No, I didn't know.'

'Eh Molly, ye do chatter,' Bill Scott teased. 'How could the lassie know what's gone on before they moved here?'

'My daddy likes to know about everything,' Avril remembered telling them. So she had got the recent history of the area while she enjoyed her scone and jam.

'Aye Eskriggholm was one o' the four farms the estate was selling to the sitting tenants because the money was needed for death duties,' Molly Scott explained. 'Bill's brother and his wife ought to have bought their place but Grizel wouldna hear of taking the money out o' the bank, even though they have a boy and a lassie to follow on. They missed a real opportunity there.'

'Aye and Grizel, that's my brother's wife, lassie, she's been jealous o' us ever since,' Bill Scott chuckled, and young though she'd been Avril still recalled seeing the glint in his eye like a mischievous schoolboy.

'She has no need to be jealous. We've worked as hard as anybody to pay for our land and they could have done the same,' his wife declared. 'We couldn't afford to buy the house and buildings at Eskriggholm so it was sold separately with the two paddocks. That's how your father bought it ye see. We'd no use for another house anyway. We've neither chick nor child to follow on.' She sighed and for a moment Avril thought she looked sad, but then she was smiling again. When she knew the Scotts better Avril had learned that Mrs Scott's one regret was that she had not been blessed with children of her own. Instead she enjoyed having people call, especially children.

'Dean is our nephew and he lives at Northsyke. He's doing well at school,' Mr Scott said proudly, 'He's a fine laddie. He'll look after you when I tell him you're our new neighbour.'

'He's fifteen though so he'll be leaving next year when he has taken his exams,' Mrs Scott said. 'The Rector thinks he ought to go on to university but he would have to go to Dumfries Academy and stay in the hostel there to pass his higher grades.'

'I dinna see him being allowed to do that.' Mr Scott looked across at his wife, then at Avril. 'His mother thinks education is a waste o' time and money,' he explained. 'She thinks he should be working on the farm by now. Where would your father have been if his mother had thought like that? It must have taken a long time to become a surgeon?'

'Oh yes, years and years, Grandma Gray said,' Avril answered readily. She was enjoying Mrs Scott's shortbread by now.

'Aye well I don't see Dean getting that opportunity if Grizel has anything to do with it. Miserable as sin she is where money is concerned.'

'Now, Bill,' his wife admonished. 'She is your sister-in-law after all.' She turned to Avril with a smile. 'Grizel is not a bit like me. I enjoy a chat so you tell your mother she's welcome to visit me anytime.'

'Thank you, Mrs Scott. I will tell her. She used to go to school every day to teach other children before we moved here but she's not going to do that any more because she's helping Daddy to make changes to the house and they're doing lots of painting. They are going to change the name to Riverview. I ought to go now or Mummy might be worried. I did enjoy your strawberry jam. Thank you very much.'

They both followed her to the pony and watched her mount easily on to Chezzie's back.

'My! I wish I was as supple as that still,' Mrs Scott said with a sigh.

'Nay, Molly, ye never were as fit as that,' Mr Scott teased and winked at Avril.

'Bill Scott, you'd better mind your P's and Q's or there'll be no dinner for ye.'

'See how badly she treats me, lassie?' Mr Scott chuckled while pretending to pull a long face, but he put an arm round his wife's ample waist as they waved goodbye.

'Don't forget to tell your parents they're very welcome any time,' Mrs Scott called.

It was the first of many visits Avril made to Sylvanside and the Scotts always made her welcome. They allowed her to help feed any new calves or pet lambs and her twin brothers also had been welcome there ever since they were able to walk.

Avril became aware of the silence in the car and that her mother was sound asleep. She leaned forward to Lindsay's right side and whispered, 'Mum seems unusually tired. Was she too excited to sleep last night?'

'Probably. We'll let her have a nap. She'll be eager to hear all your news when we get home,' he said quietly.

Avril returned to reminiscing, remembering how apprehensive she had been about going to a bigger school and catching the bus and finding her way. But the Scotts had remembered to tell their nephew, Dean, about her and he had walked to her road end and introduced himself. She had plied him with questions.

'All the first formers will be new so you'll not be on your own.' He had done his best to reassure her. She smiled at the memory. He told her about the teachers and the subjects he was studying. Once they arrived at school though he was immediately surrounded by his friends and the rest of the older boys, but if they met as they were moving between classes he always gave her a smile or a wink. In the afternoons he got off the bus at his own road end but each morning he walked along to join her and they waited together. Some of the other girls began to tease her but Avril didn't care. She enjoyed having those morning chats and when Dean discovered she was having problems with her science he sat beside her on the bus and explained things far more clearly than Mr Ratcliffe, her science teacher. He terrified her so much she was afraid to ask questions or tell him she didn't understand.

Sometimes Dean told her what he had been doing at the

weekends on the farm. He always seemed to be busy. He could drive a tractor and his father had taught him how to plough.

'You should ride your pony up our farm road,' he said one day. 'When you come to the fork take the left side and it will take you to a wee clump of trees at the top of our hill. You get a good view from there. You can see all our land spread out before you and if you look across you can see my aunt and uncle's place and your house down below. If you ride up there next Saturday afternoon I'll meet you,' he offered.

After that it became Avril's favourite haunt and they often met there even after Dean had finished at school. Avril's smile widened as she remembered her excitement when she told him about the twins being born.

'I knew I was getting a wee brother or sister but I didn't think I would get two at once. They're ever so tiny. Daddy let me hold one of them and then the other; then he told me to sit on the sofa and he put one in each of my arms and took our photograph so he could send a picture for Grandma and Grandfather Gray to see.'

Dean had looked at her curiously. 'You don't seem the least bit jealous,' he remarked.

'Jealous?' she asked, puzzled. 'How could I be jealous? I've always wanted a wee brother of my own. My cousin, Samuel Caraford, already had a sister called Tania, then last year he got a baby brother, called Alexander. I never dreamed I would get two brothers at once.'

'You are a funny one,' Dean laughed. 'My mother and our Doris both said your nose would be put out of joint and you'd be terribly jealous when the new baby arrived.'

'My nose?' She remembered rubbing it and frowning at him in perplexity.

'It's just a saying. I reckon my sister has been jealous of me ever since I was born and she was only three. You're twelve. You must have got used to being an only child.'

'I often wished I could have a father and a brother or sister when I was young but there was only Mummy and me. When we came to Scotland I often went to stay with Aunt Megan and Uncle Steven at Bengairney so I had Samuel and Tania and that wasn't so bad, but it's even better now I've got Dad and brothers of my own.'

'What do you mean, Avril? Didn't your father live with you when you were little?' Dean asked puzzled.

'No, of course not. How could he? Daddy only married Mummy last year and he adopted me and he gave both of us his name and a gold ring.' Avril shook her head now, recalling that incident and how naive she had been. She had grown up a lot since then and she had begun to understand the stigma attached to unmarried mothers. It was one more barrier which kept her from questioning her mother about her natural father.

Dean had been so good to her. He hadn't teased her and she remembered holding her hand out for him so see her signet ring. Even now it was still one of her greatest treasures.

'So is your own father dead?' he asked.

'I think he must be. I've never seen him . . .' Her face creased in an anxious frown. 'Mummy always looks upset so we don't talk about him. Anyway we don't need him now we're a proper family and I've got Callum and Craig as well as Daddy. That's what we're going to call them, did I tell you?'

'No, but they're good names for boys,' Dean said while his mind mulled over the news she had given him. He was certain his mother didn't know Avril was Mr Gray's adopted daughter. Everyone in this area thought he was her real father. He certainly cared for her as though she was his own child, Dean thought. He couldn't explain why he felt he wanted to keep that piece of news from his mother and sister but he knew instinctively it would be one bit of gossip his mother would relish, and one more reason for her and Doris to find fault with the Grays.

As Avril had anticipated Bo was sitting on the doorstep and he came forward wagging his tail as she stepped out of the car. She bent to hug him. In the car behind her she heard her mother stretch and sigh.

'Are we home already?' Ruth yawned, struggling to open her eyes. 'I must have dozed off for a few minutes.' Avril turned, smiling, her eyebrows raised. Did her mother not realize she had slept most of the way back? Lindsay avoided her questioning glance and as she looked from one to the other Avril noticed the silvery grey of her father's hair as it caught the afternoon sun. It gave him a distinguished look but surely that must have happened in the last few months or she would have noticed it before. She thought he had lost weight too, and there was a look of strain around his eyes and mouth. He caught her gaze and smiled, but she had a feeling even his usually ready smile was an effort today.

Two

When the twins were born Bessie Coulter had started coming to Riverview two mornings a week to clean but when Ruth had her operation, four months ago, she had started coming every weekday morning, sometimes staying on to give the twins their tea when they got home from school.

'Bessie will have peeled the vegetables and left the chicken casserole ready to put in the oven,' Ruth said, walking slowly towards the house and Avril realized the arrangement was still continuing. It was an indication that her mother had not regained her former health. One of her pleasures had been looking after her own family and cooking their favourite meals. She watched her father take her mother's arm, leading her to the old Windsor chair in the corner by the Aga cooker.

'You sit down and rest, sweetheart. I know how much travelling tires you.' Watching them Avril felt a frisson of fear. Her mother had always been fiercely independent and she had never been a woman who wanted cosseted. 'I'll telephone Sylvanside and ask Molly to send the boys home,' Lint said, observing Ruth's pallor with anxious eyes.

'It's good to be home. I'll see to the dinner, Mum,' Avril said. Her mother rarely wore much make-up. She'd always had a lovely clear skin but as summer sunshine streamed through the kitchen window Avril realized she had used more make-up than usual, including a little rouge. Beneath it she looked drained and exhausted as she leaned back in the chair and closed her eyes, even though she had slept so long in the car.

'It's wonderful to have you home again, Avril,' Ruth murmured, still with her eyes closed. 'We're all so proud of you, but I've longed to have you back. We all have. We do miss you.'

'Have the boys been in more trouble than usual?' Avril asked, summoning a grin and a cheery tone. She adored her twin brothers, with their cheeky smiles and sparkling dark eyes.

'They've been remarkably good lately,' Ruth admitted. 'Talking about trouble though, the Palmer-Farrs say they are at their wits' end with Rosy. Catherine grumbles because she's a tomboy and not interested in school – or so she says.' Catherine Palmer-Farr was Lindsay's half cousin and Rosemary-Lavender was their only child. Before her mother's operation the two families had visited each other often.

'Rosy was never a bad girl. She was always a bright, happy child from what I remember,' Avril said. 'She's a year older than the twins isn't she?'

'Yes, she was ten in May, a few months older than Alexander at Bengairney. The four of them get on well when they're together.'

'I'd have thought young Rosy would be eager to learn at that age.'

'I believe she is, but not the sort of things her mother wants her to learn,' Ruth said. 'Megan's father, John Oliphant, still helps with the gardens and odd jobs at Langton Tower but whenever he or Chrissie are going down to Bengairney to see their grand-children Rosy pleads with them to take her too. She loves the farm. Steven says she asks questions by the dozen about the animals, and even the crops, and he says she remembers what he tells her too.'

'Maybe her teacher at school doesn't capture her interest?' Avril suggested.

'You could be right,' Ruth said slowly. She had enjoyed teaching and always done her best, even with the most reluctant pupils.

'Maybe Rosy will want to be a lady farmer,' Avril chuckled.

'That's what her mother is afraid of,' Ruth said seriously. The Palmer-Farrs lived near Lockerbie. Langton Tower had been in the family for generations. Although most of the land had been sold the Tower House was a sort of ancient mansion and Douglas and Catherine were still regarded as local gentry. The whole place had been occupied by evacuees during the war but when Catherine and Douglas married they had made part of it into a very comfortable home. The rest was now a country house hotel and conference centre which Catherine ran with great efficiency and considerable success.

'I think part of the problem is young Rosemary doesn't fit in with her parents' expectations,' Lindsay reflected, joining the conversation, after telephoning Molly Scott. 'Alexander is at the same school. Tania and Samuel went there too and they are doing well. Megan thinks the local children treat Rosy differently because she lives at Langton Tower and has a double-barrelled name and her parents mix in a different social circle but Douglas and Catherine have worked hard to restore Langton Tower and make a success of it. I suspect the teachers also treat Rosy with more deference than she wants, or deserves. The children probably follow their example. Even Samuel and Tania think of her as being a different social class, although Alexander regards her as just another pal. I believe that's why she likes his company so much. Being an only child doesn't help of course, especially when her mother expects her to look, and act, like a miniature lady.'

'You know how much John and Chrissie Oliphant enjoy young company,' Ruth said, opening her eyes to look up at Avril. 'Rosy spends her time in the gardens with John or helping Chrissie to look after the pigs and poultry. She has a collie dog for a pet, as well as two cats and a rabbit but she still pleads with John Oliphant to take her with him to Bengairney. Sometimes he leaves her there all day and Megan drives her home at night.'

'That all sounds normal to me,' Avril said, 'I loved to go with Granny Caraford and I often stayed with Aunt Megan to play with Samuel and Tania, even though they were a lot younger than me.'

'Yes, but not even Chezzie and Bo, your beloved pets, prevented you from doing well at school,' Ruth reminded her.

'I agree with you, Avril,' Lint said firmly. 'It's normal and healthy for a child to enjoy being outdoors and getting dirty and exploring. Rosy is intelligent. I suspect Cousin Catherine expected to have a wee girl who looked and behaved like a fairy princess. The poor child hates being called Rosemary-Lavender for a start.'

'Well it is a mouthful of a name to wish on anyone, even without the Palmer-Farr for her surname,' Avril agreed. 'I can imagine the other children teasing her about that.'

'Yes, I feel sorry for the poor mite. Catherine and Douglas both went to boarding school so they are talking of sending her next year too, but they say she gets hysterical whenever they mention it.'

'I'd have hated it if I'd had to go away to school at that age too,' Avril said.

'I went when I was ten,' Lint said. 'I quite enjoyed it.' He hesitated then he added, 'as a matter of fact I've mentioned it once or twice to Callum and Craig. They're not against the idea if they get plenty of sport, and so long as they can come home for the holidays.'

'It might be easier for them when they have each other for company,' Avril said doubtfully.

'Maybe when they're older,' Ruth said. She sounded weary. 'I don't want any of my children to go away again for a while. It is so lovely to have you home dear,' she repeated fervently, her eyes on Avril.

'Do you think you'll be able to cope with Sunday lunch for everyone, Ruth?' Lint asked, eyeing her with an anxious frown. He turned to Avril. 'They are all so proud of you, my dear, and eager to congratulate you. We have invited Megan and Steven and the three children to lunch, and Mrs Caraford of course.'

'I asked Megan to bring her parents too,' Ruth said. 'The Oliphants have always been so kind to us. I shall manage. Avril will help me, won't you darling? Oh, I almost forgot. You'll have to look in the pantry and see the latest appliance your father has bought for me.'

'Oh? What is it?' Avril asked with a smile. She knew her father would buy the moon for her mother if it was possible.

'It looks like a huge chest but it's a deep freezer. You can keep beef in it for a year according to the Scotts. Molly and Bill got one from the firm who supplied their refrigerated milk tank for the dairy – in place of all those milk churns you know. Anyway Molly thinks the freezer is wonderful so Lint asked the Scotts to get one for us.'

'We bought a lamb from them to put in ours,' her father said, with all the enthusiasm of a schoolboy. 'They got it butchered for us. It's delicious. I wish we'd bought two. We shall have to wait until next year's lambs are ready now.'

'I've made some puddings and apple pies, as well as a chocolate gateau. They're all in there. Bessie helped me but she's convinced they'll go bad,' Ruth said with a chuckle, sounding more like her old self.

'I can't wait to see this latest acquisition.' Avril smiled, looking from one to the other. Sometimes they seemed so in love and so absolutely right for each other that she felt more adult than

them, especially since she had been away from home. She had
done a lot of growing up in the last four years, she realized. 'You
know I'll help with the dinner, Mum, but I don't want you
inviting people here for my sake, not if it tires you out.'

'I'd like our closest friends to come,' Ruth said. 'I haven't felt
like visiting anybody, not even Hannah, or Megan, and they've
always been so good to me.'

Avril knew there had always been a special bond between her
mother and Hannah Caraford. She had always felt that bond of
affection too. Mrs Caraford could not have been kinder if she
had been her real grandmother. Avril looked more closely at her
mother's pale face. Her skin was almost translucent. She suppressed
a shiver.

Avril thought about the many happy gatherings they had all
enjoyed at Bengairney with Steven and Megan, Samuel and Tania,
and then Alexander. Since her parents' wedding, ten years ago,
they had often congregated here, at Riverview, especially when
Grandma and Grandfather Gray came to stay, or if her father was
on call at the hospital over Christmas or New Year. Her mother
loved cooking and she had enjoyed entertaining those she considered her true friends. Sometimes they had all gathered at the
Oliphants' at Honeysuckle Cottage. John and Chrissie were
convinced her father had saved Chrissie's life some years ago and
they never forgot.

Remembering how easily her mother had dealt with these
family gatherings, and how much she had enjoyed them, Avril
felt increasingly uneasy about her lack of energy now. Her mother
would never have stayed in bed until after breakfast if she was
well but she seemed relieved to know she was here to see her
father off to work and give the twins their breakfast. She was
happy to do such simple tasks but she sensed that all was not as
it should be. Early mornings had been her mother's favourite
time of day, especially in summer.

Avril had learned to bake and to cook at an early age. At the
time she had thought she was helping Granny Caraford, little
realizing she was subconsciously absorbing her skill and knowledge. Hannah had shown infinite patience, guiding her small
meddling fingers, showing her how to make pastry or scones and
later how to cook. After so much time spent studying it was an

enjoyable change to create appetizing dishes in the kitchen. On Sunday morning she got up early to prepare an apricot stuffing for the joints of rolled shoulder of lamb. Mr Scott's lambs were young and tender so they were not large and it was her father who insisted they must take two from the freezer.

'There'll be thirteen of us,' he said, 'and at fifteen Samuel is almost a man. He can eat as much as his father, according to Megan.'

As it happened there were fourteen people by the time they were all seated round the dining table. Rosy Palmer-Farr had pleaded with John and Chrissie to bring her with them to visit Uncle Lindsay and Auntie Ruth. Chrissie found it difficult to refuse her anything when she looked at her with such pleading in her big blue eyes so she had telephoned to ask if it would be all right to include her. Avril understood Rosy's longing for real cousins and it did not worry the little girl if the twins' relationship was diluted to quarter cousins, as she called them.

'Auntie Ruth is always kind and patient,' she told Chrissie. 'I wish she had been my teacher.' Neither did it trouble her having three small boys for company. She got on well with Alexander Caraford who was only a few months younger than herself, and with the twins. They all accepted her as another member of their little gang.

When lunch was over everyone praised Ruth for giving them such an excellent meal.

'It was Avril who did the cooking,' Ruth said proudly. 'I can take no credit.'

'The recipe for the stuffed lamb came from Granny C,' Avril said, smiling across at Hannah, 'and Mum had already made the puddings and put them in the freezer. Dad and the boys helped peel the vegetables for the soup yesterday so I think you could say it was a combined effort.'

'And we made the mint sauce. Don't forget that, Avril,' Craig piped up.

'And we had to chop the mint ever so small. Tell them, Avril,' Callum insisted, 'And we set the dining room table.'

'Indeed they did. They've been very good wee helpers.' Avril beamed at them both.

'So can we go outside to show Alexander and Rosy our new

den down in the wood now? I 'spect you're all going to drink coffee and talk?'

'All right,' Lint said, 'but don't get into mischief.'

Avril was dismayed to see her mother already looking tired even though she had stayed in bed until ten o' clock that morning. She caught her father's eye and realized he was watching her anxiously too.

'Shall I show you Mum's freezer, Auntie Megan?' she asked brightly, pushing back her chair and standing up.

'Yes, I'd like to see it and then Tania and I will help you with the washing up.'

'I'll come through in a minute,' Ruth said.

'No, Mum, you go into the sitting room and chat to Granny C and Mrs Oliphant while you have the chance.' She caught Hannah's eye and the older woman nodded. Her own expression was troubled as she glanced at Ruth's wan face.

'We men will bring some of the dirty dishes through to the kitchen,' Lindsay offered, 'then maybe Steven and John would like to come for a walk up to the Scotts to see their new milk tank?'

He might be an eminent surgeon but he had never been afraid to tackle the mundane tasks, Megan thought, watching him stack the plates methodically. Her heart was heavy. He and Ruth were so well suited and they had been so wonderfully happy until illness struck in the spring. She didn't need to be a doctor to see that Ruth's condition was not improving in spite of the major operation and the radiotherapy which had followed.

'Thanks Dad,' Avril said, meeting his eyes, and understanding that he wanted to give her mother an opportunity to rest too.

'I certainly need a walk after such a lovely big dinner,' John Oliphant said with a grin at Avril, 'and I'm looking forward to seeing this milk tank I've heard about. They've got one at Martinwold now I believe. I wish they'd brought out such things in my day and saved us washing all those milk churns and hoisting them on to the lorries to go to the creamery. 'When are you getting one at Bengairney, Steven?'

'Well the landlord has given his permission at last, but only on condition that we pay for widening the door into the dairy and any other alterations we need to get a tank in place. They cost a lot of money so I needed to know where we stand if anything happened and we'd to move out of Bengairney. I asked whether the laird would take it over or whether it would count as tenant's valuation.'

'Surely you're not thinking of leaving Bengairney, are you Steven?' Lint asked.

'No,' Steven said slowly. 'But it seems none of us know what's round the corner, do we?'

'No, we don't,' Lint agreed quietly, shaking his head regretfully, 'but I think you need to plan as though you'll live forever – at least until something convinces you otherwise.'

'Yes, you're right, Lint, and we do hope to get a tank installed before next spring,' Steven said in a brighter tone. 'We're going to install a round-the-byre milker at the same time so that Megan will not need to carry the milk to the dairy any more.'

'Whatever is that?' Lindsay asked.

'It's a pipe that runs all the way round the byre and straight to the dairy. We shall connect the milking units to it instead of to a bucket then the milk goes straight from the cow's udder, up into the milk line, and direct into the bulk tank in the dairy. There will be no churns to change every time one gets filled so there'll be no fear of losing milk down the drain.'

'That sounds both efficient and labour saving,' Lint remarked.

'It will be a big advantage. I thought we should wait until we can afford to do it all at once and make a proper job while we're at it. We've so many cows now we're running out of space in the byre. The land agent is not very keen on spending money so he doesn't want to extend it.'

'I suppose the Scotts have an advantage there,' Lint reflected. 'Their farm is much smaller of course but now they own it they don't need to ask permission before they make changes, so long as they can afford to pay for them.'

'I'd like to come with you to Sylvanside as well,' Samuel said.

'You mean you're not going to help with the washing up?' Megan teased. He grinned at her.

'Not if I can help it, Mum. I must say you're a super cook now, Avril. Do you remember the mud pies we used to make and how we baked them in an oven made of stones and slate?'

'I do remember,' Avril said with a smile. 'And you always wanted to decorate them with snails. I'm glad you think I've improved since then. Tania tells me your friends at school call you Muel. Why is that?'

'It's because they think he's as stubborn as a mule,' Tania told her with a grin before Samuel could reply.

'You'd better come now, Sam, if you're joining us,' his father called. 'Steven says Dean Scott might be at his uncle's too. You can ask him about the college course he did. You'll need to make some decisions about your own future next year.'

When the men had left the house Avril showed Megan and Tania into the pantry to see the new deep freeze chest.

'I'll leave you to look while I take in a bucket of coal and mend the sitting room fire before we start the washing up,' she said. 'Mother seems to feel the cold even though it's summer.'

The room door was slightly ajar and as Avril carried the coal scuttle across the hall she could hear the murmur of voices.

'Have you decided whether to go for more radiotherapy, dear?' she heard Granny C ask. 'Have you discussed it with Avril yet?'

Avril froze on the spot, not with any desire to eavesdrop, simply because her heart seemed to have turned to ice.

'No. I'm so happy to have her home. I can't bring myself to spoil things. All I want is to enjoy having her close to me again. I can't bear to spend time away from her, or the boys, especially when there's little hope it will do any good.' Avril could hear a quiver of desperation in her mother's voice, but what was it she had to discuss?

'Avril is a sensible and intelligent young woman, Ruth,' Chrissie Oliphant said gently. 'She thinks the world of you, always has. Even if there's only a chance in a thousand of curing you I'm sure she would want you to try.'

'I agree with Chrissie,' Hannah said. 'If it was Avril who was ill wouldn't you want her to take any chance which came her way? You know how deeply we all care for you, dear Ruth. We want whatever is best for you.'

'Yes, I know you do. I'm eternally grateful for your friendship.' Her mother's voice was little more than a whisper. 'But the side effects are pretty awful. I may wait until Avril goes back to the university to start her doctorate.'

'I'm sure Avril would prefer to know the truth, Ruth,' Granny

C said quietly, sadly. 'She would help you cope with the effects of the treatment.'

Avril stepped back a pace or two and made a clatter with the bucket. The voices ceased before she pushed the door wider and entered the room with her bucket of coal.

Three

When the men returned from Sylvanside Dean Scott was with them and he and Samuel were deep in conversation. Avril made tea in the kitchen, knowing Megan and Steven would need to leave soon to get on with their own milking at Bengairney. When they had gone Dean joined her in the kitchen as she cleared away the afternoon tea.

'I think Granny C and Mr and Mrs Oliphant will be leaving soon,' she said. 'Mum is almost falling asleep in her chair. Do you feel like a walk up to our old haunt, Dean? Or do you have animals to feed?'

'I've been longing for you to come home, Avril. I hoped you might be able to go for a walk up the hill.'

'I'd like that. Dad will keep an eye on the boys. So you don't need to hurry back to feed your animals?'

'No, they're all out in the fields and the lambing finished ages ago. It's time for clipping the ewes if the good weather lasts. I wish I had a byre full of cows to milk like Uncle Bill or the Carafords though.'

'You still yearn for a dairy herd?'

'Yes, it's still my ambition,' he said with a wry smile. 'We shall be mowing hay on Monday if it stays fine so we'll enjoy a walk up the hill while we have the chance. It seems a long time since we had the opportunity for a proper chat.'

'It is.' Avril sighed heavily. 'I need a good friend right now, Dean. I'm worried about Mum.'

'Yes,' he said slowly, 'I can understand that and I'm proud you have chosen me.'

'Oh Dean, you've been my friend ever since we came to Riverview when I was eleven.'

'Riverview,' he mused with a ghost of a smile. 'Mother still insists on calling it Eskriggholm.' He didn't tell her about the ridiculous rants his mother indulged in, raving on about strangers who moved to the area and tried to change things, and considered they were above people who had lived in the area for generations. Even his father had got fed up of her tirade and told her to shut up.

'People are used to it being Riverview after all these years,' Avril said, but she guessed Dean's mother still disapproved. She resented the fact that it was no longer a farm and her brother-in-law now owned the land, as well as his own farm while she and her husband were still tenants. Although it had all happened ten years ago Mrs Scott was still bitter about it and Dean had told her his parents would never get such an opportunity again.

As they made their way up the hill above Riverview to the top of Northsyke, Dean said seriously, 'I was dismayed when I saw your mother today, Avril. She had seemed so much better after she had her operation.'

'Yes, I feel the same,' Avril said. She began to tell him about the conversation she had overheard. 'In the few days since I've been home Mother has been dreadfully tired. She seems drained of colour and energy. In my heart I knew there was something seriously wrong. Then when I overheard Granny C this afternoon . . .' Her voice shook and she turned towards Dean instinctively. 'I think Mum has cancer.' She voiced her suspicions in a whisper. Dean drew her into his arms and held her, gently stroking her hair as she rested her head against his chest. In spite of her distress Avril realized with a shock that Dean had changed in the four years she had been away. He was lean and fit and very much a man. She felt comforted by his strength and his gentleness, but after a little while she drew away with a sigh and they walked on hand in hand, in silence, until they reached their favourite spot in the shelter of the little copse.

'I don't know what to do,' she said forlornly. She reminded Dean of the tense eleven-year-old he had first seen waiting for the school bus, but she was an attractive young woman now and she tugged at his heart strings in a very different way. He had gone out with several girls while he was at college but he had never felt the tenderness he felt for Avril and none of them had attracted him physically, the way Avril did now. He had been feeling frustrated with his work even before Avril returned from university and now the feeling intensified. He was young and healthy and he had new ideas; he wanted to make changes and improvements, but neither of his parents wanted change. His mother was even more intransigent than his father. He didn't see how he would ever have anything to offer a girl the way things were, and Avril was not just any girl. She was intelligent and capable and she would be Doctor Gray in the next couple of years. She would probably end up in a research laboratory miles away from here, or even in America. She had moved far beyond his reach already, but right now she needed him and he was glad. His grip on her hand tightened and he turned to face her.

'Avril, I pray your mother doesn't have cancer as you fear, but even if she has, what can you do, except be there for her and be strong?'

'I think there must be some kind of treatment Mum could try as a last resort, but she doesn't want to go for it while I'm at home. Do you think she doesn't want me to know?'

'She will not want to upset you, or spoil your homecoming.'

'But I'm not a child any more, Dean.'

'I know that,' Dean said softly and slipped his arm around her waist, drawing her back with him to lean against a broad tree trunk. 'Perhaps your mother doesn't want to accept it herself, and talking about it, admitting it to you, will make it a reality.' He held her closer, wishing he could protect her from all her worries and the grief which he knew was going to follow.

'I suppose you're right, Dean. Dad has always said you have a wise head on you.' She looked up at him with a wan smile. 'I'm so afraid. I can't imagine what Dad will do if anything happens to Mum. It made him so happy when she agreed to marry him. Even though I was so young I could see their joy. He would do anything for her. It will be worse for him than any of us.'

'Surely it will be worst for the twins?' His arm tightened, 'and for you,' he added huskily. 'I know how close you and your mother have always been. She's not a bit like my mother,' he added almost bitterly.

'The twins are remarkably self-sufficient,' Avril said. 'Dad mentioned the possibility of them going to boarding school. They don't seem to mind the idea.'

'Maybe they don't realize how serious things are, and they have you. They've always adored you. Aunt Molly said they were terribly excited when they knew you would be home for the whole summer.'

'I may be here for longer than that,' Avril said almost under her breath. Dean waited, realizing she was speaking her thoughts aloud. 'If mother does go for more treatment sometimes the side effects can be awful. The doctors have a lot more to learn, and research to do. I must be here to give her my support. I want to help her, and care for her. Do you understand that, Dean?'

'I do understand, Avril, because I know what an unselfish and loving person you are,' Dean said gruffly.

'Dear Dean,' she laid her head against his chest and nestled closer. 'You always were my best friend. You always understand me. I couldn't possibly go back to university and leave Mum when she needs me most.' For a moment Dean's heart soared at the prospect of Avril staying here all the time, then he clamped down on such futile dreams. He had no prospects, or anything else to offer a girl like Avril.

'What if your mother decides not to have any more treatment?' he prompted gently.

'If she is as ill as I suspect . . . If − if she is dying, then that's all the more reason for me to stay at home. I want to be with her for whatever time she has left.' Her words ended in a husky croak and Dean knew she was doing her best to hold back tears. He held her in silence, his fingers stroking her upper arm. After a while he straightened. 'Want to know what I think, Avril?'

'Yes, of course I do. I suppose subconsciously that's why I wanted to come up here with you, to be on our own.'

'Right. I think you'll need to summon your courage and talk frankly to your father. He must know the facts and I'll bet he has already consulted everyone in the medical profession who may be able to help, or advise. He is a well-respected surgeon himself so he must have lots of contacts.'

'Yes, he has. You're right, of course, Dean. I have a feeling he is avoiding discussing things with me but I must make him see how important it is to me to know what's happening.'

'He knows you have the courage to see you through, Avril, and he knows how much you love your mother. I think he'll understand how important this is and he may even find it a relief to discuss things with you honestly.'

'Do you think so? I hope he will understand if I stay at home. I will talk to him,' she said lifting her small chin resolutely. 'You're right, Dean. I need to plan. I shall have to write and tell the professor I shall not be doing my doctorate. But I need to earn some money too. I can't expect Dad to go on supporting me indefinitely, especially if he is going to pay for the twins to go to boarding school.'

'There's a lot to consider then, and decisions to be made,' Dean said. 'You'll feel better, or at least more in control, when you have discussed things openly with your father.'

'You're right, Dean.' She lifted her face to his with a faint smile. 'I'm so pleased I've seen you today and that we've had this chance to talk. You always did help me get things in perspective. Usually they were never as bad as I feared.'

'I expect they were,' he grinned, 'but when you faced them squarely you always found the strength to deal with things.'

'You're a good friend to me, Dean.' Avril leaned closer and kissed his cheek before she drew away from him. She was surprised to see a faint blush on his face but he clasped her hand and grinned. 'A run down the hill will do both of us good. He set off with his long loping stride, pulling her with him.

Where the track divided he drew to a halt. 'I'd better head this way for home now,' he said, 'but you know where I am if you need me.' He hesitated. His mother could be stubbornly selective about passing on messages. He remembered Avril had telephoned once before but neither Doris nor his mother had told him. He knew they were jealous of her success at school and university, and they resented her family, still regarding them as newcomers to the area after eleven years. 'Phone Aunt Molly. She'll make sure I get your message and we'll meet up the hill, or I'll come down to your house if you want to talk.'

'Thanks, Dean,' Avril said huskily. 'I think I'm going to need a good friend in the weeks ahead.' This time he leaned forward and kissed her cheek, then trailed his fingers gently down her face.

'See you soon.'

Lindsay had a lot of responsibility and he had spent as much time with Ruth as he could in recent weeks so he was relieved to know Avril was there to keep her company and take charge of the twins while he attended to his work. Consequently it was almost a week before Avril got a chance to have a proper talk with him. Even then he looked tired and strained and her heart sank when she saw him tense.

'It's no use trying to shield me from the truth, Dad,' she said with a heavy sigh. 'I'd have to be blind and foolish not to see that Mum is seriously ill. I'm not a child any more so please talk to me and tell me the truth so that I can decide what to do about my own plans.'

Reluctantly Lindsay began to tell her about Ruth's condition, trying to be positive, but knowing Avril was too intelligent not to see for herself that her mother was dying.

'So you're saying the cancer has already spread,' Avril said carefully, keeping her voice steady with an effort. 'And another course of treatment is unlikely to help?'

'Her consultant mentioned it to offer a glimmer of hope but Ruth is like you, my dear. She is not easily fooled and she has faced up to difficult situations before. She wants to make the most of whatever time she has left, rather than spend more time in hospital, away from us all. She has greater courage than I have.' He buried his head in his hands in a gesture of despair which rung Avril's young heart, even while she shared his grief. 'All we can do is give her our love and support to see her through this – to the end.' His voice wavered into silence. Avril clenched her nails against the palms of her hands to stop herself from weeping, knowing tears could only make things worse for her father. She made her decision. She would write to the professor tomorrow. She would not tell her father until later so he could not argue or try to dissuade her.

'How long?' she asked in a low voice.

'They don't know. She is not in pain since the operation and she has had no more sickness since she recovered from the radiotherapy. Her consultant is already prescribing medication which he hopes will slow the spread of the cancer, but it is impossible to give an accurate prediction. You may not think so, Avril, but I assure you Ruth has been brighter and more positive since you returned home. It's almost as though she finds strength from knowing we are all here, together again.'

'I'm glad,' Avril said softly. Her father's words reinforced her decision to put further studies behind her, at least for now.

It was more than a fortnight later when Avril received a reply from the professor but it was an unexpectedly informal and friendly letter which did much to boost her spirits. He had been on holiday, he said, hence the delay in replying. He was genuinely sorry she would not be doing further research in his department but he did understand her reasons and he respected her for the sacrifice she was making.

'You mentioned looking for part-time work,' he wrote. 'I wonder whether you would be interested in laboratory work at your local hospital? Dr Lever and I were students together and the last time we met he mentioned that he was needing a laboratory assistant. If you are interested then do go to see him and mention my name. I think the work may be fairly routine and it will not offer you the challenge and stimulation I know you enjoy and deserve, but in the present circumstances it may suit very well and it would keep you in touch with the world of science.'

Avril waited up for her father coming home. He was later when he had spent the day in the theatre because he always checked his patients before leaving the hospital. She showed him the letter while he ate a light meal.

'Oh my dear Avril, we would never expect you to sacrifice your career! Why didn't you tell me you were writing to the professor?'

'Because I knew you would say exactly what you're saying now.' Avril smiled. 'It is my decision and I want to spend as much time with Mum as I can, while I can. But I do need to earn some money too. Do you think I could use Mum's car to travel to the hospital – that is if the job is still vacant and if I get it?'

'Of course you can. We were talking of buying you a car of your own for when you went back to university anyway.' That had been his suggestion, knowing Avril would use it to get home for weekends as often as she could, Ruth had seemed relieved at the suggestion.

'That will not be necessary now but you've already done so much for me anyway. Don't think I don't appreciate it.'

'I know you do, Avril, my dear. I could tell you there is no need for you to go out to work to earn some money. You're already working here at home, and don't think I don't appreciate that either.' He smiled wanly. 'But I know how independent you are and in any case the professor is right; it will be better

for you to keep in touch with other professionals. We will arrange
for Bessie to stay all day on the days you are working.'

'I may not get the job,' Avril reminded him.

'I'm sure you will if it is still vacant. I think you should telephone for an appointment tomorrow. I know it is selfish of me
but this will give your mother an added boost, knowing you will
be here . . .' He didn't finish the sentence but Avril nodded.

'I know,' she said softly. 'This is where I want to be for as long
as Mum needs me.'

Avril went for an interview with Doctor Lever. He was a grim-
looking man, with gimlet eyes behind steel-framed spectacles; he
moved briskly and economically and Avril guessed he did not
suffer fools gladly, if at all.

'I have already taken on a new laboratory assistant since I met
Professor Chambers,' he said, but his mouth tightened and he
scowled at some inner thought. 'However I have spoken to Fraser
since you contacted me. He speaks very highly of your abilities
and your knowledge, Miss Gray.'

'Knowledge and interest I certainly have but I don't have a
lot of experience in some of the lab techniques you probably
use,' she said.

'I'm sure you will soon become proficient. Mrs Cook is in
charge of the laboratory equipment and she will teach you everything you need. I understand you only require part-time work
so I suggest we have a month's trial if you can work Monday,
Wednesday and Friday until three thirty. The rest of my staff work
until five. In fairness to the other members of the team I must
ask you to work one Saturday or one Sunday each month on a
rota basis. We keep only a skeleton staff at weekends but it is
essential in case of emergencies.'

When Avril told her mother of her plans she saw relief and
gratitude in her dark eyes and she knew she had done the right
thing.

The village shop and the blacksmith's were the hub of village life
and there was little local news which was not exchanged and
discussed. When Bessie collected her newspapers she mentioned
that Avril would not be returning to university as originally planned.

'She has taken on a part-time job at the hospital in Dumfries so that she can spend time with her mother and help with the boys. She's a lovely lassie with a real kind heart,' Bessie said. 'I could see straight away that Mrs Gray looked happier and more relaxed, if anyone in her condition can be happy, poor soul.'

'It's a shame when Avril has done so well and with such a promising career ahead of her,' Mrs Williams, the shopkeeper murmured sympathetically. 'I expect Mr Gray would employ the best nurses available but there's no comfort like your own flesh and blood. I'm sure Avril willna regret her decision.' There were other similar comments from customers when she passed on the news. Most of them knew Avril and her brothers through the school and the Kirk and village activities.

'It seems even the best of doctors can't save their own when illness strikes,' reflected Mrs Andrews from the post office. 'I'm sure Mr Gray will have tried to get the best treatment available for his poor wife. They always look such a happy couple.'

'When it is God's will there's nothing a mortal man can do, however great his knowledge,' the Reverend Paterson pronounced as he waited patiently to be served. He knew the Gray family well. It grieved him to hear Mrs Gray's illness was as serious as the rumours had stated.

Grizel Scott listened then gave her habitual haughty sniff. She had no sympathy for the Grays, or anyone else.

'If she'd been the one who was ill she'd have expected everybody to be running after her and sympathizing,' Mrs Andrews said darkly. They had been in the same class at school and she had no love for Grizel Brown, as she had been called before she married Sydney Scott.

Grizel repeated the news about the Grays as soon as she arrived home.

'If you ask me I reckon that Gray girl didna do as well at the university as they made out. That'll be the reason she's had to get a job. And she's only going to work half the week, they say. What good is that? If her mother was as ill as she makes out she'd be in hospital,' she scoffed. Doris muttered some response, but when Dean and his father came in for their meal Grizel began all over again.

'And another thing, if the Grays were half as well off as they pretend to be they'd employ a nurse if the wife really is as ill as all that. If you ask me that girl o' theirs is bone idle. She's been spoiled, riding round on that pony instead of doing some work.'

'For goodness sake, Mother, it's years since Avril outgrew her pony. Anyway Doris always had a pony and she rode until last year.'

'That's different,' his mother sniffed. 'Our Doris is a farmer's daughter with some breeding about her.' Dean opened his mouth to protest, but he caught his father's eye and saw him shake his head. His expression said 'it's no use arguing with her in this mood.' They ate in silence.

'Anyway our Doris was a far better rider than the Gray girl.' Doris preened herself but no one commented. His sister had never been particularly good at anything that Dean could think of. She was too lazy to make any effort for one thing, yet she considered herself a cut above any of the local lads who might have asked her for a date. His mother droned on about Mrs Gray and Avril but Dean closed his ears as he often did. He wondered how much longer he could stand the situation, plodding along day after day with no plans for a better future, no real challenge. Sometimes he wondered why his father always gave in to his mother's scrimping and moaning. Aunt Molly reckoned it was because he felt he had let her down. He had been diagnosed with diabetes three years after they were married. In the beginning he had had several near death experiences due to the insulin and irregular, and often unsuitable, meals. Grizel had believed she was marrying a healthy man who farmed the biggest farm on the estate, instead she considered he was a weakling who couldn't eat the good square meals she cooked for him. Dean knew she still resented the fact that he was not as strong and healthy as his younger brother, Bill, but once his father had taken control of his illness and listened to the doctors, instead of his wife, he had lived an active and busy life, earning the respect of his farming neighbours and several times winning the regional sheep dog trials with his home-bred collie dogs. There were the two of them to work the farm now though, as well as the two men they employed, and Dean was convinced they needed to make changes to bring in more income.

'What are you dreaming about?' his mother snapped and banged her fist on the table, next to his plate, making Dean jump. 'Did you hear what I said about you and that girl?'

'What girl?'

'There! I knew you weren't listening! You're as bad as your father. I'm telling you I'll not have her mooning round here if she's going to be living at home. She'll be looking for a husband now that she's failed her exams. You look out my lad because there's no place here for her. We don't want folks who act like gentry when they're not.'

Dean had not started his pudding but he pushed his chair back so sharply that it overbalanced and clattered to the floor. His face was white with anger and there was a pulse throbbing in his jaw.

'If you're meaning Avril Gray with your wicked insinuations you can leave her and her family out of your ranting. She is way, way above me now. I wish to God I'd gone to university then I might have had a chance with her instead of slogging away here to keep *her* in idleness.' He glared at his sister. 'I don't have a car, or a wage to call my own. I'm twenty-five and I ask for money if I want a pint at the pub, or to go to the cinema. Well I've just about had enough!'

'You've had enough!' Grizel sneered. 'Drinking isna good for you. If it wasn't for me there'd be no money left. Your father made you a partner when you were twenty-one and he didna even ask me. I would never have allowed it. You didna deserve it then and you dinna deserve it now.'

'There's no advantage about being a partner when all you get is half of nothing,' Dean snapped. 'Even if Avril Gray looked my way I'd have nothing to offer her so don't go using your evil imagination to criticize her because I'll not stand for that. It's bad enough you moaning at father and me all day the way you do.' He turned on his heel and left the house.

There was silence when he had gone. It was the first time Dean had lost his temper since he was a young boy.

'You'll go too far one o' these days.' Sydney Scott spoke quietly, but his tone was firm, almost harsh, as he held his wife's eyes. 'I'm tied to you by that ring you wear on your finger, Grizel, but Dean's a man now. He's not tied to either o' us. I know you never wanted a son and I know why. You know it's the custom for a father to pass on his farm to his son if the lad wanted to farm, as my father did for me. You didn't object then.'

'That was different. Your father wasna an invalid, likely to leave his wife a pauper or—'

'Neither am I an invalid. Just because your own father died when you were young you're obsessed with hoarding money for your old age. Dean works hard and all you do is nag at him. He did well at college and he'd have no problem getting a job somewhere else. And another thing, stop harping on about the Grays. He's had a tenderness for Avril since she was a bairn and they're a decent family, going through a hard time.' He pushed back his own chair and made for the door. 'Mind your tongue, woman or you'll rue the day it ran away with ye.'

Four

Avril started work the following week and she knew at once she was going to get on well with Mrs Cook. She was a well-rounded, middle-aged woman who had worked her way up, taking examinations as she went. She described her basic knowledge of bacteriology as adequate but there was no doubt her laboratory techniques were faultless, well organized and efficient, precise to the most minute detail. Avril appreciated that and she could see why Dr Lever trusted her to be in charge. Equally she understood his disillusionment in his newest member of staff. Jake Mullen had started three weeks earlier but he was one of those people who considered it clever to avoid work whenever possible. Since she was the newest recruit he began by trying to treat her as his servant, especially when it came to cleaning and sterilizing the equipment he had used. On her first day he muddled three blood samples as well as failing to examine the Petri dishes which he should have done as soon as he arrived. He had no compunction either, even though the medical officer of health was waiting for the results relating to an outbreak of sickness and diarrhoea in two of the schools. Avril recognized him as the sort of spoiled and arrogant young man she most despised. He spoke disparagingly of Mrs Cook because she didn't have a degree. She was clearing up ready to leave on her first day when he came up behind her and grasped her shoulders.

'What gives you the right to finish work so early? I hope you realize you'll need to wash up this lot before you go.'

'You're wrong there. Mrs Cook told me we were all responsible for dealing with our own dishes, pipettes and anything else we use.'

'Ma Cook doesn't know how to make the best use of skilled people like me.'

'I'd say she has more skill and experience in the laboratory than either you or me in spite of our pieces of paper telling the world we have a degree,' she said coolly.

'You have a degree?'

'I do.'

'What in?'

'A Master's degree in science, specializing in bacteriology.' She didn't ask about his own qualifications; Mrs Cook had already told her he had scraped through his BSc after resitting examinations in his first and second years. His fingers tightened on her shoulders and she moved to shrug them away.

'How about a date tomorrow night then? Just the two of us. You'd like that.' She had not managed to shake off his hands so she stepped pointedly to the next sink and without turning round she said coldly, 'A man needs to earn my respect before I consider going out with him. From what I've seen of you today I don't think you'll ever do that.'

Neither of them were aware of Doctor Lever standing in the doorway. He had intended asking Avril whether she had encountered any problems. His habitually stern expression almost cracked into a smile as he heard her calmly giving young Mullen the setdown he needed. He fancied himself as a Don Juan, eyeing up every young woman who came near the laboratories. Doctor Lever went silently away again. He reckoned he would have no need to worry about Miss Gray. Mrs Cook had already given him a good report and she was not a woman who was easily impressed, especially with some of the younger technicians, though none of them were as lax and unreliable as Mullen. He was already regretting giving him a trial for three months.

Bessie and Avril worked out a mutually satisfactory schedule so that Ruth was never left alone in the house. The twins were enjoying their summer holidays and Molly Scott insisted they were welcome at Sylvanside whenever they wanted to come, on condition they told Bessie or Avril where they were going. Both Callum and Craig enjoyed helping with the animals and Molly and Bill Scott had infinite patience so they usually spent part of their day there. Often Mrs Scott would telephone to say they were staying for lunch because she had a big pot of broth, or stew and dumplings, a steak pie, or whatever dish she knew the boys enjoyed, which was pretty well everything she cooked as they had healthy appetites. Every evening they spent some time with their mother after they were bathed and into their pyjamas. It was the only time Avril saw them subdued. Her young brothers knew their mother was ill, and possibly dying, but she had overheard their philosophy – if you didn't talk about bad things they might go away. In their hearts they both knew life was not like that. They had seen calves or lambs die, however much you wished they wouldn't.

As Christmas approached Ruth became increasingly frail but she had already lasted longer than the consultant had predicted. Lindsay and Avril agreed they should spend a quiet family Christmas instead of the usual gathering.

'I know Megan and Mrs Caraford will understand,' he said 'and I've asked my parents to postpone their visit.' Avril understood, but her heart sank at the implication that it would not be long before they would make the long journey north for her mother's funeral.

'Granny Caraford has already said they didn't expect a family gathering this year, Dad, but Aunt Megan has suggested I should take the twins to Bengairney for Boxing Day lunch so long as you will be at home to keep Mum company.'

'That's an excellent idea. It will not be such a disappointment for the boys. Trust Megan to find a solution.' He smiled. 'Ruth would not want to deprive you, or them, of a happy Christmas with friends.'

'I don't mind for myself,' Avril said. She was finding it more and more difficult to face Christmas at all knowing this would be the last one her mother would share with them. 'Megan asked me to invite Dean as well if he is free. Samuel enjoyed having him at Bengairney when he was there as a student, even though he is ten years older.'

'You must telephone him then. I'd be pleased to know you have someone of your own generation. You must miss your friends from university.'

'No, not really. There was never anyone extra special, if that's what you're wondering.' She smiled at him.

'Yes, I did wonder. You've been wonderful with your mother and the boys since you came home. You have made my life so much easier too, my dear.'

'I'm glad to be here, and thankful I finished my degree.'

'Yes. Still I hope Dean can go with you to Bengairney. It will be good for you to have his company. I know you've always got on well with Samuel too but he is neither boy nor man at this stage.'

'I know what you mean.' Avril smiled. 'Neither he nor Tania need me to look after them as they once did and yet they are still quite young in some respects. I'll telephone Dean's Aunt Molly tomorrow. She'll pass on the invitation to Dean.'

'Why don't you phone him at home and then you'll know what his plans are?'

'His mother is not very reliable at passing on messages,' Avril said dryly. 'I don't think we Grays are the most popular people in her book.'

'I see . . .' Lindsay said slowly. 'I didn't realize. Mr Scott is always very pleasant if I run into him at Church or in the village. I wonder what we've done to offend his wife.'

'Nothing. She still thinks of us as incomers. I don't think it is just us anyway. Bessie says she's not very popular in the village. She's always complaining about somebody or something. She doesn't get on very well with Dean's Aunt Molly either and you couldn't find anyone more amiable.'

'No indeed. She's proving a very good friend to us anyway. Maybe Mrs Scott is one of those unfortunate people who can never see good in anyone, or in any situation.'

Avril was glad her father knew and understood about Dean's mother. She didn't mention that Doris had been almost as bad when Dean had taken her to the Young Farmers' Dance. There had been several times recently when she would have loved to have a walk and a chat with Dean but it seemed too complicated to telephone Sylvanside and pass messages to and fro just to arrange a casual meeting.

Dean was delighted to be invited to Bengairney on Boxing Day, and he was pleased Aunt Molly had insisted on speaking to him personally instead of letting his mother pass on a message. Later he told his father about the invitation as they were bedding the bullocks together.

'If I get all the fodder handy for feeding, and make sure the turnips are filled, for the evening feed, do you think you could manage without me for once?'

'Of course I can, son. I'm pleased the Carafords have invited you. Steven Caraford told your Uncle Bill you were the best student he'd had so far, and he has one every year.' His father beamed proudly. 'You can take the car. We'll not be needing it. I'll put the spare keys on your chest of drawers, then there's no need for your mother to spoil your day with her sermonizing.'

'Is that what you call it?' Dean grinned at his father.

'Something like that.' Sydney Scott smiled wryly. If they had not got on so well Dean knew he would never have returned to Northsyke. Sometimes he wondered how much longer he could put up with things the way they were. His father had made him a partner in the farm as soon as he was twenty-one and he was not ungrateful but he felt it was more like a shackle than the gift and trust it was intended to convey.

'Are you taking a wee gift for Mrs Caraford?' his father asked, whistling Gyp and Ben, his two collies to his side, and bending to pat them as they crouched at his feet.

'Yes. Aunt Molly offered to get me a Christmas plant for her and a bottle of whisky for Mr Caraford. She says they've received too many boxes of chocolates from their sales reps so she's sending one of them for the children. I'll pay her of course.'

'You're a good lad, Dean. You should cash a cheque for your personal expenses instead of asking your mother to bring extra when she brings the money from the bank for the men's wages.'

'It wouldn't make much difference. Mother always knows what's happened to every penny and she demands an explanation. Did she always scrutinize the accounts or only since you made me a partner?'

'She started doing the books after the second time I landed in hospital,' his father said ruefully. 'She got a fright. It's become an obsession to have money in the bank in case she's left a widow as her own mother was.'

'Is that what it is? You can imagine what she'll say if she knows I want cash to pay Aunt Molly for buying gifts then.'

'Aye.' Sydney Scott sighed heavily. 'She's always been a bit jealous o' Molly marrying our Bill and him getting the tenancy of Sylvanside. She thought he should stay here and work for me all his life.'

'Surely not?'

'Oh aye, she did. She didn't like him taking his share to buy his cows to start up but the stock was as much his as mine. Our father had always said he would help both of us get a start in farming. After that she squirrelled away every penny she could. Money in the bank makes her feel secure. She thinks animals might die before they're turned into cash.'

'No wonder she was furious when Uncle Bill and Aunt Molly bought their own farm and the land that belonged to Eskriggholm.'

'Aye, that's made relations difficult. I go over there on my own for a chat these days. We've always got on well, Bill and me and Molly always makes me welcome.'

'So that's it!' Dean grinned. 'I wondered how Uncle Bill knew everything that was going on here whenever I pop in to see them.'

'We enjoy a gossip,' his father said with a smile. 'In fact I'll drive over with you on Sunday. We'll take the dogs and I'll walk back. That will put your mother off the scent, eh lad?' His eyes twinkled as though they'd hatched a plot. Dean knew his father never would be seriously disloyal to his mother, but even his patience must wear thin sometimes.

Avril's heart gave a little flip of joy when Dean appeared at the door on Boxing Day. He was fair skinned and his whiskers were ginger when he needed a shave, but today he had a glowing, freshly scrubbed look. Even his unruly gingery brown hair had been brushed into place. His eyes crinkled as he smiled and she thought how white and even his teeth were in contrast to his tanned skin.

'Your eyes look bluer than ever with that blue shirt and your blue tie,' Avril said involuntarily. Dean was pleased he had taken care with his clothes. He and his father always bought their suits and jackets from one of the two local tailors who still came round the farms with their wares and specialized in suits made to measure. His blue tweed sports jacket fitted beautifully. His mother couldn't grumble about that. The tailors had a good reputation and his father insisted on dealing with them as his own father and grandfather had done. They had an account which his father paid by cheque. His mother had a similar account for herself and Doris at one of the stores in Carlisle.

The twins were excited about the assortment of small parcels which they had laboriously wrapped for Alexander and Rosy, as well as for Tania and Samuel, and one for Granny Caraford, whom they adored as much as Avril did.

'I hope the parcels are still wrapped by the time we arrive,' she whispered to Dean with a smile as the boys kept on squeezing and fingering them.

'It's very good of the Carafords to include me in their invitation,' Dean said, returning her smile with an admiring glance. She was wearing a new heather-coloured skirt which showed off her slim hips and shapely legs, and the matching sweater which her parents had bought her for Christmas. 'It seems ages since we had chance to see each other,' he said. 'I expect you have been too busy, what with starting your new job and everything.'

'There have been times when I've longed for a walk up the hill and a talk with you – not about anything in particular – like we used to have before I went away.'

'Why didn't you let me know? You know I'd always come. In fact there's nothing I'd like better.'

'Well it's dark in the evenings now,' Avril said with a sigh, 'and I'm never quite sure how free I shall be at the weekends. You could always come down and see me,' she added diffidently.

'Could I? To the house you mean? Wouldn't your father mind?'

'Of course he wouldn't mind, Dean. He has a high opinion of you, and of your aunt and uncle. You've no idea how kind and helpful they have been since Mum has been ill, especially with the twins.'

'They enjoy young company. They would have made super parents. So you really think it would be all right for me to come down to Riverview some Saturday evenings, or perhaps you'd prefer a Sunday afternoon?'

'Either or both.' Avril grinned, then her face sobered and she reached out to touch his arm. 'I think you would understand if you came and I was a bit tied up with – well with Mum and things.' Dean covered her hand for a moment before returning his to the steering wheel.

'You know I'd understand – so long as you promise to tell me when you've seen enough of me, or if there's a jealous boyfriend in the wings.'

'I can't imagine either of those things, Dean. We've been friends for such a long time. I feel more at ease with you, even when I'm sad, than anyone I know, and I'm so – so . . . Oh I don't know. I'd just like you to come down when you get a chance but I wouldn't like you to get into hot water with your parents.'

Dean grimaced at that. 'I'm always in hot water with my mother so that's nothing new. If it was not for my father I'd clear out tomorrow.' He sounded bitter and disillusioned.

'I'm so sorry you feel like that, Dean. It must be difficult. Mum and I have always been so close, I can't imagine what it must be like.'

Megan welcomed them warmly, hugging Avril and giving the twins a kiss. 'I'm so pleased you could come, Dean, and it's nice for Avril to have a chauffeur and some sensible conversation. I hope neither of you mind the noise –' she waved a hand towards the small sitting room off the kitchen – 'it's this group called The Beatles. Tania got a record from one of her friends and I'm sick of hearing it.'

'I'm sure I'll survive that,' Dean said smiling, 'I'm very grateful for your invitation.' He handed her the Poinsettia and turned to Steven, who had just come in from the yard. He handed him the bottle of whisky.

'Eh laddie, we're pleased to see you. You didn't need to bring anything. As a matter of fact Sam is dying for a chat with you. He's made up his mind he's leaving school when he's sixteen, as you did, and he's going to college when he's done a year's practical. He wants to know all about college life and if you think he'll manage it if he goes without staying on at school for higher grade exams.'

'Well I did so I'm sure Sam can.'

Granny C was in the sitting room watching Alexander and Rosy trying to do a jigsaw on the rug in front of the fire. It was immediately forgotten when they heard the twins in the hall.

Megan had made them a delicious lunch and afterwards Steven asked Dean if he would like to walk it off by taking a look around the farm to see the cattle. Samuel said he was going too, but Alexander and Rosemary and the twins all scampered up to the attic where Steven and Samuel had set up Alexander's new train set. Tania seemed content to listen to her records so Avril, Megan and Granny C washed the dishes and settled down in the room until the men returned. Avril knew it was inevitable that the conversation would turn to her mother.

'She's very brave but she seems to get more fragile every day,' she said. 'Doctor Lever is very understanding about my work though – thank goodness. He has taken me off all the weekend rotas until – until later . . .' She gulped. 'He has dismissed the young man who started just before me but he says it's better not to get some of the tests done at all than to have someone unreliable.'

'I suppose he's right, especially in that line of work,' Granny C said. 'One day it could be a matter of life and death. Did the young man not realize that?'

'Your father must be very relieved you're living at home, Avril,' Aunt Megan said. 'Is he still planning to send the twins to boarding school?'

'I think so. I know he and Mum have discussed it but I don't think they will go until after the summer holidays, so long as Bessie and I can continue to manage between us. Dean's Aunt Molly is wonderful at having them after school if either of us can't be there.' She sighed, then looked from one to the other. 'I don't like to upset Mum with questions when she is so frail but I had hoped she would tell me who my natural father was before – before it's too late,' she ended in a broken whisper.

'Oh Avril, my love!' Granny C shot a swift look at Megan before she moved from her chair by the fire to sit beside Avril on the settee. She put her arm around her in an affectionate hug. 'I'm sure it would be better not to mention it to your mother as she is now,' she said gently.

'If it seems very important to you, Avril,' Aunt Megan said slowly, 'then I'm sure Lint will tell you. I don't think there were any secrets between your parents by the time they married.'

'You think he knows?'

'I'm sure of it.'

'He has been a wonderful father to me,' Avril said. 'I would hate him to think I yearned for anyone else. I would never want to hurt him by asking questions.'

'If I were you my dear, I would forget about it for now. You all have so much sorrow in your hearts. One day I'm sure Lindsay will tell you when he feels the time is right. He's very wise and sympathetic about such things.' In spite of her words Hannah Caraford was relieved to hear the men returning.

'Mum, can you find a pair of overalls and some wellingtons

to fit Dean so that he can come out to the milking with us?' Samuel asked.

'Of course I can, if you're sure that's what you want to do, Dean?'

'I didn't think you would be expecting us to stay so long,' Dean said apologetically. He looked at Avril. 'Do you want to get back soon? We'll do whatever you think best.'

'Were you expecting us to stay for supper, Aunt Megan?'

'I hoped you would, dear. I know the boys like their construction set but you would see I also bought pyjamas for them and Granny Caraford bought them dressing gowns. We thought they could get bathed with Alexander and into their night clothes so that they'll be ready for bed when they get home. They'll probably sleep in the car.'

'You're always so kind to us,' Avril said softly. 'Would you mind if I phoned Dad before we decide? Just to see what sort of a day Mum is having?'

'You go ahead while I make a cup of tea in the kitchen.'

Avril was surprised when her mother answered the telephone. 'Hello, Mum. I didn't expect to hear you on the phone.'

'It's right here beside me on the settee, darling. We have enjoyed a chat with Grandma Gray and now your father has just gone to the kitchen to make us both a cup of tea.'

'You sound – you sound so much brighter. I was phoning to see what sort of day you've had.'

'It's been a really lovely day, Avril. So peaceful. We've had time to talk and to reminisce. We had our lunch in front of the fire. Here's Lint now with the tea. I'll hand you over to him, dear.'

'Dad? Mum sounds ever so much better.'

'Yes, she is.' Avril could hear the smile in his voice and she could visualize the tenderness in his eyes. 'We've had a wonderful day together.'

'I'm so glad,' she said fervently. 'Aunt Megan has asked us to stay to supper after the milking. What do you think? Should we get home?'

'No. You make the most of the day, Avril – as we have done my dear. I will help Ruth to bed when she's ready.'

'All right. We'll see you later then. Aunt Megan thinks I should get the boys ready for bed before we leave in case they sleep in the car.'

'That's a good idea. I'll come out and carry them in if they nod off. Once they're asleep they're like logs, there's no wakening them.'

'See you later then.' She turned as Aunt Megan came through to the hall to call everyone for afternoon tea before the milking began. 'Mum sounds really bright,' she said in a bemused tone. 'I couldn't believe it, and Dad says they've had a wonderful day together.'

'That's good then, Avril. Sometimes . . .' She hesitated and frowned a little. 'Sometimes when people are very ill they do have little rallying spurts. I'm really pleased they've had this day together,' she added softly. 'Right everybody!' she called briskly. 'Tea is ready.'

The twins had had a hectic day and they were asleep almost as soon as they got into the car, snuggled together under the rug which Dean had brought in case they were cold.

'I've had a lovely day,' Avril said softly. 'I'm so glad you came with us, Dean. I think I ought to feel guilty about leaving Mum, but I don't somehow.'

'No, you shouldn't feel guilty at all. For one thing we both know it is not what your mother or your father would want. For another thing, Avril, I think you're tremendous the way you manage your brothers and the household and care for your mother so unselfishly. Not many girls could do it, even if they were willing.'

'Oh Dean, I'm no saint,' Avril said, but she was glad it was too dark for him to see the flush of pleasure in her cheeks. 'Did you enjoy looking round the farm with Uncle Steven and Samuel?'

'I did. I have enjoyed the whole day. I had a long talk with your Uncle. It seems I'm not the only one who has family problems. He was telling me he had a half brother who was older than him and when he came out of the army his brother didn't want him back at the farm. He said he felt it was like the end of all his dreams at the time. That's why he started off in one of the government smallholdings. He said they'd had a lot of ups and downs and he couldn't have managed without Megan to help him, and some money from his mother to get started, but he thinks it was all for the best the way things have turned out. He reckons if he had stayed at Willowburn with his parents and brother he would never have ended up at Bengairney with a good sized dairy herd and a bright future for Samuel to follow in his footsteps.'

'I remember visiting Aunt Megan often at the smallholding. I loved to go. That was before Mum and Dad got married. They always seemed so happy but when you're a child you don't see the problems.'

'No, you're right. I don't remember my own mother nagging the way she does now, at least not until I was about eight and announced I wanted to be a farmer. Anyway Steven has given me something to think about.'

'Frustration is an awful thing,' Avril said softly, putting her hand on his arm and stroking it in sympathy, 'especially for someone who is young and ambitious and ready for a challenge.'

'I'm glad you understand, Avril. I doubt if anyone else would, even Uncle Bill.'

Dean had felt a tenderness for Avril for a long time but when she went to university he had tried to forget her, believing she would have a brilliant career and probably never return to live at Riverview, or anywhere near. Yet here she was sacrificing her career to care for her mother. It was true she already had her degree and she seemed to have a good job under Doctor Lever, but would it be enough once her mother no longer needed her? Would she go away again? He thought of the words of the musical he had been to see – 'Nothing venture, nothing gain'.

He drew the car gently to a halt in front of the house and turned to face Avril. In the faint light he saw her smile as she turned to him.

'Thank you for a lovely day, Dean.' She leaned forward to kiss his cheek but he turned his head so that his mouth met hers. It was a gentle, lingering kiss and to Dean's delight she did not draw away from him. He put his arm around her and held her closer.

'It has been the best day of my life,' he murmured as he kissed her again more firmly. They were both a little shaken as they drew apart.

'Do you still want me to come down to see you, Avril?'

'Yes, of course I do,' she said a trifle breathlessly, 'if it's what you want.'

'It is,' he said softly. 'Now we'd better get Callum and Craig inside. I'll carry one of them.'

'All right, thanks. I'll open the door to let Dad know we're home. Can you manage to take him straight upstairs, second door on the left. Mum is right at the end so you'll not disturb her.'

Dean did as she asked and her father came out immediately to carry Craig.

'Thank you, Dean.' Lint whispered as he removed the dressing gowns from his sons and kissed them goodnight.' They barely stirred. 'I'll follow you down. Would you like a nightcap?'

'Thanks, but I'd better be getting home. Avril will be tired, but we have had a lovely day.' He spoke softly as he went downstairs. Avril was waiting at the bottom.

'Both sound asleep,' Lint said. 'I'm pleased to hear you have had an enjoyable day. Your mother has had a good day too – much better than she's been recently and you left us a delicious lunch, Avril.' He laid an affectionate arm around her shoulders. 'She's quite a cook you know, Dean.'

'I can imagine,' Dean said with a smile. 'All the women around her seem to be good cooks so it must have rubbed off.'

'You must come and sample some of it soon then. What do you say, Avril?'

'Yes, of course, if you feel up to it, Dean.'

'What about Friday evening then? It's New Year's Eve and unless there's an emergency I'm not due back at the hospital until Monday. What do you say, Avril?'

'That would suit me. I'm working from tomorrow but I shall be off by lunchtime Friday until after New Year.'

Dean thanked them both and Avril went with him to the car. She was not disappointed; he drew her into his arms and kissed her tenderly, reluctant to let her go.

His heart was singing as he drove home. None of the girls he knew had attracted him as Avril did. He had always had a tenderness for her and when she had to go away to stay in the hostel to study for her higher grade exams at Dumfries Academy he had missed her terribly. Even then he had known it was more than tenderness he felt. He had almost wished she was not so clever, then she would not go away to university. It was a selfish thought and he knew it was unworthy of anyone who really cared for her. Even so he had known each step in her career took her further out of his reach. Her mother's illness was a terrible thing and he would never have wished for it, but it had brought Avril back home, and Mr Gray didn't seem to mind him keeping her company, in fact it was he who had initiated the invitation to share a meal with them on Hogmanay. His spirits soared and he was humming merrily as he entered the house.

As soon as he saw his mother waiting in the kitchen irritation replaced his happy mood.

'Where d'you think you've been all day?' she demanded, 'shirking frae the work, leaving your father to do it on his own.' Dean sighed heavily. One of these days his mother would put him off ever returning. Why did his own home seem so unwelcoming? Down at Riverview Ruth Gray was dying and yet her home was still filled with warmth and love.

Five

It was more than a New Year's resolution which made Dean vow he must live his life the way he wanted. He was no longer a schoolboy needing to account for every minute of his time and everything he spent. It was time to make a stand, but he had no inkling of how drastic that stand would prove to be.

Avril and her family welcomed him warmly on New Year's Eve. Ruth had slept a lot during the day and in the evening Lindsay helped her downstairs in her dressing gown. Dean hoped his face did not show the shock he felt at her appearance, but she still had the same sweet smile and when she wished him all that was good for the year ahead he knew her wishes were sincere. Her warmth and acceptance of him made him feel more confident about trying to win Avril's love, if only he had some prospects. He knew she regarded him as a valued friend but he wanted more than friendship. Her parents were not superior or snobbish as his mother believed. They didn't seem to mind that he was the son of a tenant farmer rather than a doctor or other professional with a university education. Farming was in his blood and even at Northsyke he felt he could make improvements if only he were allowed some leeway. He had to have something worthwhile to offer a girl like Avril, some prospects for a brighter future. He didn't blame his father for wanting a peaceful life and however much his mother nagged and interfered, his father did need her to care for him and run his household, even though she didn't always consider his needs before her own obsession.

Dean saw that Avril's mother was very tired by eleven o'clock so he elected not to wait for Big Ben to herald 1966. The new year would arrive whether he waited up for it or not but he felt a surge of yearning and expectancy. A new year was a time to be resolute. It was up to him to make changes happen in his own life. As he drove home he considered the ideas which constantly filled his head. He dreamed of the progress he longed to make and a future which included Avril. He considered his mother's obduracy, her determination that everything should stay the same – no expansion, no increase in production; a wave of frustration swamped him. Surely she must see you had to spend a little money to make a little more. The estate was on an even keel again with the death duties settled and a younger laird and a new agent. Even if they could not offer financial help they must surely welcome modernization. Silently he acknowledged that his own ambition was to have a dairy farm but his father's interest had always been sheep and training his dogs. He excelled at that.

On Sunday, the ninth of January, Ruth died peacefully just before dawn. Lindsay had sat with her through the past few nights but around four o' clock he wakened Avril. Her first thoughts were how grey and haggard her father looked. She scrambled into her dressing gown and slippers. She shivered in spite of the central heating which her father had insisted on installing as soon as he realized her mother's illness was serious. The cold was within her and no physical comforts could dispel it.

'Oh Mama, Mama,' she murmured as she knelt beside the bed and held her mother's hand in both of hers. Ruth was too weak to open her eyes but Avril felt the faint pressure of her fingers and was comforted.

'She knows we are here with her, my dear,' Lint said wearily. 'She senses our presence and she is not suffering any pain now.' Avril nodded silently. She was too choked with tears to speak. They were like a stone in her throat and chest as she strove to hold them back. A few minutes later Ruth gave a little smile, then one last long sigh. Avril glanced across at her father and he nodded silently. He was struggling to control his emotion but Avril could no longer hold back her own tears and he came round the bed and drew her to her feet and into his arms, stroking her hair and murmuring to her as though she was a child again. Eventually she found the strength to draw away and dry her tears.

'I–I'm sorry,' she whispered. 'It – it's just so – so final.'

'Yes,' Lint said quietly. 'That's it – final.' Avril sensed he was struggling for self-control and that he needed to be alone now.

'I shall be all right in a minute,' she said with a little sob. 'I know Mum would want me to be strong for the boys' sakes.'

'We'll tell them together but not until after breakfast,' Lint said, almost glad to have a decision to make.

When she heard the news of Ruth's death Molly Scott came down to Riverview and took the twins back to Sylvanside for the day.

'It will be better to keep them occupied,' she said. 'Bill will tire them out. And Avril, you know I'll be glad to help in any way I can – with a funeral tea, or looking after the boys. Just ask me when you've decided what to do, lassie.'

'Th–thank you,' Avril said, her dark eyes swimming with tears as she tried to hold them back for the sake of her young brothers. She knew the full implication of their mother's death had not sunk in yet, though they had both looked frightened when they saw the doctor leaving and heard him mention a death certificate.

After lunch, which neither of them could eat, Avril felt an overwhelming need to see Dean, to feel the comfort of his strong arms and see the kindness and understanding in his blue eyes. Her father was waiting for the minister who had promised to call during the afternoon. She tugged on her boots and buttoned up her winter coat, tucked her long honey-gold hair into a woollen hat and pulled on a pair of gloves. She looked up at the wide expanse of grey skies and scudding clouds and began to walk briskly in the cold January air. Instead of heading for the copse where they usually met Avril took the fork in the track which led straight to the farmyard. She heard the rustle of straw and movements of cattle coming from the old stone fold yard and she turned towards it. Mrs Scott saw her through the kitchen window. Quick as lightning she yanked open the back door and hurried across the yard to reach Avril before she could enter the shed.

'What d'you think you're doing here at this time of day?' she demanded. 'Skulking around like a thief!' Avril gasped.

'I came to see Dean.'

'To see Dean indeed! Don't you know the animals are housed in winter and they have to be fed? What would your boss say if Dean came to your hospital while you were working?' Avril stared at the hard grey eyes and pursed-up mouth. All her thoughts had been concentrated on seeing Dean but now her attention focused on his mother, confronting her with hands on hips waiting for an answer.

'Actually I think my boss would be understanding if the circumstances were special,' she said, her voice low but clear. She met Mrs Scott's eyes and wondered why the woman seemed to dislike her.

'Oh actually!' Grizel mocked, with a scathing sniff. 'You think—'

'Avril!' Dean came hurrying out of the shed, a fork in his hands, his face alight with welcome. He was wearing blue bib and brace overalls but his sleeves were rolled above his elbows in spite of the cold day. 'I thought I heard voices—' He broke off as Avril turned to face him. He guessed at once why she had come to the farm, what she had come to say. 'Oh, Avril . . .' He murmured softly and moved as though to take her in his arms. She had thought her tears were frozen inside her like a heavy block of ice, but at Dean's gentle tone she felt her eyes fill and willed the tears not to spill in front of Mrs Scott's gimlet glare. 'Mother,' he turned towards her, 'I think Avril has come to tell me—'

'I ken fine why she's come but she has no business disturbing ye at your work. She should have waited until ye'd finished for the day.'

'Ach, Mother you don't understand,' Dean said impatiently.

'I understand the beasts need fed, even if it is the Sabbath day. What does she expect you to do because her mother is dead?'

'You knew?' Dean's eyes widened. 'How . . . ?'

'Ach! Molly phoned after breakfast.' She raised her head defiantly and glared at him.

'Aunt Molly phoned to tell me? You knew before dinner! Why didn't you pass on her message?' Dean's eyes narrowed and his mouth set. Aunt Molly realized he would want to know, and that he would go to see Avril. 'We shall talk about this later,' he said coldly. He took Avril's arm and drew her away.

'Where do you think you're going?' Grizel demanded angrily.

'I've fed the bullocks. Old Jim will help father finish the rest of the stock,' he snapped and led Avril towards the tractor on the other side of the yard. He retrieved his jacket and pulled it on.

'When, Avril?' he asked softly.

'Early this morning. About five o'clock. Dad and I were with her.' Dean's heart filled with tenderness, she sounded so lost and forlorn. He opened his arms and she went into them like a small bird needing refuge from the storm. He held her gently against his chest and Avril felt the strength and warmth of him and the rough tweed of his jacket against her cheek and she knew this is what she had needed so badly. She had known Dean would understand how empty she felt. After a little while he asked, 'Do you want to walk or shall we take the tractor and go over to Aunt Molly's?'

'Have you time? I don't want to cause any trouble.'

'You're not the one who will ever cause me trouble, Avril. Which is it to be?'

'I'll come on the tractor with you, then you'll have it to get back here. I needed a walk and I can walk home from Sylvanside. The boys are there. Your Aunt Molly has been wonderful. She collected them first thing this morning.'

'How have they taken the news?'

'Craig wanted to know if his Mummy would be in heaven now. But Callum —' her voice shook — 'Callum said he was glad she was with the angels, b—but then he turned to me and he said —' her voice broke — 'he — he said you'll never leave us will you, Avril? Not even to see the angels?' Then he ran into my arms and sobbed. 'They're so alike in looks but in some ways they are so different. I promised I would never leave them as long as they need me, and they need me more than ever now. Dad too. He looks completely shattered.'

'I understand, Avril,' Dean said quietly. 'And I think you're being very brave, but you need to grieve too and I'm here for you whenever you need me. I promise.' He wished passionately that he could rely on his mother to welcome her or at least pass on messages.

Molly Scott heard the tractor draw into the yard and was at the door to greet them. She took one look at Avril and opened her arms.

'There, my lamb. There,' she soothed, cradling Avril against her ample bosom and rocking her like a child. Her kindness and sympathy released Avril's pent-up tears and Molly Scott drew her into the big warm kitchen and settled her in a chair beside the fire. 'The twins are outside with Bill,' she said. 'I'll put the kettle on now for a wee cup of tea.'

'I'll just wash my hands in the scullery, Aunt Molly,' Dean called, kicking off his boots at the back door.

'You've come straight frae the farmyard?' Molly popped her head round the door and raised her eyebrows. Dean nodded. 'I didn't get your message,' he said quietly, his mouth tightening.

It was some time later, after they had all had tea, when Avril rose.

'I ought to be getting home and I've kept Dean from his work too long already,' she said.

'Oh Avril, we don't want to leave yet,' Callum wailed.

'We havena helped Aunt Molly Scott feed the wee calves,' Craig protested.

'Leave them here a wee while longer,' Molly Scott said. 'I'll give them their supper after we've finished milking then Bill will run them home in the car. They'll be so tired they'll be glad to get to bed.' She met Avril's eyes over the top of the boys' heads.

'All right, if you're sure you don't mind?' Avril agreed.

'I'm sure, lassie. And I'll be there to help Bessie with the teas after the church service, as we've arranged. I'll bring the boys back to Riverview with me then while the rest of you go to the crematorium.'

'We'll never be able to repay you for all your kindness,' Avril said.

'We need no payment except to see the smiles on the faces of these two rascals. It does both of us good to have their company.'

'Molly's right, lassie,' Bill Scott said gruffly, 'We enjoy having them.'

It was only a short walk across the paddock to Riverview but Dean said, 'You'll come with me on the tractor as far as the road, will you Avril?' She nodded. The January day was already darkening.

Just before they reached the road Dean stopped the tractor and jumped down, holding out a hand to help Avril. Silently he drew her against his chest and she laid her cheek against the lapel of his old tweed jacket and found comfort in the earthy scents of it. There was no need for words between them as he stroked her hair. Eventually she straightened with a sigh.

'Remember I shall come whenever you need me, Avril,' he said softly. 'I don't know why my mother can't be more like Aunt

Molly. I can't rely on her. Leave me a message under a stone beside the old beech tree. I'll meet you at the copse or come to your house, whichever, and whenever, you say. All right?' He tilted her chin.

'I will, Dean. And thank you for being such a good friend.'

'I hope I shall always be that, Avril.' He bent and kissed her cheek then gently brushed her lips with his.

Ruth had stated that she wanted to be cremated, which meant going to Carlisle to the nearest crematorium. The Reverend Paterson suggested they should hold a service in the church for everyone who wanted to attend, followed by the cremation with only close friends and family.

'Your wife was very well liked and respected, Mr Gray. Many of the parents from the school, as well as fellow church members, have expressed a wish to pay their last respects.' Lindsay agreed wearily to all the suggestions. Even so both he and Avril were taken aback to see the old Kirk full to capacity. Grizel Scott stared in disbelief. Doris was at home with a heavy cold and Sydney was in bed with a temperature and a nasty cough so Dean had been surprised when his mother insisted on attending the funeral with him. He hadn't told her Ruth was to be cremated; it was one more thing she would disapprove of, even though it was none of her business. After the service they all stood to the side of the path to allow the main mourners to assemble. A young woman on the other side of Grizel blew her nose hard and wiped away her tears.

'She was such a lovely person,' she muttered brokenly.

'You knew her well?' Grizel asked curiously, knowing the woman was not local.

'Oh yes. She taught my wee girl when she was at Annan. She was a single mother herself so she understood when Wendy kept refusing to go to school or to do her lessons after we lost her daddy. *Miss* Vernon she was then, she was ever so patient and she gave her extra lessons. Now Wendy is at college and training to be a teacher herself, thanks to Ruth. We owe her a lot.'

'You said she was a single mother?' Grizel asked sharply. 'You called her Miss? Surely she was Mrs Gray?' Dean's heart sank as he heard his mother quizzing the stranger. The woman seemed to become aware that her interest was more than casual too. She turned to look at her and was reminded of a bird of prey she had seen at a wildlife park as it dived to catch its food – beak pointed, eyes sharp and cold. The young woman frowned. 'We were all very happy for Ruth when we heard she and Mr Gray were getting married,' she said coldly and moved away. Grizel watched her with narrowed eyes until her attention was caught by her sister-in-law.

'What's Molly doing in her car?' she demanded watching her get into the driver's seat of Avril's car.

'Aunt Molly is taking the boys back to Riverview. She's going to help Bessie with the funeral tea,' he said. 'Uncle Bill is driving their car to the crematorium. I'm getting a lift with him so I'd better get a move on. We need to follow the other mourners.'

'You're going with Bill?' Grizel asked indignantly. 'What about me?'

'I've given you the car keys, Mother. You can drive home surely?'

'Oh can I? If you're going to the crematorium, I'm coming with you.'

'You can't do that. It's only for close friends and family.'

'You're going, and leaving me here?'

'Yes, Mother. I didn't ask you to come. In fact you've neither sympathy nor respect for any of the Gray family so I'm surprised you wanted to come, especially when father is ill. Now I must be off. Uncle Bill's looking for me.' He hurried away, leaving his mother puffing out her chest like an old hen about to fight another one, but there was no other combatant at hand.

Grizel's mouth set in a thin line. 'Umph,' she muttered several times. Molly would have the run of the house while they were away, poking her nose in. Well she was a mourner too. She would go to the funeral tea. She'd been curious to see inside Riverview, or whatever they'd called it, ever since the Grays moved in. She knew they had made a great many alterations. At the time all the local tradesmen had been impressed with the improvements and said what a fine house it was when they'd finished.

Molly was surprised and flustered when she heard a car draw up so soon. She reckoned it would be an hour and a half before they all came back from the crematorium and she and Bessie wanted to have everything laid out and ready. She had been unable to hold back her tears at the Kirk and she felt as tense as a watch spring, which was unusual for her. She couldn't believe her eyes when she saw her sister-in-law get out of the car. She came straight into the house at the front door without so much as a knock or a ring at the bell.

'What are you doing, coming marching in here?' Molly demanded.

'I've as much right to be here as anyone else, including you! I expect you think you are somebody, lording it over everything while he's not here.'

'You know very well it's only close friends and family, or people who have travelled a distance, who will be expected for the tea. The Kirk was crammed full but nobody else expects to be fed. Why should you? Anyway I thought you'd want to be getting home to Sydney when he's ill in bed.'

'Doris can look after him.' Grizel was already craning her neck this way and that trying to peer into a large sitting room, then into the kitchen.

'Surely there's no one here for tea already, is there?' Bessie asked, coming through to the hall with a tray of glasses on her way to the dining room. Upstairs Molly could hear the twins and Alexander Caraford clattering around. She had sent them to change out of their best clothes hoping they would play in the garden while the adults ate their meal, and Tania Caraford had been nervous about going to the crematorium so she had come back with them and she was now in the small sitting room. Molly didn't want the children thinking she had taken advantage and invited her sister-in-law here to nose around, and she guessed that was the only reason Grizel had come. She knew instinctively that Avril would not have invited her. Dean would be angry if he found her here on his return.

'We have not got the food ready yet,' she said. 'It will be at least an hour and I'm sure you don't want to wait that long, Grizel.'

'Oh I don't mind waiting. I'll just have a look around.' Molly's tension increased as Grizel stepped forward to peer into the dining room as Bessie was coming out. Bessie had never liked Mrs Scott from Northsyke and she shut the door firmly behind her. Grizel gave an angry sniff and lifted her chin. 'Well you can hardly grudge me using the toilet,' she announced and made towards the staircase.

'No we don't. I'll show you the way,' Bessie said and moved to the side, preventing her setting foot on the stairs. 'It's round this corner underneath the stairs.' There was a small cloakroom there with toilet and wash hand basin and a row of pegs for coats. It was not the fancy bathroom which Grizel had heard the plumber talking about. Molly knew her sister-in-law well and she hovered in the hall until she came out. She felt uncomfortable having her in the house at all.

'Well aren't you going to take me into the kitchen for a cup of tea?' she demanded.

'No Grizel, I am not. Bessie and I have plenty to do before everybody gets back. If you had wanted to come into the house you could have come and offered your sympathy when Mr Gray and Avril were at home, like the rest of the neighbours did.'

'I expect they only came out of curiosity,' said Grizel with a sniff.

'People are genuinely sorry about Ruth's death. She was an asset to the church and to the school. She was always sewing costumes for their school plays and volunteering to help the slower children to learn. Why do you think there were so many people there today? That ought to tell you she was well respected and how badly she will be missed.' Molly rarely lost her temper but she could feel herself getting more and more worked up by Grizel's scornful sniffs and snide remarks, not to mention the way her beady eyes were darting around everywhere.

'Respected was she?' Grizel sneered, 'Well I learned something today. She was not the saint you think she was, Molly Scott. She was an unmarried mother when she lived in Annan. That girl is not the daughter of a surgeon at all. She could be the bastard of a gypsy for all we know. Your fine Mister Gray is not her father. I'll bet she doesn't know who her father is,' she crowed triumphantly, watching Molly's face turn pale.

'Mr Gray adopted Avril when he married her mother,' Molly said as calmly as she could. 'Bill and I have known that since the day they came here. As far as I'm concerned he is her father now and he loves her as much as he loves his sons.'

'You knew he was not her real father?' Grizel demanded accusingly. 'You knew she was a bastard and you encouraged my boy to be friends with her. You—you're no better than she is – was.' She was furious to think Molly had known all along and never told her.

'For goodness' sake, Grizel, Dean knew Avril was adopted. Mr

Gray is the only father she has ever known and she loves him. Dean likes her for herself, not her pedigree.'

'Bah humbug! We shall see how much he loves the cuckoo in his nest and who he favours now. Whatever happens she needn't think she'll get her claws into Dean or get her hands on my money. I'll put a stop to all that, you see if I don't.'

'Grizel control yourself. You'll lose Dean altogether if you carry on dictating to him. He has a mind of his own and he has genuine affection for Avril – maybe even more than affection for all we know. She's a lovely-natured lassie, and clever too.'

'I'll show her who is clever,' Grizel snapped. 'I'm not having my son marrying a bastard who doesn't know who her father is. He might have been a German prisoner of war! He might have been a thief, or a—'

'Aye and he might have been the King of Siam!' Molly snapped. 'Pull yourself together, Grizel and stop talking nonsense or you'll drive Dean away altogether.'

'He knows which side his bread is buttered,' Grizel declared confidently. 'He'll not leave a good home for her. Anyway she wouldn't want him if he was only a labourer.'

'I wouldn't put it to the test if he was my son,' Molly said. 'Dean is a man now and you've thwarted and frustrated him long enough. Now I think it's time you went home and calmed down.'

'I don't know who you think you are to order me around, Molly Scott. You needn't get above yourself because you own a bit of land, and you needn't come whining to us when you can't pay the bank interest.'

Molly gasped and stared open-mouthed for a moment. 'We don't owe a single penny to anybody but if we did you'd be the last person I should ask for help, Grizel. Now get out of here before I really lose my temper with you,' she said tightly. Bessie slid past her and opened the front door.

'It's this way, Mrs Scott,' she said and held the door open. Grizel had no option but to go through it with Molly barring her way into the house and Bessie looking ready to pick her up bodily and put her out. She strode through the door, her head high, but she was seething inwardly.

'You'll regret your high and mighty airs, Molly Scott,' she called in a parting shot.

'Whew,' Molly muttered and breathed a sigh of relief as Bessie closed the door firmly behind her.

'You can say that again. She's getting worse in her old age,' Bessie said. 'She caused enough trouble when she was a member of the Rural. We were all pleased when she took a huff and left. Now we'd better get cracking before everybody gets back.'

'Yes, you're right,' Molly agreed, but her mind was on Dean and Avril. She knew Grizel was both selfish and ruthless. She had proved that in her determination to marry Sydney as the eldest Scott son. She had been disillusioned when the doctors discovered Sydney was diabetic, even though he had never allowed it to hold him back, but Grizel had been bitter ever since. The sad thing was Sydney had really loved her, and probably still did. How else could he have put up with her? What devious scheme would she hatch to come between the young couple, especially now, when Avril needed a good friend. It troubled her to think that at twenty-one Avril had promised to take on the responsibilities of a mother for her young brothers, even while grieving for her own loss.

Six

Dean ran upstairs to change out of his best suit and white shirt. He would have liked to stay longer with Avril and her family but with his father confined to bed he needed to get home to attend to the animals. His heart sank when he saw his mother waiting for him at the bottom of the stairs. The look on her face told him she had some grouse or other. Even so he was surprised by her abrupt question, although it was more of an accusation.

'You knew Mr Gray is not that girl's father?'

'If you mean Avril, Mother, of course I knew. She was adopted by Mr Gray when he married her mother. Why? What difference does that make?'

Grizel almost spat with fury as she stated her opinion in no uncertain terms, as she had done with Molly earlier.

'So who is her father then?' Doris came to join them in the hall.

'I've no idea, nor can I see that it has anything to do with you,' Dean snapped, losing patience with both his mother and his sister. It was typical of Doris to add fuel to his mother's anger.

'Can't a man be ill in peace,' Sydney croaked from the top of the stairs. 'Grizel, I'm sick of hearing you going on about that bit of gossip you picked up. Can't you let the dead rest in peace?'

'You're as bad as he is, Sydney Scott. You've known all along. It's the living that concerns me and you'll not be so calm if your only son wants to marry a bastard!'

'If I thought there was any chance of Avril marrying me I'd go to her tomorrow whoever her father might be,' Dean snapped. 'No girl in her right senses would want you for a mother-in-law though. Now let me pass. I'm going to get the beasts fed. I'll leave the pigs for Doris to feed since she doesn't seem to do anything else.' He brushed past them and headed for the back door, welcoming the chill January air to cool his anger.

'I'm going back to bed,' Sydney Scott told his wife in a hoarse voice, 'but take my advice for once, Grizel, leave the lad in peace and stop slandering that lassie. I reckon she means more to him than you realize. Remember I went against my mother's wishes when I married you and there's nothing to say he'll not do the same. Be warned.' Grizel scowled at his retreating figure. She didn't like being reminded of her own past. Her father had been a labourer at Northsyke. Old Mr Scott had allowed her mother to stay on in the cottage when he died in return for helping in the house and seasonal work outside. They had always been short of money and Grizel was determined the same thing would not happen to her. It wasn't often Sydney openly criticized her, but she knew he often disagreed with her opinions.

'If you ask me Dad likes her as much as Dean,' Doris muttered, which did nothing to soothe her mother.

One of the bullocks had got his leg stuck through the wooden partition dividing one pen from the next. Dean knew if pulling had been a solution the animal would have freed himself. He spoke softly, rubbing the sensitive bit of his spine where it joined the tail, trying to calm him.

'Jim, I'll need a saw, please? I need to cut a wider gap to release his leg before he breaks it in his efforts to be free. Bobby if you feed the rest of the animals with their turnips it will draw them to the troughs instead of them milling around and knocking this fellow over and me with him.' Both men hurried to do his bidding, respecting his quiet manner and decisive tone. Dean did his best to soothe the frightened beast but he had clearly been stuck for some time, judging by the deep scars and blood running down his leg. It took time and patience but eventually the animal was released, albeit with a badly bruised and swollen leg. They guided him to a single pen to allow him to feed and recover from his ordeal without being bothered by the other bullocks. By the time the rest of the work was done Dean was more than an hour late going in for his supper. At least his Mother would have joined Doris in the room by now, he thought with relief. In the evenings they spent ages watching the television, even when it only showed the black and white test card.

It had been a stressful day. Avril had been very brave but it had been impossible for her to hold back her tears at the crematorium when the twins were no longer there to need her comfort. He had longed to be near her and give her his support. Old Mrs Caraford and Megan had been very upset too; they had known

Ruth a long time. As for Avril's father he had borne up well but he seemed to have aged ten years in as many days. His eyes were hollow and his face looked gaunt.

Dean had been surprised to see Mr Turner from Martinwold at the funeral. He didn't know he had once hoped to welcome Lindsay Gray as his son-in-law if his own daughter had not been so spoiled and selfish. His appearance had sparked a discussion between Steven and Mr Oliphant later when they gathered around the dining table at Riverview. Dean mulled over their comments. He respected the opinions of both men. He had got to know them well while he worked as a student, and lived with the family at Bengairney. His thoughts scattered and he almost groaned aloud when he found his mother sitting at the table waiting for him.

He had barely started to eat his meal before she began firing questions about Avril, ranting furiously when he had no satisfactory answers to offer. He was hungry and he ate in silence, his thoughts moving to Avril and her father. He had almost finished when she banged her fist on the table, making the cruet and cup and saucer jump. 'You can sit there and sulk in silence,' she hissed, 'but I'm telling you I will not have that girl anywhere near here again.'

'There's no fear of that so you can stop raving,' he muttered wearily.

'Raving! I'm telling you for your own good. You deceived me. Even your father knew she was not the surgeon's daughter.'

'You're the only one who thinks it's important. I can't see that it makes any difference, you didn't make her welcome when you thought she was Mr Gray's own flesh and blood.'

'She'll never be welcome. She's a bastard. Do you know who her father is? Does she know? I'm not having any gypsy's brat marrying my son.'

'She is not a gypsy's brat, but even if she was I'd marry her tomorrow if she would have me,' Dean said bitterly. What sane woman would ever want to marry him with a mother like his, he thought bitterly, and what had he to offer? Nothing he could call his own.

'Any more of that talk and you'll be finding fresh lodgings, my boy!' Dean pushed back his chair so violently it clattered to the floor. 'Maybe that's just what I ought to do!' he snapped back. He snatched the car keys from their usual hook and strode out of the house, grabbing his old overcoat as he went.

'Where are you going?' Grizel demanded. There was a trace of alarm in her eyes.

'Anywhere but here,' Dean retorted and shut the door behind him.

Molly Scott sighed when she heard a car draw into the yard. She had had a busy day and a stressful one and she was tired. She got up to glance out of her kitchen window.

'It's the Northsyke car,' she said. Bill had settled down for the evening with his paper on the opposite side of the kitchen range. Molly switched off the little television on the dresser. They cooked and ate and sat in their big kitchen and only used the sitting room on special occasions. 'I half expected there'd be a row over there tonight, the mood Grizel was in. If she'd had any sense she would have kept her own council, especially today. There's been enough sorrow.'

'When did Grizel ever have sense pray?' Bill asked. 'Sydney will still be recovering frae the flu so I expect it will be Dean seeking a bit o' respite frae her sharp tongue. Come in, laddie,' he called, 'the door's never locked as ye should know by now.'

'Have you had your supper, Dean?' Molly asked.

'Yes, I've just finished. We had a bullock with his leg stuck so I was late in.'

His uncle eyed him intently. 'But not so late your mother got tired o' waiting to deliver one o' her sermons, eh lad?'

'No, not late enough for that,' Dean said heavily. There were no smiles, no glint of laughter in his blue eyes tonight Molly noticed. In fact his face looked set, almost grim for such a young man.

'Your mother must have been talking to one o' the other mourners at the Kirk,' she said slowly. 'She came to Riverview after the service. She was going on a bit because she'd only just learned Avril is adopted.'

'She had the cheek to go to the Grays' house?' Dean asked in angry surprise. 'Why did she go there? She has never expressed a word of sympathy for them, not even for the wee fellows, losing their mother while they're so young.'

'I've never known Grizel have any sympathy for anybody except herself,' his uncle said dryly.

'I can't stand much more,' Dean muttered. 'I only came back home after college because Father wanted me to. Recently I've been thinking he could manage easily enough with Bobby and Jim to help him if he stops growing corn and reduces the number of ewes. What do you think, Uncle Bill?'

'I reckon he could manage but he enjoys your company, lad.' He eyed his nephew shrewdly, noting the angry flush which still lingered on Dean's cheeks, and the disillusion in his eyes.

'He might like my company but not enough to make any changes to make it worth me staying. There's four of us to keep, as well as the two men to pay. Father finds satisfaction with his dogs. He's training two collies for men he knows and he's talking of breeding from Ben and rearing one or two collies to train and sell.'

'Aye the sheep dogs have always been his real interest,' Bill acknowledged. 'He's good at it too.'

'I know.' Dean sighed. 'I think he's disappointed I haven't inherited his talent.'

'Your grandfather was pretty good but I didn't inherit the gift either. I always liked dairy cows best, so you're like me, Dean.'

'If we had a dairy herd at Northsyke maybe I'd feel some satisfaction,' Dean said bitterly. 'I'd be doing the extra work but it would bring in more income.'

'Do you want to know what I think, laddie?' Bill asked slowly, reaching for his pipe and his tobacco pouch from the mantle shelf.

'I always value your opinion, Uncle Bill,' Dean said. 'You know that.'

'Aye.' Bill hesitated, frowning. 'The way you look tonight, laddie, I reckon it's a good job your father has not spent his capital to put on a dairy herd at Northsyke.'

'You never thought it was a bad idea before.' Dean's voice was sharp with disappointment. 'I know Northsyke is not ideal for a dairy but you've always said it pays better than the beef and sheep, even though it's a lot more work.'

'That's true, but I reckon your father knew there was a risk your mother would drive you away with her nagging and her need to be in control, then where would he be with a dairy herd he never wanted.'

'It's come close to that tonight,' Dean muttered.

'I thought so.' Bill Scott nodded. 'And I canna blame ye. Grizel was always possessive but she's got worse. Your father is tied to her and he's more dependent on her than he might have been if he'd had better health, but you're a free man.'

'I don't feel free. Mother keeps her beady eye on everything.'

'Maybe, but you'll want to marry one day. Grizel will never welcome the lass, whoever she is. If you were milking cows seven days a week you'd need to live on the spot. You couldn't ask a young wife to move in with Grizel and I don't see her—'

'Good lord, no!' Dean exploded.

'Your father knows that, and he realizes a young man needs to run his own life.'

'Then why can't mother understand that? The way I feel tonight I could leave home and never return!' Dean said grimly. 'In fact I'm thinking about it!'

'Then be thankful your father didna spend his capital equipping a dairy and buying in dairy cows. You'd have felt compelled to stay then, and your mother would have reminded you about the money at every opportunity. If you're going to leave better to do it now. As you say, Sydney could manage without you if he cuts back a bit.'

'I see what you're getting at,' Dean said slowly, 'and you're right.' He sighed heavily. 'Mother has such a vicious tongue. She's calling Avril a bastard and going on and on about her father. Avril has never done her any harm.'

'I had enough of that from her today,' Molly said. 'I nearly lost my temper with her. But what would you do, Dean, if you left home? I often wished you'd been my laddie. You'd be more than welcome to come to us but that would cause a terrible rift in the family. I can't say I'm worried about your mother for we've never got on, but your father and Bill have always been close.'

'Don't worry, Aunt Molly,' Dean said, 'I wouldn't involve you in a family quarrel. I heard Steven Caraford and his father-in-law talking about Martinwold at the funeral tea this afternoon. They were saying Mr Turner is looking for another dairyman to take over his herd. Maybe I should try for something like that. The money is good and the experience would be beneficial.'

'Martinwold,' Bill Scott said slowly. 'That's where John Oliphant and his wife used to work isn't it?'

'Yes. Steven's wife, Megan, spent her childhood there until she married. Mr Oliphant said Mr Turner had always demanded high standards but he was a good boss and a fair man. He keeps up with the times too. He's converted his byre into a milking parlour and the cows sleep in cubicles in a big shed. They can walk about freely and feed from silage when they want instead of being tethered in their stalls.'

'That's certainly a change from carting hay and turnips to them in the byre, the way we do, and mucking out twice a day,' Bill mused. 'I don't like to think o' ye working as a farm labourer though, Dean, but it would be grand training at a place like that.'

'Experience is what I need,' Dean agreed. 'I don't want to stay a labourer for the rest o' my days though. I'd like to rent a farm of my own some day. The trouble is I've never had a wage so I've no money of my own for anything. It didn't matter much before; I've had all I needed in food and clothes and the use of the car, but when it comes to setting up house I need money.'

Bill was silent for a while, drawing on his pipe while he sorted out his thoughts.

'It's always been the way for most farmers' sons, at least in my day. We never got a wage but we knew our fathers would try to set us up in a rented farm when the time came, and then we'd be on our own and have a chance to make our mark. Maybe things are changing now. You've worked hard since you came home from college and I reckon your father will help you if you get a wee farm to rent. Sydney will not let your mother rule the roost over something as important as that. He told me they had enough money in the bank to buy Northsyke as sitting tenants. Maybe he was right about not buying it though if he guessed you might not stay.'

'You'd need to make an appointment to see Mr Turner,' Molly said, 'if you're seriously considering the job.'

'Aye, why don't you phone now, from here?' Bill urged 'At least you'll know if the job has gone.'

'Oh it hasn't gone. He hasna advertised yet,' Dean said. Then more eagerly, 'Would you mind if I use your phone?'

'Go ahead,' Molly said. 'You'll need the directory to look up the number. It's on the shelf below the phone.'

When Dean had gone into the hall Molly said quietly, 'I hope

Sydney willna be too upset, or think we've put him up to this, even if we have encouraged him a bit.'

'Sydney willna blame us, or Dean. So long as he has his dogs I reckon he'll jog along until he's age to retire, then he'll give up the tenancy if Dean doesna want it. He might be relieved if Dean can make his own way into dairy farming. I'm convinced Syd would put his foot down with Grizel if he was convinced he was making the right move. I'm certain he'll help Dean if he does get the tenancy of a dairy farm.'

'Maybe you're right. You always had more ambition than Sydney, even before he had the diabetes. That gave him a real shock.'

'It gave us all a shock. Remember we thought he was a goner a couple of times when he landed in hospital.'

'I used to think Grizel had her eye on you but she set out to get Sydney because he was the eldest son. I reckon she regretted that when he developed the diabetes.'

'Well I haven't! I wouldn't have married Grizel if she'd been the last woman on earth,' Bill declared. 'There was only one lassie I wanted and you know who she is.'

'Aye, we've been lucky together, even though I've never managed to give ye any bairnies, Bill. Grizel thought we were crazy to buy our farm. She'll never forgive us for becoming landowners.'

'She has no need to be jealous. They could have sold Northsyke with vacant possession and made a good profit. Even the good Lord can't manufacture extra land so it will always be in demand, even if the price does fluctuate a bit.'

Dean came back into the kitchen, his face flushed and his eyes bright.

'I'm to go for an interview on Saturday afternoon. Mr Turner says he prefers a married man but he'll consider me because he knows Steven Caraford thought highly of me when I was a student at Bengairney. He asked if I'd mind having Samuel to stay in the house with me when he starts as a student next June, if I got the job.'

'And would you?' Molly asked.

'Not a bit. We got on well when I lived at Bengairney for a year. It would be company.' His eyes clouded and he frowned. 'If I do get it the problem will be buying some furniture to get by. I'd need a bed and a chair and a table at least.'

'We could let you have a bed, Dean, and I've plenty of blankets and a spare eiderdown,' Molly offered.

'We'd better wait and see whether he gets the job first, Molly,' Bill warned. 'If you do get it, Dean, and if you're sure it's what you want, we'll lend you a couple of hundred pounds to tide you over. You'll need food and clothes and coal to see you through until your first pay day.'

'Aye, it'll not be easy,' Molly said slowly. 'You'll have your own meals to make and a cold empty house at the end of the day. Think about it carefully, Dean. I'd hate to see you miserable.'

'I will,' Dean nodded, wondering if he could be any more miserable than he was at home.

Seven

Dean lay in bed that night thinking about Avril and her family, knowing how much they would be missing her mother. Had he acted wisely in making an appointment with Mr Turner because he'd lost patience with his mother? Was he foolish to feel so frustrated and unsettled? His thoughts moved to the forthcoming interview. If he was offered the job at Martinwold he would need to live at the farm, yet he had promised Avril he would be here for her if she needed him.

His mind went round in circles. If he continued to work for his parents at Northsyke he would be near to Avril, but what prospects did he have? What could he offer a girl with her education and background if their friendship blossomed into the love he longed for. Working at Martinwold would mean having more cash in his own name than he had ever had and he would gain valuable experience managing a large dairy herd, and working in some of the most modern premises in the area. But the cows would not be his own. Would he still feel the same frustration when he couldn't do things his own way? Was there more of his mother's genes in him than he had realized? He sat bolt upright in bed at the thought. Surely he would not grow into a grumpy old man who moaned and criticized everyone else? Heaven forbid. He lay down again and pulled the blankets over his head. In his heart he knew his greatest doubts were about moving away from Riverview and Avril. So why was he even considering going for an interview? Dean slept badly that night, filled with doubts when waken and troubled by muddled dreams when sleeping.

When he wakened Dean decided he would telephone Steven Caraford and ask his advice about working as a dairyman for Mr Turner, then he would call at Riverview and discuss things with Avril. He telephoned Bengairney while his mother was down at the village collecting the daily paper and other odds and ends. It was Megan who answered and she was immediately enthusiastic when he explained about the interview.

'Steven is just across the yard, Dean. Hang on while I call him in.' Steven was also positive and supportive.

'We've sensed for a while that you needed more of a challenge, Dean. Megan and I always thought you were cut out to be a dairy farmer. If you can get the job at Martinwold it would be excellent experience for a year or two. I'm sure Megan and her parents will agree with me. They always had respect for Mr Turner as a fair employer and I know your own standards are high enough to please him.' He chuckled and added, 'after all you were well trained at Bengairney. Just a minute, Dean, Megan is asking me something.' Dean hung on, waving Doris away irritably when he saw her lingering in the kitchen doorway hoping to overhear his conversation. Then Steven was speaking again. 'Megan suggests you come here for lunch on Saturday before you go for your interview. She's asking if you could bring Avril and the boys with you for the afternoon. What do you think?'

'It's very kind of her and there's nothing I'd like better but I shall need to consult Avril. I suspect she may not want to leave her father on his own so soon. Can we let you know?'

Megan realized Dean was right and she lost no time in telephoning Lint herself. Avril had inherited her mother's kind and considerate nature. She would put Lint and the twins before her own interests at a time like this. Megan had known Ruth and Lint for a long time. She knew neither of them would want Avril to sacrifice her young life, especially when she had already given up her doctorate. She needed friends too. If her friendship with Dean deepened into something more then Megan would be happy for them. She had liked and respected Dean when he had lived with them during his year as a student.

Lint watched Avril as she served their evening meal. Megan was right. He must not allow her to put him and her brothers before her own happiness. She looked pale but her face was calm and gentle as she gave the boys their meat and encouraged them to try the vegetables. She had matured rapidly during the past few months and already the boys looked to her for guidance as they had looked to their mother. Indeed he found himself consulting her on various matters too.

'Avril, my dear,' he said, striving to sound casual, 'I shall be back to my full quota of patients next week. I was wondering if you would mind looking after the boys while I go down to the infirmary for a few hours tomorrow. There are several things I need to check up on as well as some paper work which needs my attention.'

'On a Saturday?' Avril queried. 'Are you sure you feel up to it, Dad?' She looked at him anxiously. She knew he was sleeping badly. She had heard him go downstairs during the night more than once and she suspected the privacy of his bedroom was the only place he could give way to his grief. His face was strained, almost haggard.

'You know some of my colleagues were at the funeral but I feel it might be easier to meet the others while the hospital is relatively quiet. My work has always given me satisfaction and I think it may prove to be my salvation now.'

'Yes, I see,' Avril murmured. 'I think I can understand that. It will be no problem looking after these two rascals, will it boys?'

Later that evening Dean knocked at the door soon after the twins were in bed. Lint had read them a story and tucked them up as he did every night but instead of joining Avril in the sitting room he had gone straight to the small room he called his study. Dean was pleased they were alone for a while as it gave him a chance to explain about his interview and the reasons he had applied for the job.

'Oh Dean, I'm sure I am the cause of any trouble. I shouldn't have disturbed you at work.'

'Dear Avril, my decision has nothing to do with you coming to Northsyke. Any of my friends should be able to visit me without my mother getting herself into a stew. Please don't blame yourself. I've felt frustrated and stifled ever since I returned from college. I hoped we would make changes and improvements but my father is content the way he is and my mother is against anything which needs money.'

'I've heard Uncle Steven and Aunt Megan say more than once how good you were with their dairy herd.'

'It isn't just that. I don't believe in waiting to step into dead men's shoes. I need to do something for myself. Between my father's health and my mother's avarice I feel stifled. Do you understand, Avril?'

'Yes, I think so. I had no idea you were so unhappy, Dean. I'm really sorry.'

'My only regret is that I shall be so much further away if I get the job at Martinwold and I promised to be here if you need me. I want to be near you, to see you.'

'Oh Dean –' Avril's pale cheeks flushed with pleasure – 'you've always been so thoughtful. Maybe I could call to see you on my way home from work sometimes. It's not much of a detour. Martinwold and Bengairney are much nearer to Dumfries than we are here.' She blushed. 'That is if – if you wanted me to call,' she added uncertainly.

'Avril, I always want to see you,' he said gruffly and moved from his chair to sit beside her on the big settee in front of the fire. He took both her hands in his and looked into her dark eyes. 'I have to tell you though there will not be much comfort in my house if I do get the job. Not for a while anyway. I shall need to buy furniture and stuff and I need to earn some money first. Do you understand?'

'Of course I do, Dean. I have not always had the luxuries which Dad provides for us now,' she said glancing round the comfortable, beautifully furnished room. 'In fact we all had to rough things a bit when we first moved here. Dad and Mum enjoyed the challenge of making this place a home together,' she added sadly. Then on a determinedly brighter note, 'The most important thing is for you to be happy.'

'Well it would make me very happy if you called on me whenever you can. I would really appreciate that,' Dean said softly. Avril looked into his earnest blue eyes and her heart gave a flutter.

'You've always been my best friend, Dean,' she said, 'and now I wonder what I should do if I didn't . . . if I couldn't see you.'

'It's a relief to hear you say that. If you had minded me going to live away I was going to cancel my interview. As it is Megan has asked me to go to lunch with them tomorrow. She asked me to take you and the boys if you would like to come? That is if you are free to come?' he added uncertainly.

'I wouldn't have liked to leave Dad on his own all day but he is going down to the hospital tomorrow so I'd love to come. As for Callum and Craig they always enjoy a visit to Bengairney to play with Alex, or to follow Samuel and Uncle Steven round the farm.'

'That's super!' Neither of them suspected Megan and Lint of manipulation.

Dean arrived to collect them on Saturday morning, helping the boys stow their old coats and wellingtons in the boot of the car and taking care with the box of cheese scones and the fruit loaf which Avril was taking for Megan.

'You seem a wee bit subdued,' he said quietly to Avril as he closed the boot. 'Do you still want to come?'

'Oh yes, I do,' Avril said quickly. 'It's just such a strange feeling, being without Mum. Some of the time I feel as though she's standing beside me in the kitchen; other times the house seems empty because she's not there, even though we're all in it. Then this morning when I wakened I felt happy because we were coming with you to Bengairney, but a bit of me feels guilty for being happy when Mum has just died. I expect you think I'm stupid to feel this way.'

'I'd never think you were stupid whatever you say, Avril. I have no experience of losing someone so dear to me so it would be shallow to say I understand. I remember Grandma Scott after Grandfather died. I was only eight at the time so I didn't understand what she meant then. She said there has to be some rain before we can see the rainbow. She missed Grandfather terribly but she was not sad all the time. I'm certain your mother knew how much you loved her, Avril. You have had the rain and she would want you to enjoy the sunshine now, and the rainbows if you're lucky enough to see them.'

'That's a lovely way of putting it, Dean,' Avril said gratefully. 'And you're right of course. I need—'

'Aren't you two coming,' Callum shouted, knocking on the back window of the car.

Avril smiled. 'I was going to say I need to act as normally as possible for the sake of the boys. '

'Will Rosy be at Bengairney?' Craig asked as soon as they got into the car.

'I don't know,' Avril said smiling, 'but I wouldn't be surprised if she's heard you two are going to be there.'

Rosemary-Lavender was there, prancing up and down with excitement and looking as unlike a flower as it was possible in a pair of badly patched trousers and thick woollen jumper and with her mop of blonde curls bundled into an old Fair Isle tammy. Callum and Craig would have disappeared with her and Alexander immediately but Avril insisted they change into wellingtons and old coats.

'She's far worse than any boy,' Samuel said with an affectionate grin as he and Steven came round the corner from the barn.

'Hey don't disappear too far, you lot,' Steven called, 'It's nearly dinner time and I've a big stick waiting for anyone who is late.' None of the four youngsters paused.

'How are the boys getting on without their mother?' Steven asked, turning to look keenly at Avril.

'They're not too bad so far but it's early days yet. They will be back to school on Monday and I shall be back to work, as will Dad. Bessie is going to meet them from school each day and stay with them until I get home. That suits me better than having her working in the mornings and she says it doesn't matter which end of the day she works so long as she has a wee job to earn some money.'

'At least you know Bessie is reliable,' Steven said gravely. 'I know it's not the same as having their mother at home but young children thrive on a regular routine, much the same as animals.'

'I hope they will,' Avril said fervently.

'Come and see the twin heifer calves, Dean,' Samuel said. 'They were only born an hour ago.'

'I know what you're like, Samuel Caraford,' Avril said with a grin. 'Remember Dean needs to keep his shoes clean until he has been for his interview with Mr Turner.'

'Oh yes, I'd forgotten about that,' Samuel said. 'I do hope you get the job, Dean. It will be great if you're there when I start my student year at the end of June.'

'I'll just put my wellingtons on,' Dean said. 'I'm hoping Mr Turner will show me round the cows and the farm steading.'

'I expect he will but if he doesn't offer you must ask him, laddie,' Steven advised. 'It's always better to show you're interested and I believe Martinwold is worth a look even if you don't get the job.'

Lint decided to leave for the hospital soon after Dean had collected Avril and the boys.

'I'll spread you a cheese scone, Dad,' Avril said. 'They're freshly baked,' she added quickly, knowing he was about to refuse. She worried about his lack of appetite. When he had come downstairs in one of the dark suits he kept for the hospital she realized how much weight he had lost. She spread two scones, leaving them open and each with a generous wedge of cheese on top.

'Goodness Avril, this a is a meal, not an elevenses. They are delicious though,' he admitted after he had demolished one half of a scone. 'Are you taking some to Megan?'

'Yes, I thought I ought to with four extra people to feed. Granny Caraford always baked something to take when Mum and I went with her to visit Aunt Megan at the Schoirhead smallholding.'

'I think it became a custom on account of the food rationing during the war and Mrs Caraford was always a great one for feeding everyone. I'm sure Megan will appreciate your thoughtfulness. I expect young Rosy will be there today as well since it's the weekend.'

Later Lint had good reason to be grateful for Avril's cheese scones. He rarely used the lifts at the hospital and he was making his way up the stairs to the surgical wards when he met Sister Allan coming down.

'Mr Gray! Oh Lint,' she gasped. 'I didn't know they had sent for you as well, but I am so thankful you were able to come, and Mr Burgess will certainly be relieved to see you.'

'No one sent for me. Is there an emergency?'

'Oh yes. There's been a crash at a level crossing. A car with six young people in it stalled on the line I think. The train driver couldn't stop and one of the carriages turned on its side. They're bringing in the injured now but there are at least two fatalities.'

'I see. In that case I'll come with you. I shall need to scrub up and . . .' Already his mind was alert as his training and experience took over. Three hours later Sister Allan brought him a cup of coffee. There were more patients awaiting his attention but he scribbled Megan's telephone number on a notepad. 'Will you ask someone to telephone this number and explain what has happened. Say I may be very late home this evening. I don't want my absence to alarm my daughter or the boys, especially so soon after . . . In the circumstances.'

'I understand. They would be worried. I'll see to it.'

Dean had already left for his interview when the call came

through from the hospital. Megan passed on the message to Avril, explaining that Lint had arrived just as the victims of the crash were being brought in.

'He is operating on the worst cases himself. He didn't want you to be worried if he is delayed, Avril. He may be very late home according to the nurse who telephoned.'

'Oh, I am glad he let us know,' Avril said with feeling. 'I would have been worried, but I know he doesn't like to leave any of his patients until he has made sure they are stable and no complications after he has operated.'

'Well now that we know Lint will not be back you must all stay for supper, that is unless Dean needs to be back to feed his animals?'

'No, I don't think so. He told his father where he was going and why he wanted the car, but he didn't tell his mother. His father agreed she need never know if he didn't get the job and if he does Dean says the less time she has to nag him the better.'

'She does seem to be a miserable sort of woman,' Megan mused.

'I suspect it has become a habit to moan.' Avril shrugged philosophically.

'Well I think it will be good for Dean to get away from her,' Megan said firmly. 'I do hope Mr Turner offers him the job, although I realize it will be a big change and a lot of responsibility.'

'Yes,' Avril said slowly. 'I shall miss him when he has to live further away.'

'He will not be so far from us if he gets the job at Martinwold and you know how much we like you to come here, Avril,' Megan said reassuringly. 'We'll sort things out, my dear. I'm sure we shall.'

Yes,' Avril agreed quietly, but her thoughts were on her young brothers and on her father. She had promised her mother she would be there for them, and even if she had not promised she knew in her heart she could never neglect them, not even for Dean.

Eight

The twins had enjoyed a hectic day but they were tired by the time they arrived back at Riverview. Although it was after eight o'clock Avril saw there was no sign of her father's car.

'Shall I come in and help you get these rascals to bed?' Dean asked.

'Haven't you had enough of them?'

'Of course not. I reckon they're too tired to be any trouble tonight anyway.'

'They've enjoyed their day with Alex and Rosy. They'll do without a bath tonight. Aunt Megan washed their hands and faces and scrubbed their knees before we left. They stood as still as wee statues and never made a murmur.' Avril smiled at the memory. 'They wouldn't have let me do that without a protest.'

'I don't blame them.' Dean grinned. 'Come on then, boys.' He put on a deep gruff voice. 'If you're not into your pyjamas and your teeth cleaned in seven minutes I'm going to—'

'Eat us all up like the wolf in Little Red Riding Hood?' Callum suggested.

'We'll give you indigestion if you do that,' Craig giggled, but they were content to get to bed and by the time Avril had heard their prayers and collected their dirty clothes they were almost asleep.

'I think you have a magic touch for dealing with them,' she said with a smile at Dean.

'I would like to stay with you until your father gets home. What do you think, Avril?'

'I'd like that but he may not be back for ages. I remember once when there had been a pile up on the road he slept at the hospital.'

'He'll not do that without letting you know though?'

'No. I'm sure he'll come home tonight.'

'If I wait with you until eleven o'clock, will you promise to go to bed then, if he's not back?'

'It would be lovely to have company until then,' Avril said but he noticed she avoided any promises. 'The room is warm with the central heating but I'll put a match to the fire. It feels cosier on a winter's night.'

'Mmm, I wouldn't be surprised if we get hard frost tonight. Aunt Molly is already fretting about me going into a cold house if I take the job at Martinwold but I shall be able to tell her Mr Turner modernized his dairyman's house when he built the milking parlour. It still has an elderly Aga cooker which needs coke twice a day but he has installed central heating in the downstairs rooms and on the upstairs landing and in the bathroom. It's run from an oil boiler.'

'That's the same as ours. I'm glad you'll be warm, Dean.'

'It's more comfort than we have at Northsyke and more than Aunt Molly has either. Mr Turner seems to consider his men well.'

'You do think you'll take the job then?'

'There is only one thing which makes me hesitate,' he said, meeting her eyes. 'That's the thought of moving away and not being able to see you so often, Avril.'

'I know. I wish it was not so far away too,' Avril admitted, 'but both Uncle Steven and Mr Oliphant think it is a good opportunity for you.'

'They're probably right. You will call to see me sometimes on your way home from work?'

'Of course I will if you want me to, and so long as I know Dad will be at home for the boys. I know he'll cooperate but he does have a responsible position at the hospital and he has had a lot of time off recently. He insists he doesn't want the boys to tie me down, but oh Dean, they're so young to be without a mother. They're not ten until November. I miss her terribly myself and it's worse for them.' Her voice was suddenly thick with tears. Dean moved across to sit beside her on the settee and put his arms around her drawing her close. To his delight she laid her head against his shoulder and he felt the silky softness of her hair against his cheek.

'Did you know my father was once engaged to Mr Turner's daughter?' she asked.

'No. No, I didn't know that. What happened?'

'I was only a child. Mum and I didn't know Dad or the Turners then. Aunt Megan was at Dumfries Academy with Natalie Turner but she was too much of a snob for them to be friends. One night Mrs Oliphant was taken seriously ill. Apparently Dad saved her life by getting her to hospital and beginning the operation himself until the senior surgeon could get there. Natalie Turner threw a tantrum and told him he had to choose between her and his work immediately, even though she knew Mrs Oliphant was desperately ill and she had known them most of her life. Dad chose his work and drove Mrs Oliphant to hospital. Aunt Megan was there and she said that was the end of their affair as far as Dad was concerned. Later he told her it would have ended anyway. Natalie was getting too demanding and he had discovered she had no intention of having any children.'

'Where is Mr Turner's daughter now?' Dean asked.

'She lives locally I think. She married another doctor soon afterwards. He was divorced. He's only a few years younger than her father. He already had three children older than I am. Apparently Mr Turner and Doctor Wright-Manton don't get on, although he did buy them a house when they got married. Mrs Oliphant reckons that was because he didn't want them moving into Martinwold with him and his wife.'

'Mr Turner told me he had no family to carry on after him,' Dean mused, 'but he said he had no intention of retiring for a long time yet. He looks very fit and healthy.'

'I think he's about five years younger than John Oliphant and he was born in 1900. I remember him and Granny Caraford discussing their ages. She is seventy-two so Mr Turner must be about sixty-one.'

'Joe Lang, that's the dairyman who is leaving, says he rides his horse every day. He goes around the farm checking up on stock and fences and whatever work is going on. I think that's a good thing for an owner or a good manager to do, but Joe and his wife think he's spying on his workers.'

'Maybe some of them have a guilty conscience,' Avril said. 'I think it is better to have a boss who is interested. If he was not he wouldn't care about their houses either.'

'I agree. Aunt Molly has offered me a bed and some blankets but there's a few other things I shall need to buy. The kitchen has more cupboards than I'm ever likely to need, as well as a large pantry and wash-house. Mrs Lang said one of the bedrooms has built-in wardrobes and there's an old table in the wash-house too, and a couple of chairs. I haven't seen them but they might do for me if I give them a good scrub. One thing I shall have to get used to,' he added ruefully, 'is doing my own washing. There'll be no chance of bringing it home to Mother. I doubt if she'll speak to me for months when she hears I'm going to work for somebody else. She was angry enough when I did my student's year at Bengairney instead of staying at home.'

'We have a twin tub washing machine in the old wash-house,' Avril said, sitting up. 'It was still working but when Mum had her operation Dad got one that is plumbed into the water supply to make it easier for her. It washes and rinses all in the same machine. It's super. You can do other work while it does the washing. But we used to think the twin tub was good until Dad bought this automatic machine.'

'I would like to buy the twin tub then if your father is agreeable,' Dean said eagerly. 'I shall need some cooking lessons from Aunt Molly too.' He grinned. 'I get free milk and a dozen eggs a week and as many potatoes as I want. I shall have to learn how to make good use of them. I want to save as much money as I can. I do intend to have a farm of my own one day, Avril, though it seems a long time away at present,' he added dejectedly.

'Oh Dean, I'm sure it will all happen for you one day,' Avril said, and snuggled closer, reaching up to stroke his cheek in a gesture of comfort. 'You deserve some good fortune.' Dean turned his head so that his mouth was against the palm of her hand. He kissed it gently and met her eyes.

'You have the darkest eyes I've ever seen, Avril. They're like those beautiful dark pansies.' His arms tightened and he kissed her cheek, then her lips, allowing his mouth to linger. When Avril did not draw away he deepened the kiss, parting her lips gently, feeling her response with a sense of elation. He traced the line of his jaw with his lips and nibbled gently at her ear lobe. It was some time before they drew apart and Avril's cheeks were flushed with more than the blazing fire. Dean glanced at the clock.

'It's quarter past ten. I wouldn't like your father to come in and think I take advantage of you in his absence, Avril. You must guess how I feel about you.'

'Yes,' she whispered, 'I do. When I was at university I was always wary when boys got aroused.' Her colour deepened. 'I don't know Mum's circumstances or how she came to have me without being married, and I don't suppose I shall ever know now, but I'm certain she was not a wicked person. I've vowed not to let that happen to me but I love being with you Dean, and held close to you. I feel safe with you. I–I'm glad you find me attractive enough to – to rouse your emotions but I know I can trust you.'

'Thank you,' Dean said gruffly. 'I hope you will always feel like that. I wouldn't be human if I didn't long to make love to you, but until I have some sort of prospects and something to offer you I don't want to take any chances with your reputation or your happiness.'

'I know that, Dean,' Avril responded softly. She gave him one more kiss and stood up to smooth her skirt over her slender hips and pat her hair into place. 'I'll go and heat some milk for a cup of cocoa. What do you think?'

'That would be—' Dean broke off at the sound of a car door slamming. Moments later Lint came into the house, blinking in the light as he entered the room. He sank wearily into his big armchair, closed his eyes and stretched out his long legs.

'You look absolutely exhausted, Dad,' Avril said with concern.

'It's been a hell of a day,' he muttered without opening his eyes. 'Two young women killed outright, and a young man died before they could get him into theatre.'

'How awful,' Avril murmured with real sympathy. 'Are there many seriously injured?'

'Yes. Mr Fraser, the senior orthopaedic surgeon, had to amputate a young man's leg above the knee. He was a professional dancer.' He sighed heavily. Avril crept out of the room, motioning to Dean to stay where he was.

A little while later Avril returned, wheeling the trolley.

'I know you'll say you're too tired to eat, Dad, but Aunt Megan made a caramel custard specially for you. She says exhausted men are like patients – they need a light and nourishing diet.' Her tone was gentle but firm, reminding Lint painfully of Ruth. He had always found comfort in her arms after a stressful day at the hospital. She had been so gentle and understanding. He groaned, opened his eyes with an effort and sat up.

'What else have you brought? Something smells good.'

'It's chicken soup, proper chicken soup with a little rice. It's quite light so I hope you'll try it?'

'I will, my dear. Food was the last thing on my mind but it smells delicious and it reminds me I haven't had anything since your cheese scones this morning.' He drew the trolley closer and began to eat the soup slowly, savouring it.

'I should be going now, Mr Gray,' Dean said quietly, rising to his feet. 'I offered to wait with Avril until eleven o'clock. I hoped she would go to bed herself then. I should have guessed she was waiting to make sure you had a meal.'

'Yes,' Lint looked from one to the other. 'I do appreciate your thoughtfulness, Avril.'

'We're glad you're safely home, Dad, but you do look shattered.'

'I am, but I need to unwind before I go to bed if I'm to get any sleep. Please wait a little while, Dean. Tell me about your interview?'

'It went very well thanks. Mr Turner has offered me the job but I have to telephone and confirm my acceptance by Monday lunchtime, after I've had a chance to discuss things with my father.'

'That's excellent. Congratulations. Will your father object?'

'I don't think so. The present dairyman has three weeks' notice still to work and Mr Turner would like me to work with him for the last ten days to get used to the milking parlour. That will give me time to help Dad sort out our own sheep and sell any with poor mouths or feet. We'll reduce the numbers a bit. He and the men can manage the beef cattle, and I shall suggest he cuts out the cereals. That will only leave the turnip field for ploughing and he'll have no harvest to worry about. I'm sure he'll agree. Uncle Bill thinks he may even be relieved if he doesn't need to consider my future.'

'Where will you live until the other man vacates the house?' Lindsay asked, glad to have something else to think about.

'I'm to lodge with the present dairyman and his wife. They seemed quite pleased with the idea. They're having a few problems with hygiene and Joe thought I might have some idea what's wrong. Neither he nor his wife like working in the parlour after being used to the byres.'

'And do you think you'll like it?' Lint asked with interest. He remembered walking down the long byre at Martinwold with cows tied on either side. That was where he had first met Ruth.

He had had several women friends and even been foolish enough to drift into an engagement, but he had never felt the instant attraction he had felt for Ruth from the moment they met. Her apparent indifference to him and subsequent wariness had intrigued him. It had taken some time to win her over but Ruth had been the best thing that had ever happened to him in this life. There would never be anyone to take her place.

'Dad? Did you hear what I said?' Avril prompted, removing his empty soup plate and pushing forward the crème caramel. She smiled at him. 'You were miles away and you said you wanted to forget about the hospital for a while.'

'My thoughts were not on the hospital. I do want to put it aside for now but I'm afraid I shall need to go down there in the morning.'

'That's all right. The boys will be happy enough here with me. It's Sunday so there's nothing planned. But Dad, I was asking you if Dean can buy the twin tub washing machine to take with him to Martinwold. His Aunt is giving him a bed and some bedding but he needs a few things for the house.'

'Of course you can have the washing machine, Dean. I don't want any money for it. You're a good friend to this family.'

'Oh but I must pay—'

'Not at all. There's a pair of comfortable armchairs you can have as well if they'd be any use. They're upstairs on the landing but we never use them, do we Avril?'

'No we don't.' She beamed at Dean, pleased that her father was being so helpful.

'I don't know how to thank you . . .' Dean began, flushing with pleasure.

'Then don't try, lad. We wish you well and if there's anything else we can help you with just tell Avril.'

'A lesson in using the washing machine from Avril,' Dean said smiling ruefully, 'and a few cookery lessons from Aunt Molly. I think they're the things I shall need most. Mrs Lang is leaving the stair carpet and the sitting room carpet because they are moving to a cottage and it only has two bedrooms and a living room. The house they're in was the original farmhouse and it's quite big, but of course you'll know that, Mr Gray.'

'Yes, I remember Megan and her parents living there,' Lindsay acknowledged. 'John and Chrissie moved to Honeysuckle Cottage after Chrissie had her operation. They had to give up the Martinwold Dairy. John Oliphant has helped my cousin Catherine and her husband with the gardens and maintenance at Langton Tower ever since. That's why Rosy manages to invite herself down to Bengairney so often. She adopted the Oliphants as surrogate grandparents as soon as she could talk. I can't imagine how she'll settle at boarding school but her parents insist they will be sending her after the summer.'

Dean's father accepted his decision almost as though he had expected it sooner or later.

'I hear Martinwold is one of the best dairy farms in this region so the experience will be good for you,' he said, 'but I shall miss ye laddie.' It was Sunday morning and they leaned together over the gate, gazing absently at the pen of bullocks which would soon be ready for market. 'You're like ma brother, Bill. He always yearned for a dairy herd but ye'll come to realize Northsyke is not the best of farms for a dairy. We might have more acres than Sylvanside but all of theirs is good fertile pasture, especially since Bill bought the Eskrigg land. It's all ploughable. He has a good farm now, although he is a bit short of shed room.'

'Mmm, I hadn't considered that aspect,' Dean said, 'but surely—'

'I did consider making changes, laddie, when you were coming home after college, but we only have forty acres as good as the Sylvanside land, and another fifty that's mediocre; the rest is hill land and more suited to sheep than anything else. Our house and steading are all at the south end. When dairy cows are coming in and out twice a day it's better if the steading is in the middle with the grazing land more accessible. Remember that, Dean, when ye're looking for a farm of your own to rent.' His eyes twinkled. 'Oh aye, laddie the experience will be good for you, but you're too much of a Scott to want to stay there forever. When the time comes for ye to rent a farm of your own then I'll do what I can to help, never fear.'

'So you really don't mind me going, Dad?' Dean said with relief.

'All fledglings have to learn to fly sometime. Mind you, your mother willna see it that way,' he warned. 'If ye take my advice ye'll tell her the night before ye're ready to leave.'

'I expect Mother will do a bit of grumbling but surely I ought to tell her?'

'You please yourself, laddie, but the older ye get the more ye learn about handling people and being up front isna always the best way with some.'

'I'll see what mood Mother is in this week. I don't really like deceiving her over something this important.'

'That's up to you, Dean. You'll need some sort of transport.'

'Yes. I thought I might try to buy a second-hand motorbike as soon as I can afford one,' Dean said.

'Ach, I dinna want ye riding around on one o' them,' Sydney said. 'I'm thinking o' letting ye have the car. I was at the garage in Langholm last week and they have a nice wee Austin for sale that would suit us fine. We'll go and take a look at it tomorrow afternoon. If we think it is as good a bargain as Phil Roland makes out, then we'll make him an offer. You could drive it back to Sylvanside and leave it there. I'll collect it when you take this one away next Sunday.'

'That's generous of you, Father. Thank you.' Dean was delighted and his spirits rose. His father grinned and Dean thought he seemed to treat his secret plans like a game of hide and seek with his mother.

Dean felt his mother was in a reasonable mood and there were things he wanted to discuss, like having his clothes back from the wash in time to pack on Sunday morning. He told her his plans on Wednesday while there were only the two of them in the kitchen but his heart sank when she spun round and glared at him. The tirade started; threats and names poured out. He sat in silence, knowing it was useless to argue or interrupt. Then to his horror his silence seemed to have a totally different effect and she burst into tears, asking how they were to manage without him and his poor father an invalid.

'Dad isn't an invalid, Mother! You shouldn't pretend he is. It's belittling him. He will manage perfectly well, as he did when I was away at college. We're sorting out the sheep to reduce the number of ewes for lambing and he's agreed to cut out the cereals. You'll not have me to feed and clothe any more; look how much better off you'll be.' But Grizel was determined to disagree with everything he said.

'She was like that with me,' his Uncle Bill told him later that evening when Dean went to Sylvanside to get peace from his mother's constant haranguing. 'She didn't want me to leave Northsyke, even though Molly and I were getting married. God knows why she wants to control everybody. She said Sydney wouldn't manage and it was my place to stay and help. She should have more faith in him. He was always a good manager and he's a first-class stockman. Since he learned how to control his diabetes it hasna hindered him too badly.'

'Well mother is being as contrary as possible and Doris is just as bad. Mr Turner is paying the Langs for my board and lodging but I can't arrive with a load of dirty washing and I shall not have the house to myself for a fortnight.'

'Bring your washing over here, laddie,' Molly Scott said. 'I'll have a washing day on Saturday and have it dried by Sunday ready for ye to take with ye. Does your mother know you're taking the car?'

'No. Dad said he would tell her when he was ready. I should have taken his advice and not told her anything until I was leaving,' he said unhappily. 'I'll drive Dad over here on Sunday morning and he'll collect the new car. That will be a surprise. At least Doris will be pleased. She's always wanted a smaller car.'

Nine

Dean settled in well at Martinwold but he was relieved when the Langs moved on and he had both milking parlour and house to himself, even though it did echo with emptiness. He had discovered the problem with the hygiene in the milking parlour.

'I'd like to strip down all the clusters and renew the rubber liners,' he said to Mr Turner the first morning he was on his own. 'I'm fairly certain Joe has not been circulating the right detergent around the parlour and there's a build up of milk stone and some of the tubes are perished. It will cost a bit to renew all the liners,' he added uncertainly, catching his boss's speculative look.

'You think that will solve the problems we've been having with the milk samples failing the tests?'

'I'm pretty sure it will. Joe admitted he didn't understand the difference between detergent, which we use for the initial cleaning, and the hypochlorite we use in the final rinse. I can show you how perished the tubes are if you like?'

'No, I'll take your word for it. Joe and his wife had been used to putting everything in the steam chest for sterilizing when we milked in the byre. They can't do that with the fixed equipment in a parlour. I'll give Bradshaws a ring and ask if the liners are in stock. They'll probably deliver them tomorrow. They send a van round once a month so you can get the detergent supplies, brushes, waterproof aprons and such like from the van. They send the bill to me. I don't like waste or extravagance mind you, but it's false economy to risk having penalties for dirty milk samples.'

Dean had the milking parlour and the premises up to his own standards by the following week. Murdo Turner had a good look round. He made no comment but he was pleased. Dean saw him keep nodding when he noted improvements.

'If you can keep it up Dean, I think we are going to get on splendidly.'

The house was a different matter but Dean was grateful to his Uncle Bill. He had hired a cattle trailer and driven over with the bed and other items of furniture from Aunt Molly, as well as bringing the washing machine and chairs from Riverview. Megan had invested in a larger fridge for herself and she sent her old one down with Steven, plus bacon, butter and cheese, a meat casserole, some scones and a large fruit cake. Dean was delighted.

'I suspect this is a good excuse for Megan to get a new fridge like they have in the kitchen at Langton Tower,' Steven said with a grin, 'but at least the old one is coming to a good home.'

'I'm really grateful,' Dean assured him. 'Would you like a cup of coffee?'

'I'd rather have a look round the milking parlour and the cubicle shed if that would be all right?' Steven admitted.

'Oh certainly. I'm sure Mr Turner will not mind but I'm glad you waited until I'd got it cleaned up a bit. The Langs had been having trouble but I think I've got to the bottom of it.'

Avril called in on her way home the first Friday he was alone in the house. Dean was delighted.

'It will be six o' clock before I finish milking and clearing up,' he said diffidently. 'Will you be able to wait?'

'Oh I think I might,' Avril teased and saw his eyes light with pleasure. 'I made a chicken casserole for our supper. It has been in the car boot all day but the weather is so cold it is as good as a fridge.'

'What about the boys?'

'Bessie is collecting them from school and making supper. Dad is always home earlier on Fridays unless there's an emergency and he would have let me know.'

'So he knows you're here? He doesn't mind?'

'Of course he knows and why would he mind?'

'Well the house is a bit of a dump, especially compared to Riverview.'

'It's the people who live in the house who make it a home,' Avril said firmly. She had brought a few groceries and fresh bread. She found the remains of a loaf which was getting stale so she made Dean a bread pudding with dried fruit and syrup soaked in eggs and milk with a crunchy brown sugar topping. He had a can full of milk in the fridge so she made a large jug of custard, knowing he would eat the remainder tomorrow.

'I could get used to being spoiled like this,' Dean said when he came in from work. He washed and changed quickly then came to steal a kiss before Avril dished up their meal.

'I wondered whether you would have any spare plates,' she said with a twinkle but I see you have a cupboard full of assorted sizes.'

'They're from Aunt Molly. I think she has been clearing out her cupboards. I suspect she thought I would fill the sink full of dirty dishes before I did any washing up.'

'And do you?'

'I do not!' Dean said indignantly, then saw the teasing in her dark eyes. 'I prefer to do it as I go along. I keep things tidy if I can, but I'm not much of a cook yet. Megan sent Sam down with a big pot of soup. It lasted four days. I have porridge and bacon and eggs when I come in for breakfast. I'm always famished then. Aunt Molly showed me how to make the porridge and I skim the top off the milk. It tastes like nectar when you're really hungry.'

It became a regular thing for Avril to call on Dean on Friday evenings but he always visited her and his Aunt and Uncle on Saturday or Sunday afternoons and when it was his free weekend he and Avril went to the cinema or to a dance.

'We see as much of each other now as when I lived almost on your doorstep,' he said a few weeks later. He felt he was fortunate that Avril seemed happy with their arrangements but he longed for more and there were times during the long winter evenings when he wondered if he would ever be in a position when he could ask her to marry him.

At Easter Lint arranged to take the boys down to visit his parents for five days over a long weekend.

'Are you sure you'll not come with us, Avril?' he asked.

'Not this time, but tell Grandma I will come down and stay for a few days when Callum and Craig start boarding school in September. I can't believe they're looking forward to it. I'm dreading them being away.'

'They'll be fine. You're not nervous about staying here on your own? I'm sure Mrs Caraford or Megan would be happy to have you to stay with them.'

'Don't worry about me, Dad. I shall be all right,' Avril assured him, firmly believing what she said.

Usually Lint called in at the village shop to collect the newspaper on his way to work; he liked to glance through it if he had a coffee break. On the Friday morning he and the boys were leaving early to avoid the Easter traffic so Avril collected the newspapers herself later in the morning. She was on holiday and she planned to spend the morning cooking and then have the afternoon and evening with Dean. She was leaving the shop after making her purchases, but she stood aside to allow someone to enter. It was Grizel Scott, Dean's mother. She was neither tall nor fat but as she stood blocking Avril's exit she seemed to expand like a fighting cock about to go into battle.

'It's you!' she hissed accusingly. 'You're the one responsible for breaking up my family. You've driven away my boy! My only son!'

'I–I . . .' Avril could only stare at her in astonishment. Mrs Williams, the shopkeeper, and the three waiting customers all turned to stare but Grizel was oblivious to her audience. This was the first time she had seen Avril since Dean left home. He had not visited his parents since he moved to Martinwold, knowing he would only get more bitter recriminations. Grizel blamed Avril for that too, unaware that he met his father at least once a fortnight at Sylvanside and twice they had met at the market in Annan and had had lunch together.

'Mrs Scott,' Avril managed in a reasoning voice, 'Dean has only gone to work to gain experience in—'

'He had work! He doesn't need experience. He doesn't need a bastard like you to tell him what to do. You're an evil influence! The daughter of a whore, that's what you are!' There was an audible gasp in the shop. The colour drained from Avril's face.

'My mother was not a – a . . .' Her voice was hoarse.

'Do you know who your father is?' Grizel snapped. Without giving Avril time to speak, even if she had known what to say she ranted on. 'I'll bet your mother didn't know who he was either. He could have been any o' the Germans from the prisoner o' war camps. Or more likely a gypsy. You, with your big dark eyes and your . . .' Avril swayed slightly and put her hand out. Her heart was pounding and she thought she was going to be sick.

'That's enough! Mrs Scott, you've said enough.' Mrs Williams had come round the counter. She took Avril's arm. 'Do you want a seat, lassie?'

'N–no. Thank you.' All she wanted was to get past Mrs Scott and outside into the clean fresh air.

'Stand aside and let her past,' Mrs Williams ordered. 'And if you can't keep a civil tongue in your head, Grizel, then you can take your custom somewhere else.'

'Why should I? It's true. Ask her!' She glared at the shop-keeper and then again at Avril, her small eyes hard and challenging. 'You don't know who your father is, do you?' She almost spat the words at Avril as she leaned closer. 'Well I'm not having a gypsy's brat getting her claws into my son . . . You'd be the ruination of him. I want to know who my grand-children are and—'

'Excuse me. Are you going in or out?' A man, another customer, was now standing behind Mrs Scott, impatient to collect his news-paper. She had no option but to move and Avril was thankful to escape.

Afterwards she couldn't remember who else had been in the shop. She had no recollection of driving home. She collapsed in a heap at the kitchen table and burst into tears, shivering with shock. She hated quarrels and there had been very few of them in her life so far to prepare her for Grizel Scott. She wanted to curl into a ball and hide. She felt she would die with humiliation. Normally she might have accused Mrs Scott of trying to shift the blame for her son's departure from Northsyke to assuage her own guilt, and excuse her own failings as a mother. Bessie had known her before she was married and she said Grizel Scott needed help because she was growing more neurotic.

Although she hid it well Avril was sensitive about the iden-tity of her real father and the circumstances of her birth; she had hoped desperately that her mother would talk to her about it before she died, but she had remained silent on the subject. Today Grizel Scott had struck out viciously at Avril's most vulnerable feelings. Her usual calm control and common sense had deserted her in the face of Mrs Scott's bitter aspersions. The dishes she had planned to cook for Dean no longer mattered. The morning passed in a sea of misery. She roused herself to heat some soup for her lunch but she couldn't eat it. The thought of food sickened her.

She had never doubted that Dean was her friend, a very good friend, and she didn't doubt that friendship now, but friendship and marriage were totally different relationships. Since her return from university they had grown closer and several times passion had flared between them. He was a wonderful companion and he had been kind and understanding about her mother's illness and her death. He was considerate and patient with the twins too and they liked him. He never complained when she needed to put their needs before his. Oh yes, Dean was a genuinely kind and thoughtful person who shared many of her own interests. She knew he enjoyed their kisses as much as she did. She was not so naive that she didn't know when a man was sexually aroused but that was a natural reaction, wasn't it? Even animals enjoyed sex, but that didn't mean they loved their mate. The more Avril analysed her relationship with Dean the more uncertain she felt. Grizel had done a good job of planting seeds of doubt and fear. His ambition was to have a farm of his own. Perhaps her companionship helped him pass the time while he worked at Martinwold. He often said he wanted more of her but he never mentioned marriage. Perhaps he shared some of his mother's doubts about her background, even if only subconsciously. Could she blame him if he wanted a wife whose family history was an open book – one of the local farming families known to his own family through the generations. Maybe he wanted a wife who came with a modern dowry – a father with influence in the farming community, someone who might give him cows or machinery as a wedding present and help him on his way up in the farming world.

Avril's brain went round and round but it always came back to the fact that Dean's mother was right – she didn't know who her father was. Did he know about her? Had he seen her? Had she met him and not known? Whose blood did she have in her veins? What evil traits did she have in her? However much he tried to resist his mother's influence Dean must surely have been affected by her constant ravings. Avril shuddered, remembering the silence in the shop, the people listening. There was no way she could face Dean today, nor any other day. Perhaps she should move away, maybe emigrate? Yet how could she leave her young brothers, or break the promise she had made to them and to her mother that she would always be here for them.

Ten

Dean was bitterly disappointed when Avril didn't turn up on Friday afternoon. He knew she had the day off and she had suggested doing some cooking and bringing food for their evening meal. He had done his best to make his bare front room look clean and comfortable, drawing up the two armchairs and pulling forward the coffee table Aunt Molly had given him. He felt the house could be made into an attractive and comfortable home, even though it was tied to his job. Perhaps he ought to spend some of his newly acquired savings on more furniture, he thought, looking around. He lit the fire and made it look cosy and inviting. Time dragged on. He made a cup of tea then went out to do the milking. Surely Avril would be here before he finished?

At six o' clock the house was still in darkness and there was no sign of Avril, and no appetizing meal. The fire had burned low and the room was chilly. Despondently Dean wondered if she was ill. Perhaps she had been called in to work? But she would have let him know. What if she'd had an accident in the car? His heart beat erratically. He hurried to the telephone. The Riverview number rang and rang but no one answered. Several times that evening he tried to phone but there was no reply. Surely Avril would have let him know if she had decided to go down to Gloucestershire with her family? His mood alternated between anxiety and annoyance, but worry about her safety was his overriding emotion.

When there was no reply the following morning he telephoned Sylvanside and spoke to his Aunt Molly.

'That doesn't sound like Avril,' she said slowly. 'I'm sure she was not going with Lindsay to see his parents, but I don't think he would have gone either if Avril was ill. I'll go down for the newspapers and call at Riverview on the way. Don't worry, Dean. Maybe there's been a misunderstanding. You two haven't had a quarrel have you?'

'Definitely not. We enjoy a spirited discussion now and then but we've never had a quarrel, or even angry words.'

'All right, laddie. I'll see what I can do.' Molly felt her own concern mounting as she tidied her hair and put on her coat and hat ready to go to the village shop.

At Riverview there was a vestibule before entering the main hall so the front door always stood open except in the wildest weather. Today the house looked shut up and deserted. Perhaps Avril had gone to stay with Mrs Caraford, but why hadn't she let Dean know? Unless the old lady had been taken ill suddenly? And what about Bo? The collie dog was getting old now; Avril would never neglect him. Molly walked slowly round to the back of the house. There was Bo eating his food beside the open door of what had been the wash-house. It was now a boiler room cum coat and boot store. Molly pushed the door wider and called in.

'Avril? Are you there, lassie? Are you all right?' Avril's eyes darted hither and thither wishing she had locked the back door too. She really didn't want to face anyone. She ought to have guessed Mrs Scott, kindly woman as she was, would come to the house. 'Hello! I'm on my way to get the newspapers. Shall I bring yours?' Molly tried to sound as normal as possible but every instinct told her there was something wrong.

'C—come in,' Avril called, feeling utterly defeated. 'I'm in the kitchen.' Molly was shocked by Avril's pale face. Her huge dark eyes looked haunted and it was clear that if she had slept at all it had not been a refreshing slumber. Yesterday's papers lay unopened on the table, along with the flour and other groceries she had purchased. There was an untouched cup of cold tea. Avril was still in her dressing gown and slippers.

'Are you ill, lassie?' Molly Scott asked with such genuine concern that Avril felt tears spring to her eyes. She had been too stunned and destroyed by Grizel Scott's onslaught to give way to tears. When she had eventually drifted into sleep she had been plagued by a dreadful nightmare. Now her neighbour's kindly concern swept away her defences and hot tears coursed down her cheeks.

'Avril? Oh my lamb.' Molly Scott came round the table and pulled her into her plump arms, rocking her like a child. 'Has there been an accident? Is it your father? The boys . . .?' Molly caught her breath on a stifled sob at the possibility of either of the beloved twins being hurt.

'Th–they're fine.'

'Then what is it, lassie? What can have upset you so badly? Dean was worried sick about you when you didn't go yesterday and when he couldn't get a reply on your telephone. Tell me what's wrong. Maybe I can help.'

'No. N–nobody can help now Mum's gone,' Avril said, scrubbing at her eyes, furious with herself for giving way to tears.

'Ah . . .' Molly murmured, but she felt perplexed. Avril had grieved badly for her mother, while she was so ill and she had been unable to help her. She had appeared to accept her death and had set herself to caring for her young brothers with admirable courage. Perhaps the loss had hit her when the house was empty with the boys and her father away. 'It is natural to grieve,' Molly said uncertainly, 'but you look so ill, lassie. Let me make you a fresh cup of tea then I'll leave you to get dressed. I'll call in on my way back from the shop and bring your newspapers, then if you feel like it, you can come and have your dinner with me and Bill.' Avril shook her head but Molly was already finding the teapot and pushing the kettle on to the hot plate to boil. Avril felt too drained to argue, or to explain she needed her mother because she was the only one who could tell her who her father was and explain the circumstances of her birth. She knew in her heart that Grizel Scott was totally and completely wrong when she had called her mother a whore who wouldn't know who had fathered her child, but the fact remained that even she didn't know who her own father was. She had always known her mother loved her dearly and their circle of friends had accepted her and loved her too, including her adopted father. She had been happy and sure of their love and their respect – until now when Grizel Scott's furious outburst had rocked her world to its foundations.

At the village shop Molly said, 'I'll take the Riverview papers please. I shall be calling in there on my way home so I'll drop them off.'

'Well I canna say I blame the lassie for not wanting to collect them herself after yesterday,' Mrs Williams said. 'She looked as though Grizel had struck her a physical blow. White as a sheet she was. We all felt so sorry for Avril. I was furious with Grizel, causing trouble and distress like that, and in my shop. I told her not to come back here if she couldna keep a civil tongue.'

'I don't know what you're talking about,' Molly said, frowning at the shopkeeper. 'Surely my sister-in-law didn't start ranting in public?'

'Oh but she did.' Mrs Williams lost no time in telling Molly about the confrontation and Grizel's wild accusations. She added a few embellishments of her own. 'Mrs Black was waiting to be served at the time and she thinks Grizel should see the doctor and get something for her nerves,' she added, 'but Mrs Sharpe reckons some women are affected like that at a certain age, but it hasna affected me like that.'

'No, nor me,' Molly responded absently, her mind going over what she had learned. 'Thanks Ida. I'll be off now.'

'Don't forget to pass on my best regards to Avril.'

As soon as Molly arrived back at Riverview and plonked the newspapers on the table with a thump Avril knew she must have heard about Mrs Scott's angry tirade. Molly pulled out a chair and sat herself down at the table, then she jumped up again.

'I need a cup of tea,' she said tightly. 'It's taking all my will power not to go to Northsyke right now and tell Grizel exactly what I think of her. As for Sydney he would be downright ashamed if he knew his wife had caused such a stushie – and in the village shop of all places!'

'A–a stushie?' Avril repeated, looking up with a frown.

'An uproar – in public too.' She brought the pot of tea to the table and stirred vigorously, but her mind was not on the tea. 'As I understand it Grizel was ranting on about your natural father, lassie? And that's why you didn't go to see Dean? Or answer the telephone?'

'Yes,' Avril whispered, and willed the tears not to start again. 'I don't think I should see Dean again. His mother is a horrid woman, but she is right. I don't know who my real father is. She is afraid we might marry and she doesn't want her grandchildren to be – to be contaminated or—'

'Nonsense! When has your father's identity ever made a difference to any of us who love you, lassie?' Molly was seething inwardly at the damage her sister-in-law had done. 'We're all privileged to know you, we love you for the kind and considerate person you are, and we admire you for the clever young woman you've proved to be. Lindsay Gray once told me he could never have wished for a better daughter and he said you – more than anyone – helped him break down your mother's defences and win her love.'

'Maybe other people do love me – as I love them, b–but it's different for Dean. Mrs Scott is his mother, she is his own flesh and blood.'

'You wouldn't think so the way she has treated him. She never wanted another baby after Doris, and when she knew she was expecting again all she wanted was another girl.'

'Even so Dean is bound to share some of his mother's views and – and her doubts. She really doesn't want me to be the mother of his children. How can I blame her? How do I know what sort of children I might have? I've decided it's best if I don't see Dean again.'

'Oh Avril, lassie, don't say that. Dean has always known Mr Gray was your adopted father, and it's never made any difference to the way he feels about you, now has it?'

'No, but we were only children then. Now we're – we're adults and I think I love him. I couldn't bear to hurt him or for him to be disappointed in me.'

'Don't you think he should make his own mind up about who he wants for a wife?'

'I know he thinks of me as a good friend. I think it would be better to part now before – before it's too late . . .'

'Before he falls in love with ye, lassie? I think it's a bit late for that. If you'd heard how upset he was when he telephoned me this morning you would know he's more than half way in love with ye already. He tried to telephone last night. Didn't you hear it?'

'Yes,' Avril whispered. 'Yes I heard it. I didn't want to talk to anybody. I feel as though I want to hide from the world. If it wasn't for Callum and Craig I think I should go right away from here.'

'That bitch really has gotten to you,' Molly said through tight lips. 'I could throttle her for what she's done. Don't you see lassie, you're doing exactly what she wants if you split up with Dean. There isn't a girl in the whole of Britain she'll consider suitable to be her daughter-in-law. Now drink up your tea. I shall have to get back and make some dinner for Bill. Will you come up and join us?'

'Thank you, you're always so kind, but I don't feel like going anywhere, or seeing anyone today. I need to think.'

'All right.' But Molly bit her lip and shook her head, uncertain what she could say or do to help. Avril spoke so firmly and with such dignity it was difficult to argue. 'All right, but you know where I am, lassie, and remember there's very few folk in the world like Grizel. You should pity Dean for having such a mother, and love him all the more.'

Avril gave her a wan smile as she accompanied her to the door and thanked her for calling.

When Molly arrived home it was to find Dean already there and marching restlessly round her kitchen while Bill sat at the table looking anxious and relieved to see her. She explained that Avril was well but too upset to see anyone. Dean was furious when he learned of his mother's outburst. Bill was outraged and threatened to go over to Northsyke and 'sort her out' himself. Eventually Molly persuaded them to calm down and wait until she had made them both some dinner.

'Avril is seriously upset, Dean. She's considering you, and any future you might have had together, but I can tell she's hurt because her mother never told her who her real father is. I suggest you take things slowly for a while, give her time to sort out her own thoughts and feelings. She needs to know you're still her friend.' Dean groaned inwardly. He tried to be patient because he felt he had nothing to offer Avril yet, nothing like she deserved anyway, but he felt far more than friendship for her.

'Meanwhile I wondered whether you could have a talk with Mrs Caraford, Megan Caraford I mean,' Aunt Molly said. 'She's known Avril since she was a wee girl. Even if she doesn't know who her father is she may be able to help Avril get things in perspective, and the sooner the better. I have a feeling your mother's accusations may have opened old wounds and it will make things worse to let them fester in Avril's mind.'

'All right,' Dean said slowly, considering, 'but it's not the easiest subject to talk about, is it?'

'No. You'll need to get her on her own.'

'I need to be back home by three o'clock for the milking but I might call in at Bengairney on my way by. There'll be no opportunity for a talk but I could always let them know Avril is on her own, and a bit down in spirits.'

'Good idea, lad,' his uncle said approvingly, then deliberately changed the subject. 'When Lindsay Gray comes back from seeing his parents he's talking about doing up the row of sheds at Riverview. One o' them used to be a wee byre when Eskrigg was a farm. They face east towards us. I told him I'd be interested in renting them from him so that I could rear all our heifer calves.'

'All of the calves?' Dean asked, his thoughts diverted, if only temporarily.

'Yes. I could sell the ones I don't need as replacements in our own herd. They are nearly all first cross between my Ayrshire cows and Friesian bulls from the Artificial Insemination Centre. There's plenty of demand for them.'

'Yes, I know. Mr Turner is upgrading some of his to pedigree Friesians. I think it's the third or fourth generation before they're accepted as fully pedigree but a lot of them are neater, nicer cattle than the pedigree Friesian cows with ugly udders.'

'Aye, I'd agree with that. Anyway I wondered whether you could suggest to Mr Gray that it would be an advantage to open up this side of the buildings so that I could get in with a tractor for feeding and cleaning them out. It's only a few hundred yards across the paddock. Maybe we could make a track for a tractor and trailer to save going round by the road. Did I tell you we have young Dick Forsythe helping us now? He's the only one of the three Forsythe boys who wants to farm but his father is drinking their place into the gutter. The lad doesna stand a chance.'

'It's a wicked shame,' Molly said. 'Dick is a hard worker and nicely mannered.'

'Aye, takes after his mother. She was a genteel woman. The oldest boy is an electrician and Jim is a builder.'

'Mrs Forsythe's father was a builder,' Molly said. 'Maybe the boys take after him.'

Dean was sorely tempted to call at Riverview and try to see Avril but he took his aunt's advice to give her time and drove on to Bengairney.

'Why hello, Dean,' Megan greeted him in surprise. 'Steven and Samuel are both away at a pedigree sale in Ayrshire today. They'll be back for milking of course. They would have asked you to go with them but we thought you would be spending your spare time with Avril when Lint and the boys are away.'

'That was the plan,' Dean said morosely.

'You two haven't quarrelled have you? I know Avril hates quarrels.'

'No,' Dean shook his head and glanced at Tania who had returned to her book after greeting him with a smile. Alexander and Rosy Palmer-Farr were sprawled on the rug in front of the fire building some sort of Lego construction but Dean knew they had sharp ears. Megan sensed his unease.

'Come into the kitchen and talk to me while I set out the tea. You'll be ready for a cup before you start the milking.'

'Thank you, I'd appreciate that,' Dean said but a small frown still creased his forehead.

'Now tell me what's bothering you and Avril if you haven't had a quarrel.' Dean explained about his mother's outburst. He didn't try to defend her or hide his bitterness. How dare she try to come between himself and Avril. He was afraid she had struck Avril's most sensitive feelings.

'I see,' Megan said slowly, thoughtfully. 'Avril did mention something about this before Ruth died. Personally I think she ought to have been told the circumstances of her birth years ago but Ruth found it a very painful subject. She thought – indeed we all thought Avril was happy after Lint adopted her. In fact I know she was but something like this is bound to make her wonder and consider. It's only fair that she should know everything but you have to understand, Dean, it's not my business.'

'I'll never forgive my mother for hurting Avril like this,' Dean burst out. 'Isn't there anyone who could tell Avril the truth and convince her it doesn't matter who her father is?'

'Was. He's dead now.'

'So you know?'

'It's not my place to talk to Avril, Dean, and I don't think I could. I don't know the whole story.' She broke off, frowning. 'I think the best person to explain everything would be Granny Caraford. Steven's mother has known Ruth and Avril longer than any of us, but she wouldn't interfere without Lint's permission.'

'So there's nothing we can do to help Avril until he returns,' Dean said flatly. 'Aunt Molly says she's terribly down. She doesn't want to see anyone and she believes we should split up and stop seeing each other.'

'Oh Dean, that's awful!' Megan said. 'I didn't realize it was so serious. I don't know if I can do anything but I'll certainly try, even if it's only persuading Avril to come over for her Sunday dinner tomorrow. I'll invite Granny Caraford too. She hasn't been too well since she had the flu so that might help persuade Avril to come.'

Dean had to be content with that but he was young and impatient and he longed to see Avril and reassure her that he loved her even if she was the daughter of the devil himself. Only his Aunt Molly's warning that he should be cautious and not rush her held him back.

Eleven

Megan was concerned about Avril. She told Steven about Dean's visit when he returned from the sale.

'I can understand Avril being upset. She must have been mortified to be confronted like that in front of other people, especially when she has no knowledge or defence. The poor lassie would be utterly bewildered. I think you should telephone Lint. He loves her and he'll not want her brooding on her own. I'm sure he'll agree to my mother telling her the truth. He likes Dean too and he seems to encourage their friendship, even though he knows Mrs Scott is a bit neurotic.'

'A bit neurotic! She sounds totally vile to me. All right, I'll phone Lint.'

'Avril deserves to have her questions answered for her own sake. You know I've thought so for a long time,' Steven said firmly. 'Mother will be able to explain things and she will be fairer than anyone else, certainly she's less prejudiced than I would be,' he added darkly. 'Avril will not want to hear her father was a brute and a bully, will she?'

'No, but it will be difficult to explain that he raped Ruth. I hope we don't make things worse than ever for Avril,' Megan demurred, anxious and uncertain about the best course to take.

Megan had difficulty persuading Avril to come for Sunday lunch and only the news of Granny C's slow recovery from the flu and her desire to see her persuaded her to accept.

'Steven is going down to get her as she's still easily tired. She has always had tender feelings for you, Avril dear, so I hoped you would be free to come and see her while your father and the boys are away.' She had left Avril with no plausible excuse.

Megan was dismayed at the sight of her pale, strained face and the dark shadows beneath her lovely eyes; they seemed to hold a haunted look. She uttered a silent prayer that they could restore the girl's confidence and give her the reassurance she so obviously needed. She had always been such a happy, lovable child,

accepting everyone at face value and being accepted in return
for her ready smile and affectionate nature. Megan couldn't understand how anyone could treat her as cruelly as Grizel Scott, even
if she did think she was protecting her son. Steven's mother was
the best person to explain but Megan hoped she would not find
it too harrowing going over the past.

Lint had agreed immediately that she should be told. He
sounded upset and he had promised to telephone later to see
how Avril had accepted the news.

'We'll come back early if she is upset,' he said. 'I don't want
her brooding alone.' There was no doubting Lint's genuine concern
but he knew Granny Caraford loved Avril as much as she did
Samuel, Tania and Alexander. Surely between them they could
restore Avril's self-confidence.

Dean was impatient and desperate to see Avril but Megan had
given him the same advice as his Aunt Molly – to bide his time
and wait for Avril to contact him. It was not what he wanted to
hear. He longed to hold Avril in his arms and tell her how much
he loved her, to convince her he shared none of his mother's
warped opinions. Then he remembered how little he had to offer
a girl like Avril. She deserved more than being the wife of a farm
labourer, and that is exactly what he was now, however well paid
he might be. He mooched around the house, closing the door
on the echoing empty dining room and the unoccupied bedrooms.
He didn't even have a properly furnished house to offer and Avril
was used to such a beautiful home. Her parents had tastefully
modernized Riverview, and they had had the money to carry
out their ideas, whereas he was saving every penny towards renting
a farm of his own.

Megan ushered Granny Caraford and Avril into the sitting
room when lunch was over. 'Tania will help me wash up, won't
you dear,' she smiled at her daughter, who had already been
primed. 'You keep Granny company until we're finished, Avril.
It's ages since you saw each other for a proper chat.' For once
Avril was glad to obey. She felt drained and exhausted.

'What are these?' she asked lifting the books Hannah Caraford
had set on a side table.

'They're photo albums. Some of them go back to when I was
a girl. Do you want to see some of them, Avril?'

'All right. I don't think you ever showed them to me before, did you?'

'I didn't think you'd be interested in old photos when you were a child.'

Hannah began to leaf through the oldest album, explaining some of the pictures of her own parents and her home. 'This was my cousin, Eleanor,' she said pointing to a picture of a girl with long fair hair and features similar to Avril's own. 'Her mother died when she was still at school so she often stayed with us, especially during the holidays. We were as close as any sisters could be.'

'You obviously loved her,' Avril said, hearing the nostalgia in Hannah's voice. 'She looks vaguely familiar, yet you're not alike.'

'No, not in looks. We married within a few months of each other but we remained close friends. This is the house where I lived before my husband was killed. We had not been married long. I had no children. I gave up the smallholding and took a job as housekeeper. Months later Eleanor had a baby boy. She developed an infection and died soon after the birth.'

'How awful,' Avril whispered, looking down at the pretty young woman.

'Yes, I was dreadfully upset. Her husband was devastated. He was Edward Caraford of Willowburn. We called him Eddy. As soon as I was free from my job he asked me to keep house for him and take care of his baby son Fred.'

'I–I don't understand. I thought Willowburn was where you and Uncle Steven used to live?'

'It was. When Fred was four years old Eddy and I decided to get married. It was second best for both of us but we had always been good friends. We felt it would give Fred stability. He was a lovely wee boy and I loved him dearly, but he was prone to tantrums even then, like his maternal grandfather. Sometimes I blamed myself. I had had no experience of bringing up babies.' She sighed heavily. 'Fred was five years old and he had just started school when Steven was born. He grew jealous and difficult. He wanted to stay at home with me, like his new brother. Of course he had to go to school so he became convinced we loved Steven more than him.' Hannah sighed again. 'The jealousy increased as Fred grew older. We were sorry for him because he had never known his own mother. Perhaps we gave in to him too often. I truly did my best . . .'

'Oh Granny C, I'm sure you did,' Avril said, patting the wrinkled hand affectionately.

'These are mostly photos of the boys growing up at Willowburn.' She flicked through several pages more quickly. 'And these are of Steven and his best friend, Sam Oliphant. He was Megan's brother. He was killed during the war. Neither Steven nor Sam wanted to go to war but the government needed as many young men as possible and they drafted in landgirls to take their place.' Avril stiffened. Her mother had been a landgirl after she left school. She had once said she wanted to do her bit for king and country, but when Avril asked her more about it she had clamped her lips shut and refused to talk about it.

Hannah reached for another album, a thinner one.

'This was Steven and Sam in uniform. Fred refused to go to fight so Steven had no option . . .' She paused as though choosing her words.

'Is that how you met my mother? When she was a landgirl?' Avril prompted gently, seeing Granny C turning her wedding ring round and round on her finger. It was something she did when she was agitated.

'Yes.' She took Avril's hand in hers and held it tightly. 'We had had several others before Ruth. They never seemed to settle, or they were no use at the work. Ruth was splendid. We got on together from the day she arrived. If I'd been blessed with a daughter I would have wanted one like your mother.'

'I'm glad,' Avril said huskily, her eyes filling with tears.

'I must have been blind not to realize what a challenge she was to someone like Fred. This is Ruth in her land army uniform. She was lovely – so fresh and young, so innocent, brought up in a vicarage by her father and an elderly great aunt. I should have known . . .'

'Known what, Granny?' Avril asked tensely, her voice little more than a whisper.

'Fred always expected to have his own way – with Steven, with his father, with everyone. I have to be honest. He was a lazy bully in those days. He didn't earn respect but he couldn't bear your mother ignoring him . . .' Her hand tightened on Avril's and she was silent for a few moments. Avril felt her tension mounting too. 'Ruth ran into the kitchen one day in a terrible state,' she said jerkily. 'She couldn't speak to me. She packed her bags and left,' Hannah finished in a rush.

'My mother ran away?'

'I realized something had frightened her, but I never dreamed Fred would – would force himself on her. He knew how innocent she was. Oh Avril, my dearest child,' she drew her close and held her tightly. 'I blame myself.'

'Fred . . .?' Avril whispered, her dark eyes wide with shock, 'This man Fred is my father?' She struggled from Hannah's arms but she gripped both her hands, holding them as though she might run away.

'Yes,' Hannah admitted huskily. 'I never knew Ruth had borne his child. We exchanged cards at Christmas. I knew she had been ill, and later that she was training to be a teacher, but she didn't tell me about you, my dearest Avril . . .'

'Then when . . .? How?'

'Fred went to Canada so I had to leave Willowburn. I wrote to Ruth to give her my new address and explain why I was moving. That's when she told me about you, my dear. I longed to see her again and to see you too, but she was uncertain about bringing you to Scotland in case Fred returned and tried to claim you. Ruth loved you so very much, Avril.'

'Yes,' she whispered, 'I know. B–but why, oh why didn't she tell me?' Her mouth trembled.

'She had been badly shocked. She wanted to forget. When your grandfather died the vicarage went with his job so your mother had to make a new home for both of you. Fred had behaved atrociously and you were the grandchild of my dearest friend and cousin, and Eddy's grandchild too. I persuaded Ruth to bring you to see me. The rest you know, or most of it. Mr Patterson drew up the plans to convert my shop into a house for me and an apartment for the two of you.'

'Yes, I remember. I loved being there, helping you with the hens and the pigs and gathering apples in the autumn,' Avril said. 'B–but I should have known! Mother ought to have told me who I was, and – and . . .' She bit back a sob.

'You did meet your father once, Avril,' Hannah said carefully.

Gwen Kirkwood

'I did? When? And where is he now?' She didn't know whether she wanted to meet a man who had forced a young and innocent girl to have sex. That was rape. It was not a word Granny C would use but her father had raped her mother and she was the result. She shuddered.

'Do you remember I was unable to come to the wedding when your parents got married, Avril? You were a bridesmaid. I wanted to see you both so much, but Fred had returned from Canada. He had cancer. He didn't have long to live. I couldn't turn my back on him Avril. I had loved him as a child. I had to do my best for Eleanor's son. He was a changed person, quiet, humble, grateful for anything I could do for him. I couldn't cast him aside. Do you understand?'

'I–I suppose so. I do remember a man being with you that time we came to collect my bantams when we returned from Gloucester to live at Riverview. He was sleeping in a chair. He didn't seem to be aware we were there.'

'That's right. Lint thought it was better that you should see him, however briefly. He understood you would want to know who your natural father was one day.'

'So Dad knew who he was? He knew what he had done to my mother – but he still loved us, both of us.'

'Of course he did, my love. You were an adorable child. Now he is proud of you and he couldn't love you more if you had been his own flesh and blood, Avril.'

'He's always been wonderful to me,' Avril whispered brokenly.

'You said my cousin, Eleanor, looked vaguely familiar. That's because she was your grandmother and you resemble her very much, except that she had grey eyes and you have your mother's beautiful brown eyes. Her hair and her features were very like yours, my dear. She would have loved you dearly, as I do. She was a very gentle person.'

'So . . .' Avril rubbed her temples; her head was beginning to ache with tension and lack of sleep. 'I called you grandmother because Samuel called you that and I wanted a grandmother too, but you really are – in a way. You are my step-grandmother. Uncle Steven really is my uncle.'

'Yes, that's right. He and Fred were half-brothers.'

'Why oh why didn't someone tell me? You all knew who my

father was. I should have known too.' She could hear her voice rising hysterically but she couldn't help herself. 'Mother never once mentioned him. I had a right to know! Why did everyone keep it a secret from me?' Avril couldn't stop the tears which were pouring down her pale cheeks. She stared wildly at Hannah. 'I–I'm glad he's dead!' she said vehemently. 'I suppose you think that's terrible, but he must have been a horrible man.' Hannah forced herself to speak calmly.

'Your mother would be badly shocked by her ordeal, Avril. She never talked to me about it either. I believe she pushed it to the back of her mind and tried to forget it ever happened. Dearest Avril, it wasn't that she wanted to deceive you. She never meant to hurt you. She loved you. You were the most precious thing in the world to her. It took a long time before she learned to trust another man. I shall always be grateful to Lint for his patience and for loving her so dearly.'

'Yes.' Avril gulped and brushed away her tears with an effort. 'I miss Mother terribly but so does Dad. I hear him up in the night, prowling around the kitchen, making a drink, or in his study.'

'It is early days yet and time is a great healer. I realize that is a platitude, but there is truth in it. I grieve for your father too because their time together was so short, and yet very few couples experience a love like theirs. Try to remember that, my dear, and be thankful that your mother loved you so much and that she found happiness too eventually.'

'There's so much to take in. I really, really wish she had talked to me about everything, but I thank you for telling me. I'd like to go home now. I–I want to be alone.' Hannah's heart ached at the sight of her forlorn young face.

'I understand my dear, and so will Megan. She felt we should have told you some time ago but it was not my place to tell you while Ruth was alive.'

'No, I suppose not.'

'Avril, I do hope you will not allow any of this to come between you and Dean Scott, if you truly love him.'

'We'll see,' Avril said, non-committally.

Twelve

Avril was thankful she had the house to herself. She did not sleep well that night. Her mind kept going over every detail of what she had learned and trying to remember anything she had heard of Fred Caraford, the man who was her father. She struggled to recall the only time she had seen him but she had paid little attention to him then and he had paid none to her. She still felt hurt that her mother had not felt able to talk to her about her birth and her identity before she died, but she could understand why she had tried to block such a trauma out of her mind. What sort of evil brute would force himself on an innocent girl? He must have been horrible, yet the dying man she had seen at Granny Caraford's had left no such impression on her young mind. Granny Caraford had loved him once and she had taken him in and given him a home when he needed help so surely he couldn't have been all bad, or so she tried to comfort herself. At least she knew who she was now. Uncle Steven and Granny Caraford really were her relatives, and Samuel, Tania and Alexander shared the same grandfather as herself.

When Molly Scott called in on her way to the village Avril was dressed and had nibbled a slice of toast while her mind continued to revolve around her discovery.

'Shall I bring your newspapers, lassie, and is there anything else you want from the shop?' Molly called cheerfully.

'Only the papers, thanks,' Avril said, then frowned. 'No. On second thoughts I'll come with you and you can drop me off at the end of the drive on your way home, if that's all right?'

'Suits me fine, Avril.' Molly smiled. 'You're looking better today.'

'Yes,' Avril's mouth firmed. 'I don't want the people in the village to think I'm afraid to venture into the shop because of Mrs Scott. Dad will be back and collecting his own papers after tomorrow.'

'That's the spirit,' Molly said approvingly.

Mrs Williams was her usual pleasant self and the shop was busy so Avril was relieved to be handed the papers with nothing more than the usual greeting and a smile. She was only one of millions of people in the world with problems she realized, glad she had come in person.

'Is your grandmother recovering from the influenza, Avril?' Molly asked on the way home.

'Yes, though she still looks pale and tired,' Avril responded readily. She hesitated, then added, 'She showed me some of her family photographs, including one of my real grandmother. She says I resemble her except that I have my mother's dark eyes and eyebrows.'

'Your – your *real* grandmother?' Molly echoed.

'Yes. She and Granny Caraford were cousins and very close friends when they were young. She had a little boy called Fred, but she died soon after he was born so Granny Caraford brought him up at Willowburn. Later she married his father, Edward Caraford, and they had Uncle Steven.' Avril kept her voice flat and expressionless when she added, 'Fred forced his attentions on my mother while she was a young landgirl at Willowburn. She ran away home to Westmorland to her father. Granny Caraford didn't know about me until Fred went to Canada. He did come back. I met him once but he was dying with cancer. Granny Caraford was looking after him. I wish I had known who he was,' she added vehemently. 'I would have paid more attention. They should have told me!'

'So,' Molly said carefully, 'the Carafords are your blood relatives? Do you – do you feel better about things?' she asked diffidently.

'I–I don't know. I need time to take it all in. I have not told anyone else. I'd rather tell Dean myself, but I need time . . .' She raised her dark eyes to Molly Scott's kindly gaze. 'At least I'm not a gypsy's brat,' she added bitterly, 'or any of the other things his mother accused me of.'

'Don't you fret about Grizel. She has an evil tongue. This never was anyone else's business and I'll not be passing it on, except to Bill. Ye'll not mind that? We don't have any secrets from each other ye see.'

'I know.' Avril gave her a faint smile. 'It's just that so much has happened recently it's hard to take everything in.'

'I can understand that, Avril, but I hope you'll not wait too long before you talk to Dean. He's worried about you.'

'I shall be back to work tomorrow, but I–I will tell him eventually.'

In her heart Avril still wondered what sort of man her father had been. Maybe Mrs Scott was justified in trying to protect Dean from a wife who had bad blood in her – not that Dean had ever asked her to be his wife. Maybe he never would now.

When Lint returned he saw that Avril had not been sleeping. He did not shy away from the subject.

'There's little more I can tell you, my dear. Your mother and I only discussed it once. She wanted to put it out of her mind. Mrs Caraford would know Fred better than anyone and I know she loves you as she loves her other grandchildren. There was a deep bond of affection between her and your mother. She wished passionately that things could have been different, but from a selfish point of view I'm thankful you both belonged to me.'

'Yes, so am I. I feel so mixed up inside though,' Avril said unhappily.

'It will take a little time but as far as I'm concerned, Avril, you are as dear to me as if you had been my own child. I hope you will remember that?'

'Oh I do, and I have never wanted anyone else as my father. Please don't ever think that.'

'I'm glad you feel that way too. There were other aspects which hurt your mother and made her even more reluctant to talk about the past. When she returned home to her father some of his parishioners – people they had both known and respected for many years – shunned her when they realized she was expecting a child out of wedlock. They condemned her without ever knowing the circumstances. I believe that really hurt both Ruth and your grandfather, because we both know she was never a woman without principles and self-respect.'

'I must have caused her a lot of sorrow,' Avril said softly.

'No. She told me she worshipped you from the moment she saw you and held you in her arms. Until then she had never believed the saying – every cloud has a silver lining. She said Fred Caraford was the blackest cloud that had ever entered her life but you were the silver lining and she had never wanted to be parted from you.'

'We were very close,' Avril admitted. 'She must have hated my father for what he did but she never held it against me.'

'Of course she didn't. She loved you dearly and she was so

happy when she saw how delighted you were to have Callum and Craig for your brothers.'

'I loved them from the first moment I saw their crumpled wee faces,' Avril said with a reminiscent smile.

'They're lucky to have such devotion, especially now. They love you very much Avril, and they're beginning to depend on you, but I don't want you to make sacrifices for them. I want you to live your own life, and hopefully find someone to love as your mother and I loved each other.'

'If someone loved me enough they would love my young brothers too, as you loved me.'

'Maybe, maybe not. Two boisterous boys can be a handful and most young men would be quick to tell you they are my responsibility. I took them to see the boarding school I attended while we were down in Gloucestershire. They seem to think they will be happy there so they will start after the summer holidays. I shall have to make provision for when they have holidays of course. It is vital they know this is their home. I hope I shall be able to come to some arrangement with Bessie. What do you think?'

'Yes. I'm sure we shall manage between us. Bessie thinks the world of them. She's helped look after them since they were born.'

'Yes, that makes a difference, especially when she has no children of her own. But Avril, you must remember I do not expect you to put the boys before your own happiness.'

'I wouldn't be happy if I thought they were homesick or miserable, wherever they are.'

Lint had received a great deal of cooperation from his colleagues during the last few months of Ruth's illness and he was doing his best to repay them. The surgeon who had been seconded to them for the past six months was returning to Birmingham so he knew there was a busy time ahead. He welcomed the prospect. He had always found satisfaction in his work and it helped him set aside his personal grief. He was usually free at the weekends and he dreaded being in the house without Ruth. He still found himself planning to tell her things, or share a private joke, only to remember she was no longer there. He knew he was fortunate that Avril had taken over the running of the house with Bessie to help but it was not that sort of comfort he craved and no one on this earth could fill the void which Ruth's death had left in his life.

He enjoyed physical work as an antidote to his life in the hospital but he needed it now to tire him and make him sleep. He resolved to make a start on the alterations to the row of farm buildings which bordered one side of their yard. He knew Bill Scott was keen to rent them.

Avril was restless and uncertain. Another week passed and she had not called on Dean, but neither had he been in touch with her. She was beset by doubts and misgivings, certain that Dean must be influenced by his mother's opinions. Then there were the boys. Maybe her father was right, maybe they were too much for a young man to accept in his life but she knew she could never desert them while they needed her.

'I think I'll go to Annan and get some fresh beef and maybe a chicken,' she said to her father on Saturday morning. 'I would like to make the best use of the freezer now we have it. If I prepare some casseroles it will make our evening meals quicker and easier to prepare when I'm working.'

'You're not going over to see Dean then?' Lint asked.

'He'll be busy working,' she said briefly.

'Well I think I'll go over to Bengairney to see Steven and discuss the alterations to the buildings before I start,' he said. 'Bill tells me young folk don't want to use a fork and wheelbarrow for cleaning out sheds these days. They all want to sit on tractors. I'd like to make a proper job of the conversion. I'll take the boys with me. They'll enjoy spending an hour or two with Alexander.'

Both Steven and Megan seemed pleased to see him and Lint was grateful for their welcome. Callum and Craig had had no doubts about theirs. They pulled on their wellingtons and scampered off with Alexander.

'Is Rosy not here today?' Lint asked.

'Not yet,' Megan said with a wry grin. 'She has a bigger bicycle now and she has cycled here twice without even telling her mother. She only telephoned once she'd arrived because I insisted.'

'It's quite a distance for her to come on her own,' Lint whistled.

'Yes. Steven gave her a lift home and put her bike in the back of the Land Rover. She's a hardy wee thing for all she's small for her age.'

'I think we should give Dean a ring,' Steven said when he joined them. If he's free he'll probably have some ideas about the best way to convert the sheds to make the most use of them. Wasn't one of them a byre at one time?'

'Yes, it was. The nearest end to the house. We made the old dairy into a boiler room and cloakroom. The wooden stalls are still in the byre. They need knocking out. The partition walls are wood too so it will not be difficult to make one empty shell, but I don't know whether that's what Bill would want and he's very diffident about telling me.'

As things turned out Dean was working but he said he would be free by lunchtime.

'We'll come down to see you instead then, Dean,' Steven said. 'It will save you time. Just a minute. Megan is calling me.' Steven listened to his wife's suggestion. 'She says she will send down a pot of broth and some sandwiches and then we can talk while we eat. Is that all right? I think Lint would be interested to see some of the sheds you have at Martinwold. It might give him some ideas of his own.'

Dean was unsure whether he wanted to see them or not. He knew from his Aunt Molly that Avril had learned who her real father was from Mrs Caraford so why hadn't she called to tell him? He missed her terribly but both Megan and his Aunt advised him to give her time to sort out her feelings. Silently he cursed his mother for her interference and the humiliation she had caused Avril. She had succeeded in driving a wedge between them.

Lint observed the sheds at Martinwold with genuine interest.

'The new sheds are not as substantial as the traditional stone and slate buildings which we have but I can see how light and roomy they are for getting in with a tractor and trailer. Our sheds are very low inside because there is a hay loft above for storing the fodder. The whole floor will need to be replaced.'

'In that case,' Dean said quickly, 'it would be better to remove it altogether, if you don't mind me offering an opinion?' he added uncertainly.

'Of course not, Dean. That's why we came to see you, to get ideas,' Lint assured him.

'The young animals thrive better if they have plenty of ventilation.'

'That's true,' Steven agreed. 'They don't get so many breathing problems. If the boards are rotten anyway I'd agree with Dean. Remove the lot. Besides they need to be fairly high to get inside with a tractor.'

'When I see how the Martinwold byre has been converted to a milking parlour we could almost have done the same,' Lint mused.

'Mmm, you're right. It would have been ideal, but, apart from the expense, I don't see Uncle Bill changing to a milking parlour,' Dean said. 'Though I believe most dairy farms will change in time. Numbers are so much more flexible with a parlour.'

'All this lets me see what can be done,' Lint mused thoughtfully. 'The buildings are in good condition at Riverview. I'll gut out the insides but you'll have to come over and tell me where I should make the new doors. Bill wants them facing towards Sylvanside.'

'I reckon one wide door in the middle would be adequate,' Dean suggested. 'Wide enough for a tractor and trailer to get in. If it is in the middle you can work from either end.'

'But what about partitions for the animals?' Lint asked.

'Bill Scott could make his own pens with gates,' Steven said. 'They'd be movable and he'll be able to change the sizes according to the sort of cattle or calves he puts in.'

'Do you think he'd want that?' Lint asked doubtfully.

'He would need a hand to sort things out but he'll see the advantages when I've discussed it with him,' Dean said. 'Versatility is important these days.'

'Especially if you can save on labour,' Samuel chipped in. 'Isn't that right, Dad?'

'It is where you young folk are concerned,' Steven agreed. 'This generation barely know how to wield a brush and shovel,' he added with a grin at Lint.

'We use our brains instead of brawn,' Samuel declared.

'Mmm, I get the picture,' Lint said. 'Come over and see us next weekend if you're free, Dean, or the one after. We can discuss it more then. Meanwhile I shall concentrate on removing all the wooden partitions. I shall only be working at it at the weekends. I'll get a builder to help with the new doorway. It will need a big lintel for support. I intend to have it ready before the winter so your uncle can get his animals housed.'

★   ★   ★

Avril didn't know whether she was glad or sorry when her father told her Dean was coming to see them next weekend. As the week wore on her nerves and her excitement increased. She did want to see him and she needed to talk to him and find out whether he shared any of his mother's opinions but the longer the silence between them the more her uncertainties increased. It would be better on her own territory. On Friday evening she washed her hair and took more time that usual setting it into a style Dean liked. Mentally she planned their meals.

Thirteen

On the Wednesday following Lint and Steven's visit to Martinwold Mr Turner came to the yard in search of Dean.

'I've a favour to ask of you, Dean,' he announced. 'I know it is your free weekend coming up but I would like you to change it. I'm concerned about my wife. I'd like to take her away for a few days. She's too stressed and she's not sleeping well. I think a change of scenery might do her good.'

'I'm sorry to hear Mrs Turner is not well,' Dean said.

'Och I expect it's Natalie's fault, but she's old enough to stand on her own feet and we've been more than generous to her and that man she married.' Dean had noticed he never referred to Natalie's husband by name, or as his son-in-law and his mouth always tightened whenever he was mentioned. 'I changed my Will about a month ago and I made the mistake of telling my wife what I'd done.' He shrugged. 'Not that I should be telling a young fellow like you about wills or families. In fact I should have known better than to tell my wife. I expect she's told Natalie and now she's plaguing the life out of her mother. Anyway what I wanted to know is whether you'd mind swapping your weekend off. I'd feel easier about being away if I knew you were here to keep an eye on everything – and I mean everything.' Again his mouth tightened and he looked Dean in the eye. 'We used to leave a key for the house with Natalie if we were away but I vowed I wouldn't do that again after the last time. They moved in for the weekend and threw a party; must have been a big one. They emptied the drinks cabinet and left me to pay a huge bill at the butcher's and another at the grocer's.' His face was grim but he relaxed as he looked at Dean, noting his concerned expression. He might be young but he was trustworthy. He was conscientious too and intelligent. He would use his initiative if anything did go wrong. 'I know you'd get the vet or ask Steven Caraford for advice if you were in doubt about any of the animals.'

'Yes, of course.'

'And you'll not let the bull out unless you have somebody with you?'

'I never do that, not with this fellow anyway. He's not to be trusted.'

Dean had been looking forward to spending most of his free weekend at Sylvanside, hoping to see Avril and have a real talk, but he knew he could not refuse his boss's request. Mr Turner treated him well and he seemed genuinely worried about his wife.

'I'll do my best to see that things run smoothly,' he promised.

'Good lad, I knew I could rely on you. I plan to leave tomorrow until Tuesday or Wednesday of next week.' He hesitated then shook his head almost despairingly. 'I shouldn't be burdening you with my family problems but I know you're not a gossip. You have a key to the farm office and the filing cabinet where we keep all the animal records, haven't you?'

'Yes, I have, but the only thing I'm likely to need would be the pedigrees if any of the cows we selected for AI come on heat. I'd need to phone the insemination centre and have the cow's details ready.'

'That's no problem. But Dean, I'd like you to keep this key as well until I get back. It's for the door from the office through to the house. There shouldn't be anything to worry about but you never know. If we get a power cut or anything like that perhaps you could go through and check the freezer and make sure everything else is in order? I'd like to know there's someone to keep an eye on things.'

'Thank you, sir.' Dean flushed at the compliment.

'You're a good fellow, Dean.' Mr Turner patted him on the shoulder. 'I'll make it up to you.'

At Riverview Saturday came and went but there was no sign of Dean.

'Perhaps something came up,' Lint said. 'Maybe a cow calving or something like that. It didn't occur to him that Mr Turner might be the unwitting cause. Sunday also passed without Dean's arrival.

'I'm not sure if we fixed which weekend exactly . . .' Lint said, sensing Avril's tension and disappointment.

He could have telephoned at least, Avril thought. Was he paying her back for not calling on him at Martinwold? Or had he changed his mind about wanting to see her at all now that he'd had time to consider his mother's point of view?

One of the cows had come on heat for the second time. It was Sunday evening but Dean knew if he telephoned and left a message at the AI Centre tonight they would get one of the first visits by the inseminator in the morning and the cow would be more likely to be receptive to the semen than if she had to wait until later in the day. Artificial Insemination could still be a bit hit and miss and some of the selected semen was expensive. He decided to go up to the farm office to phone and get the information required for the form filling to save time in the morning.

It was about seven in the evening when he unlocked the office door. He almost jumped out of his skin when a bulky figure spun round to confront him. He recognized Doctor Wright-Manton, although they had never been introduced. What had the man been doing poking around Mr Turner's safe, and why was he here at all? It was clear he had come through to the office from the house because the door was wide open.

'Who are you? What business have you coming creeping in here?' Wright-Manton demanded angrily.

'I am Mr Turner's herdsman. This is the farm office and I understood I was the only person with a key during Mr Turner's absence so I might ask you what business you have in here?'

'Don't be impertinent! I am Turner's son-in-law. I'm checking everything is in order as he asked me to do in his absence.' He scowled when he saw the disbelief on Dean's expressive face. Dean turned his back and went to unlock the filing cabinet. He searched for the pedigree of the animal he wanted. Wright-Manton watched with narrowed eyes.

'Do you have a key to both filing cabinets?'

'No, only this one with the records for the animals. Mr Turner deals with the men's wages and tax and any other business so he uses the other cabinet.'

'You'll know the combination to the safe though?' Wright-Manton suggested slyly.

'The safe? Of course I don't know the combination. Only Mr Turner has access to that.'

'Oh come on, don't tell me you haven't peered over his shoulder and made a note of it,' Wright-Manton said with a sneer.

'I have no reason to do such a thing,' Dean said indignantly.

'But you'll know what he keeps in there?'

'I know he keeps the cash for the men's wages there after he has been to the bank.'

'So there will be cash in there now?'

'I shouldn't think there'll be much. He paid the men early, before he went away.'

'Including you?'

'No. I get mine once a month and he pays me with a cheque. I prefer it that way and then I'm not so tempted to spend it all.'

'Another of the thrifty Scots, like Turner himself, eh?' Wright-Manton sneered again. 'Is that how you're worming your way into his favour? What else does he keep in his safe then? Does he keep his Will in there?'

'I wouldn't know anything about that,' Dean said coldly. 'That's none of my business.' He would have liked to add 'or yours either,' but he suspected the doctor had had quite a bit to drink and he might turn nasty. 'You'll have to excuse me I need to get this information written out ready for morning.' He turned back to the desk, leaving the other man prowling around the office. Dean made the task last far longer than he needed. Eventually Wright-Manton went back into the main house, locking the door behind him. So he did have a key after all, thought Dean with a frown, and yet Mr Turner had been adamant that only he would have access to the house via the office. He gathered his information and closed the cabinet but still he lingered. He heard footsteps in the room above, then Wright-Manton stumbling on his way down the stairs. Dean lingered for over an hour in the office. He felt uneasy about leaving until he knew the other man had left and locked up properly behind him. Eventually he heard a car driving away and realized Wright-Manton had parked round the back, obviously not wanting to be seen around his father-in-law's house during his absence.

Dean felt uneasy and he didn't sleep well that night. Supposing Mr Turner's son-in-law had taken money, or more drink? Would his boss think he'd taken it, or disturbed anything else? Wright-Manton had certainly been searching for something. He worried about it all next day. It was a lovely summer evening and he decided to walk through the in-calf heifers and then over the next field to Bengairney. The exercise would do him good and he might tell Steven about his encounter with Wright-Manton.

As it happened Steven and Samuel were strolling round one of the Bengairney fields near the Martinwold boundary. They were also inspecting a group of in-calf heifers but when Samuel saw Dean he waved enthusiastically and they came to meet him.

'Were you just out for a walk, Dean or were you coming down to see Megan?' Steven asked.

'I was doing the same as you and kept on walking.' Dean frowned.

'Something bothering you? Mr Turner will not be back yet, is he?'

'No, he's not due back until Wednesday or Thursday.' He hesitated then decided to tell Steven about finding Wright-Manton prowling around the house. 'Mr Turner definitely said he was not leaving a key with them after the last time. If he has taken anything, even if it is only a bottle of whisky I wouldn't know but I'll bet Mr Turner will. I'd hate him to think I'd taken anything. I don't even like the thought of going into the house when the Turners are away.'

'I reckon I'd feel the same,' Steven said slowly. 'It's a bit tricky when Wright-Manton is his son-in-law. It may be all right for him to express his opinion but he might not like anyone else criticizing his daughter's husband.'

'I'd tell him that man had been in his house,' Samuel said with youthful indignation. 'Anyway you said Mr Turner had never liked him, Dad.'

'That's true and Lint can't stick the man and he's not one to criticize as a rule. Maybe Sam's right, Dean. Try to mention it casually but let him know you met his son-in-law at the house. Apart from anything else he ought to know Wright-Manton has a key. Maybe Mrs Turner left one with Natalie.'

Dean felt better for discussing things with Steven. Everything else went well and when Mr Turner returned he seemed more cheerful.

'Did any of the cows need AI while I was away?'

'Oh yes, Martinwold Jess came back again. It's her second service so I asked for the same bull – the one we'd chosen.'

'Good lad. Did you find the details all right?'

'Yes, I went up to get them on Sunday evening. I was a bit surprised to see Doctor Wright-Manton in the farm office. Is he interested in the pedigrees?' Dean managed to sound reasonably innocent, or so he hoped.

'You saw Natalie's husband in the office? Did you let him in?'

'Oh no. He was already there when I arrived. He had come through from the house. I haven't checked anything in the house myself, by the way. We had no power cuts or anything else to worry about.' Mr Turner stared at him.

'Hell and damnation!' he muttered. 'Nothing to worry about? That sly rat must have a copy of the back door key. He must have had one made when Natalie had it the last time. I'll get the bloody locks changed before I leave my house again – in fact I shall send for the joiner and do it today. What was he looking for in the farm office anyway? Did he say?'

'N–no, not really. Well he asked what you kept in the safe. I told him you kept the cash for the wages there but that you'd paid them before you left. He asked if you kept your Will in there and if I knew the combination. I'm glad I didn't know anything about the safe.'

'The sly bugger.' Murdo Turner rarely swore and he looked ruefully at Dean. 'Sorry lad. I shouldn't take out my irritation on you.' He looked a bit shamefaced.

'It seems I'm not the only one who has trouble with family,' Dean said dryly.

'Surely you don't have any trouble? I met your father, didn't I? He seemed a very decent man.'

'That was Uncle Bill, my father's brother. There's nothing wrong with my father either though. It's my mother who causes trouble.'

'I don't suppose she's happy about you coming to work for me, is that it?' Mr Turner asked shrewdly.

'Something like that,' Dean admitted. 'The trouble is she voices her disapproval wherever she is, even in public. She has a bitter tongue.'

'Ah, I see.' Mr Turner nodded and looked keenly at Dean. 'I

haven't seen Avril round here for a few weeks. That wouldn't be due to your mother, would it?'

'She hurt Avril badly.' Dean didn't really want to talk about that so he changed the subject. 'You wouldn't need to change your locks if you put a bolt on the inside of the doors but you would have to leave by the office door if you were locking up the house for a while.'

'That's not a bad idea, Dean,' Mr Turner said, considering. 'It's not a bad idea at all in fact. If I did get new locks I wouldn't be surprised if my wife gave a key to Natalie. Mmm, I'll get some bolts fixed and I'll put a stop to that rogue prowling around my house when I'm not here.'

Avril had waited all weekend to see Dean. He hadn't even bothered to telephone. The longer the silence went on between them the harder it was to break. She was restless and unhappy but she was no longer sure of a welcome if she called at Martinwold. The following Friday evening she decided to make a different detour and call on Granny Caraford instead.

'Oh Avril, I am pleased you've come,' Hannah Caraford greeted her with relief.

'Is something wrong, Granny C? You seem upset.'

'I am, but I'm angry and disappointed too. You knew I had rented the apartment to a young couple who said they had come up from Manchester and were looking round to buy a house?'

'Yes. What have they done?'

'They got behind with their rent before I was ill and I didn't have the energy to check my bank statements for a while. They have not paid anything for the last four months so I went round to tell them they would have to start paying a bit extra each month to clear the debt. The young man was really abusive and the girl sulked and said they couldn't afford to pay.'

'This is awful. You shouldn't be having worries like this. Could Steven help you deal with them?'

'It's too late,' she said flatly. 'They've packed up and gone. He must have used one of the vans from his work and loaded it up during the night, otherwise I would have seen them. They not only owed four months rent they have taken all the small pieces of furniture, the mirror from the bathroom, even the curtain rails and the light bulbs.'

'Oh Granny C that's terrible!' Avril put her arms round the older woman and hugged her warmly. She was surprised when Hannah leaned against her, almost as though she was too weary to cope with such troubles. Avril knew she used the rent from the apartment to supplement her pension since she had stopped keeping her hens and the two sows. 'Should we tell the police?' she asked diffidently. 'When did it happen?'

'They must have gone the night before last. I don't want to involve the police. I don't know where they have gone and you can't be sure whether they might come back and take revenge of some sort. The worst of it is they have left the place in an awful mess. It will all need redecorating and they have ruined the carpets with stains and oil, I think he must have worked on his motor bike in the living room.'

'Surely not! Can I go in and have a look?'

'Aye, you do that lassie. I'll make a cup of tea. Would you like to stay for a meal? I have some nice ham and salad and I'd appreciate the company.'

'That would be lovely. I've left supper for the boys. Dad said he would be home early since it's Friday.'

Avril took the key and went to look at the apartment. It was even worse than she had anticipated. Anger boiled in her. People shouldn't be allowed to get away with such things but she could understand how nervous Granny C felt, especially since the man had been nasty already.

'Do Steven and Megan know?' she asked when she rejoined Hannah.

'No. To tell the truth I feel foolish for letting them get away so long without paying and I expect Steven will be angry on my behalf, or think I'm a silly old woman.'

'I'm sure he'll not think that but I don't blame him for being angry about the mess they have left and the way they have cheated you out of the rent.'

As they washed up together Hannah was silent for a little while and then she said quickly, before she could change her mind, 'Do you remember Mr Paterson, Avril, Angus Paterson?'

'Yes, of course I remember him very well. He was always so

kind to me and Mum when we lived here. And I remember him drawing the plans for Megan's parents when they converted Honeysuckle Cottage. It was lovely when he'd finished wasn't it? We haven't seen him for a while. Is he keeping well?'

'Quite well but he has given up driving now. He will be eighty this year but his brain is still as active as ever.' She hesitated again then went on. 'He thinks I should sell this house and the apartment and build a small bungalow for myself in the orchard. He says there's any amount of land for two houses, let alone one, though he knows I wouldn't want two of course. He wants to draw up some plans for me to consider. He says he would like to do it as one last project.'

'I see. What do you think about it?'

'I'm not sure. I had never considered such a plan. Shall we go out and have a look before it gets dark? There is plenty of room at the side for me to have my own drive in and Angus says it wouldn't be expensive to screen it off with some trellis if I couldn't afford to build a wall. His idea is that I should have spare capital from the sale of this house and the apartment and I could use it, or the interest, when I need anything extra.'

'Mmm, well that does sound a reasonable suggestion,' Avril said slowly.

'Angus thinks it would be less of a worry for me than having tenants.'

'He could be right about that,' Avril said with feeling. They walked down the garden to the orchard which had been so loved and familiar to Avril as a child. 'Oh yes,' she said, 'I can see what Mr Paterson means. It would be so secluded and private here and yet not too far from the road or neighbours. It's a lovely view across the fields too and you would still have your garden.'

'There's just one thing I'm not so sure about,' Hannah said slowly. 'It would cost quite a bit to build a bungalow. Angus has suggested paying for everything until it is finished and then I can repay him when I sell the house and the apartment. He has been a very good friend for a long while now but I'm not sure I want to be in his debt. If anything happened to him I would need to repay the money immediately, but of course I can't say that to him.'

'No, I can see that,' Avril said slowly. 'Don't you think you should discuss it with Steven?'

'If he thinks I'm short of money he will be offering to pay for things and I don't want that. I'm sorry, lassie. I shouldn't be burdening you with my problems but I do feel better for your visit.'

'You used to tell Mum that a problem shared is a problem halved,' Avril said with a smile. 'Anyway I've enjoyed my visit, except for seeing the state of the apartment, and I think Mr Paterson's idea is an excellent one.'

'Yes, I'm coming round to thinking so too and I'm sure I shall find a solution.'

'Couldn't you sell the apartment separately instead of letting it again? That would release some capital.'

'I hadn't thought of that. Whether I sell or let, it will need redecorating first,' Hannah said glumly, 'but we'll forget about that for now. Don't be too long before you come to see me again, Avril. I always enjoyed your company, even when you were a wee bairnie.'

'Yes, I loved following you around the hens and the wee pigs, and you awakened my interest in cooking too.'

'Aye, the last time I spoke to Lint he was telling me what a good job you're making of running the house for them all, but he's worried in case he deprives you of your freedom to enjoy your own life. How is Dean Scott getting on?'

'I–I haven't seen him for a while,' Avril admitted.

'So you havena told him who your real father is yet then? Not that I think it will make the slightest difference to him. Don't leave it too long, lassie. I'd like to see you happily married.'

Happily married, Avril thought as she drove home to Riverview. Marriage was one thing Dean had never mentioned, and he didn't seem likely to either. Even if he did, how could she desert the boys after promising she would be there for them?

Fourteen

The twins were getting ready for bed when Avril arrived home. They greeted her as though she had been away for a week instead of an evening. Their obvious affection warmed her heart but Lint looked at her shrewdly. She was home earlier than he had expected and she seemed preoccupied. When he had tucked the boys up in bed and heard their prayers he joined her in the little sitting room.

'Did you call to see Dean this evening?' he asked. 'Will he be coming over tomorrow?'

'I don't know. I called on Granny Caraford.' She told him about the trouble Hannah had been having and the awful mess her tenants had left behind. 'She'll never be able to deal with it herself; the walls in all the rooms need painting.' She went on to tell him about Mr Paterson's suggestion to build a small bungalow. Lint was silent for a while, considering.

'I can understand Mrs Caraford feeling let down and taken in by people she has treated kindly, but I'm sure Steven wouldn't consider her foolish. I think he ought to know. It's not good for her to have things preying on her mind at her age. The sooner she gets the place cleared up and habitable again the better she will feel. Then she can put it all behind her and decide whether to put it on the market or relet.'

'I agree but do you think she'd feel I've been telling tales if I telephoned Aunt Megan and told her. I er . . . I did wonder if Samuel is free if we could go down and do some of the clearing up this weekend but it would mean leaving the boys at home with you.'

'Ah Avril, you must not let the boys hold you back from doing the things you want to do. Besides we're going to work on the shed and I've half promised to make them a cart with the wheels from their old pram if any of the boards are usable and I'm sure they will be.'

'I see. So you think it would be all right if I phone Aunt Megan?'

'I think it's a good idea.'

Megan was dismayed by the news and insisted they would all help clear up the mess.

'I'll talk to Steven when he comes in,' she said. 'If he's not too busy we'll bring Sam and Tania down in the Land Rover and we'll lift whatever carpets need to be dumped and bring them here to burn. Granny C had the apartment papered with that Anaglypta paper after Ruth moved out didn't she?'

'Yes, she thought it would be easier to emulsion the walls if they needed to be smartened up between tenants but this couple seem to have deliberately made a mess in every room. The whole lot needs painting.'

'I have plenty of paint brushes and a big tin of cream emulsion to get you started. I could run into Annan and get whatever colour Granny Caraford wants for the living room. Are you sure you don't mind giving up your Saturday to help, Avril?'

'I'd be happy to do it and I would feel a whole lot better if Granny C puts this nasty episode behind her. She really is upset.'

'Yes, it's not good for her,' Megan agreed. 'She's seventy-three and she shouldn't be cleaning up after useless tenants.' Avril didn't mention Mr Paterson's proposal. She felt that was Granny C's affair.

The following morning Avril arrived first as she had intended.

'I hope you don't mind Granny,' she said diffidently, 'but I've come to help you clear up the apartment. I told Aunt Megan what had happened and they are coming down to take away the wasted carpets. Tania wants to help too and Samuel will help me emulsion the walls to freshen everything up. Do you mind?' Avril looked at her, her brown eyes wide and anxious.

'Mind, lassie? Oh Avril . . .' Her voice shook and she hugged Avril warmly. 'I didn't expect you to do anything like this, but I should have known you're just as kind and considerate as your mother always was.' Her voice shook. 'I really wondered how I was going to cope with it all.'

'Well that's fine then. We're all young and fit so we'll get cracking as soon as Sam and Tania get here. Shall we have another look? I think the spare bedroom carpet might be all right with a good brushing, and the linoleum in the bathroom, the kitchen and the passage should come up all right with a good scrub and a polish, although the rugs will have to go. They must have walked everywhere in muddy boots.'

'Yes. The living room and the main bedroom carpets are the worst.'

'If you do decide to sell the apartment soon the living room will look better bare than with a filthy carpet. Someone buying will want to choose their own carpets anyway.'

'Yes, you're right, Avril and the more I think about it the more I think I should sell. Angus Paterson is right about a bungalow and it is a good idea of yours to sell the apartment so that I have enough capital to make a start. Maybe I should tell Steven and see what he thinks. Meanwhile I'd better start peeling some vegetables for a big pot of soup and I'll ask Megan to bring me some fresh rolls if she is going to Annan.' She smiled. 'Hungry workers will need to be fed. Ah, here they come.'

In spite of the work there was a lot of laughter and satisfaction. At fourteen Tania was as tall as Avril and she proved herself more capable than her elders had thought possible considering she usually had her nose in a book. Between them they transformed the apartment. Hannah telephoned Angus Paterson and he came round with what he called a rough draft of his suggestions for Steven to see. The two men and Hannah spent some time viewing the proposed site in the orchard. Steven and Megan thought the bungalow was an excellent idea and Steven offered to provide the rest of the capital. Hannah objected strongly.

'It is nothing compared with what you did for me when I wanted to start farming,' he reminded her. 'I shall only be repaying what you gave me.'

'I don't want repaying, Steven. You know that, but maybe it would be better to borrow the money from you than from Angus and I will pay you back when the bungalow is finished and I sell my own house.'

'So it's all decided,' Steven said with satisfaction as he and Angus Paterson squeezed into Hannah's kitchen to join them all for soup and ham rolls and generous wedges of the apple pies which Megan had brought with her.

'We hadn't meant to stay this long,' Steven said, 'but I'm glad that's all decided. 'I need to be getting back now though. I have a cow looking like calving and a few other jobs to do.'

'I will give Tania and Samuel a lift home,' Avril offered. 'We've agreed we'll all come back tomorrow and paint the hall and the spare bedroom if Granny C doesn't mind us doing it on a Sunday?'

'Sometimes it's better the day, better the deed, lassie and you'll never know what a weight you've taken off my mind.'

Megan insisted Avril should stay for supper when she dropped Tania and Samuel at Bengairney.

'Mother and Father will be bringing Alexander home soon and they hoped they would see you.'

It was much later than Avril had expected by the time she got home.

'All I want now is a hot bath and bed,' she said, smiling at her father. 'It's been a satisfying day but we need to finish the painting and scrub the linoleum tomorrow. I can understand now why you and Mum got so much enjoyment and satisfaction making this house into such a lovely home.'

'We did, didn't we?' Lint sighed heavily, looking around. 'Dean was here for quite a while today. I think he had hoped to see you but he went back to Sylvanside to help Bill Scott with the milking. He seems concerned about him being more breathless than he used to be, but Dean said himself he'd forgotten how much more work there is milking in a byre, emptying the buckets and wheeling the churns to the dairy to be emptied into the bulk tank.'

'I see,' Avril said coolly. 'It's not much of a weekend off for him then.'

'No. He should have been here last weekend but Mr Turner asked him to swap while he and his wife went away for a few days.'

Dean was bitterly disappointed that Avril was away and he wondered if she was avoiding him even though common sense told him she couldn't have known he had changed his weekend off.

He was even more disappointed on the Sunday to find that she was away again, helping Mrs Caraford. They needed a long talk about themselves and he had wanted to tell her he was going to look at a farm to rent. It was on the same estate as Bengairney. He knew he had no hope of getting it but Steven felt it would be good experience for both him and Samuel, who was taking a day off school to go with them. The outgoing tenant had told Steven he was fairly certain the agent had already made his mind up the new tenant would be the elder son of an existing tenant with a good reputation both as a stockman and for paying promptly. Dean had told his Uncle and Aunt about it and they agreed it would be good experience even if nothing came of it.

'We looked at several farms before we were lucky enough to get Sylvanside,' Bill said. 'I reckon we only got it because we were already tenants on the estate. I told you young Dick Forsythe from South Rigg comes to help us during the week, didn't I?'

'Yes, how is he doing?'

'Fine. He'd have made a good farmer. He labours for one or other of his brothers at weekends if they're needing an extra pair of hands but his heart is in farming. He reckons his mother would sell their land tomorrow but she's afraid his father would drink away the money. If you ask me he's doing that anyway. He's owing money all over the place.'

'That's one problem with parents I didn't have,' Dean said, 'so maybe I should count my blessings.'

'If I'd been a younger man, or if I'd had a son to follow on, I reckon I might have borrowed the money to buy the Forsythe's land. They'll not sell the house and buildings because the two older boys have set up their own business premises there and the elder laddie has converted one of the barns into a house for him and his wife. Dick says his other brother is saving up to do the same.'

'It doesn't sound as though there'll be anything left for Dick.' Dean reflected on the unfairness of life and knew he was luckier than many. He was saving quite a bit each month since he had been working for Mr Turner but he would still need some help from his father to buy stock if he did get a farm to rent. Although he was enjoying his work at Martinwold, and getting on surprisingly well with Mr Turner, he knew his life's dream – or half of it – would always be to have a farm of his own to run. Mr Turner knew that was his ambition too but he seemed to understand.

'You can't hold a good man down,' he'd said one day when they were discussing things, 'but from a selfish angle I hope it will be a few years before you get a place, Dean.' He had chuckled aloud and Dean couldn't help but smile. Although Turner was his boss he often found it as easy to discuss things with him as with Steven or his Uncle Bill.

Avril had driven Samuel and Tania home and stayed for supper at Bengairney again. She felt satisfied with their weekend's work but now she was grubby and tired as she drove home. As she cut across country along one of the narrow roads she was astonished to see Dean coming in the opposite direction. They both slowed automatically and before she could gather her wits Dean had screeched to a halt and was reversing; swiftly and precisely. She thought his blue eyes widened with pleasure as he brought his car level with hers. His window was already down and one tanned, muscular arm lay along it, the fine golden hairs gleaming in the evening sunlight but he lowered his eyes now and they looked warily at each other.

'Dean . . .' Her breath caught unexpectedly.

'I've been hoping to see you all weekend, Avril,' he said. 'Have you been avoiding me? Not that I could blame you after my mother's outburst,' he added bitterly.

'Didn't Dad tell you we've been helping Granny Caraford clean her house?' She shrugged and held up her hands. 'See how grubby I am. I'm ready for a bath and bed but we've had a satisfying weekend.' She was chattering, and it was not like her.

'We need to talk, Avril,' Dean said firmly. 'I can't wipe out the trouble and pain my mother caused you. God knows I would if I could. I don't care who your father is or was. I never have. You are you.'

'Maybe I am,' Avril said slowly, giving him a troubled look. 'But there's no denying some of what your mother said is true. I don't know what bad blood flows in my veins, or what traits may come out in my children.' She shuddered, recalling the horror and humiliation she had felt at Mrs Scott's accusations. 'She's afraid her grandchildren may turn out to be a bad lot if you marry me.'

'I'd give anything for the chance to find out,' Dean muttered almost under his breath. Then he looked her in the eye. 'You could feel the same about the blood in my veins with a mother like mine. Maybe you do? Is that it?'

'No of course not, but she is your mother, Dean. She wants what's best for you.'

'I know and I feel guilty about being so angry with her but even Uncle Bill thinks she needs help – from a doctor I mean. I have not been back home since I went to Martinwold. Dad comes to see me if there's anything he wants to discuss about the farm, and we meet at Uncle Bill's and at the market. We can't choose our relations, Avril but we can choose our friends. Can't we at least be friends again? Damn!' he muttered as a car drew up behind him and peeped the horn. 'We need to talk, Avril,' he said urgently. 'When can we meet?' The car horn blared more loudly, impatient as another car drew up behind it. There were two young men in each car and Avril guessed they were probably competing with each other. 'When?' Dean repeated, stubbornly refusing to budge as the car nudged up to his bumper.

'Friday evening. I'll call on my way home.'

'Promise? We'll go out for a meal—'

'I promise, but I'll cook and we will talk.' Only then did Dean grin and his blue eyes lit up as she remembered. He pulled away and the car behind drew level with her.

'Didn't he have time to give you a kiss love? Shall I give you one instead?' the young driver called cheekily. He didn't look any older than Samuel.

'No thanks.' She put her car into gear and drove on but her heart was lighter. Dean really did want to see her.

It seemed a long week to Avril but on Thursday evening she made two steak pies ready for Friday, one for the boys and her father and the other to take to Dean's.

'They look good,' Lint said, coming into the kitchen to make them both a drink of hot chocolate. 'Can I assume you're taking one of them to Dean tomorrow evening?'

'Yes.' Avril felt the colour rise in her cheeks. 'We met on the road last Sunday on our way home.'

'Mmm, I guessed as much. You've looked brighter and happier all week. I think you care for Dean more than you realize, Avril, and you've always been good friends. Friendship is a good basis to build on for a long-term relationship you know. I hope you'll not let any nasty gossip come between you.'

'We shall have to see about that. We're going to have a good long talk tomorrow. It may clear the air.'

'I hope it will. Er . . . there is another thing you might consider.'

'What's that?' Avril asked more sharply than she intended.

'Dean spent quite a bit of time here at the weekend, helping me remove the wooden partitions in the long shed. I get the impression he feels a bit inferior to you, especially now that he's

working as a farm labourer, while you have a university education and a career.'

'I'd never consider Dean inferior whatever he did for work,'
Avril said indignantly. 'And I wouldn't call my present job such
a wonderful career, although it is well enough paid.'

'I know how you feel, my dear, but does Dean? Anyway, to
change the subject. Why don't you take the insulated box I bought
for bringing home food for the freezer? It will keep your pie
cool now the weather is so warm.'

'That's a good idea. Thanks, Dad. How are you getting on with
Grandfather's books on tropical diseases?' she asked, changing the
subject.

'They're remarkably interesting. In fact we had a long discussion on the telephone the other evening. If my father had
been younger I believe he would have gone out to some of these
countries to see what he could do to help the children. I may
even consider it myself one of these days but I shall wait until
Callum and Craig are a bit older and we'll see how they settle
at boarding school.'

'Speaking of boarding school Aunt Megan was saying young
Rosy gets really hysterical whenever her mother mentions it now
the time is drawing nearer. She's adamant she doesn't want to go
away. Megan says Mrs Oliphant gets really upset when Rosy sobs
in her arms and pleads with her to talk to her mother.'

'The Oliphants have seen as much of Rosy as her own parents,
probably more, and Chrissie Oliphant is a kind-hearted woman,
but I'm afraid neither Catherine nor Douglas are likely to listen
to anyone over this. They both went to boarding schools so they
can't see why Rosy shouldn't enjoy going too.'

Fifteen

It seemed a long week to Avril waiting for Friday evening. Dean wished the time would pass more quickly too but he was working long days helping the other men gather in the hay between the morning and evening milking so sleep claimed him as soon as his head touched the pillow. Mr Turner welcomed every pair of hands and he paid Dean overtime for working extra. He wondered what his mother would say if she knew he was earning more each month than the income for the four of them at Northsyke. He knew it would take a lot more than he had saved to stock a farm of his own and keep a wife. It had been a valuable experience viewing the farm with Steven, even though he had not been successful. Steven had mentioned a thirty-acre holding which was coming to let on another estate. Steven and Megan had started off with no more than thirty acres but Steven admitted they had been lucky to get the use of their neighbour's land too. Dean discussed it on the telephone with his Uncle Bill.

'If you want to keep dairy cows, Dean, I reckon you should wait for a bit bigger place than that, unless it's already equipped for dairying?' his uncle advised. 'Steven Caraford and his wife milked their cows by hand when they started off. They must have put in some long hard days but things have moved on since the war. It takes a lot of capital to set up a dairy now, apart from buying the cows. You'd need a byre and a milking machine and a refrigerated tank to hold the milk. Soon there'll be no lorries lifting milk churns at farm road ends and those who canna get a milk tanker into the yard, or afford to buy a bulk tank to hold their milk, will go out of dairying. Be patient laddie. Something will turn up.' Dean knew he was right but he longed to have something more to offer Avril than being a farm labourer.

On Friday evening Dean kept looking out of the milking parlour to see whether Avril's car was parked outside his house. He grinned with pleasure when he saw she had kept her word.

'Mmm, that's a lovely smell of cooking,' he greeted her when he eventually finished his work for the day and entered the kitchen. Avril turned to greet him with a tentative smile. She need not have worried. Dean was so obviously pleased to see her. 'I'll have a quick bath and change my clothes,' he said.

'You look tired, Dean. Are you sure you want me to stay this evening?'

'Of course I want you to stay.' He explained about the hay and extra hours. 'And one of the cows decided to calve last night so I was up at two o' clock to check on her.'

'Was she all right?'

'Yes, she would have managed on her own but I suspected she might be having twins and I was right. I was rewarded with a fine pair of heifer calves.'

'Samuel told me that if you get a heifer and a bull calf as twins the heifer will not breed. Is that right?'

'Yes it is. Speaking of Samuel he has finished school. He's going youth hostelling for a week with his friends but he'll be coming here to live with me after that.'

'I see. I expect you're looking forward to the company,' Avril said, knowing she sounded stiff and wary.

'Oh Avril,' Dean came closer. 'I expect I smell of cows but I've missed you so much. All I want is to hold you in my arms and never let you go.'

'I–I thought when you didn't phone or call . . . I thought maybe you shared your mother's opinions. If–if you do, Dean, I'd rather know now, because—'

'God Avril, I've never shared my mother's opinions over anything and certainly not about you.' He stepped close and took her face in his hands. They were rough and he did smell of cows but Avril didn't care when he bent his head and kissed her hungrily. She was short of breath by the time he released her. 'I'm sorry, I shouldn't have done that – at least not until I've washed and changed.'

'I'm glad you did,' Avril said huskily and her brown eyes were shining as she looked up at him. 'I don't care how mucky you are so long as I know you want me to be here.'

'If I had my way I'd want you to be here all the time – all day and especially all night.' He chuckled when he saw Avril blush. 'It will be good to have Samuel here but that's what I was trying to say – we may not have many more Friday evenings to ourselves and I want you all to myself.'

'We'll be able to go for a walk or to the cinema if it's wet so we can be on our own.'

'Yes, and he'll be going home every second weekend. As a student he'll need to have a go at everything, not just the dairy. Avril . . .' Dean bent and kissed her again, a slow, lingering kiss. 'Now I'll go and change. The smell of your cooking makes me ravenous. Give me ten minutes. Don't run away will you?'

'Not until I've had my dinner anyway,' Avril teased. 'I'm afraid I've raided your garden. You've made a good job of it. I dug some new potatoes and young carrots and I pulled the few beans which were ready. I hope that's all right.'

'Of course it is, it's what they're for but I'm not so good at cooking as I am at growing. Is that rhubarb crumble I see?'

'Yes, you have a good crop of rhubarb. I'd like to take some home with me for the freezer if you don't mind?'

'You're welcome. Mrs Oliphant planted that when they worked here.'

It was a pleasant meal and Dean obviously appreciated her efforts but as they cleared away Avril began to feel nervous. They really needed to talk. Dean came up behind her as she washed the dishes. He put both arms around her and drew her back against him, gently kissing her ear lobe and then her neck, before he rubbed his cheek against her silky hair.

'Whatever you have to tell me, Avril, it will not make any difference to the way I feel about you,' he said softly. 'Leave the dishes. I'll do them later. Come and sit in the garden with me.'

'I–I . . . This is the last of the plates. I'll leave them for you to put away though.' He led her through to the garden to a wooden seat beneath the old apple tree. Without any preliminaries Avril blurted out her news.

'Fred Caraford was my father.'

'Caraford?' Dean couldn't hide his surprise. A dozen questions sprang to his mind, but for a moment he was silent. 'Is he a relative of Steven Caraford?'

'They were half brothers. M–my f–father is dead.'

'But if he was a Caraford surely that's good news, isn't it, Avril?'

'Any man who rapes a young, innocent girl can't be a decent man,' she said bitterly.

'You're sure that's what happened?'

'Granny Caraford told me. She had no doubts. She didn't use the word rape, but she wouldn't would she?' Avril went on to tell him what she knew of Fred and his background. 'I brought some photographs which Granny C has given me. He looks a nice wee boy but even Granny C admits he grew up to be jealous and a bully, taking what he wanted – even from her.'

'But she did forgive him and take him in at the end you say?'

'Yes. She's a good woman. I met him once but he was very ill by then. He never knew he had a daughter.'

'So Steven really is your uncle if they were half brothers,' Dean mused. 'And Mrs Caraford is your grandmother too, in a way. No wonder she has always loved you so much. I see now why you wanted to help her with her house last weekend.' Dean drew her into his arms and held her close, smoothing her hair with a gentle hand. 'I was so afraid you were avoiding me,' he said gruffly. When Avril looked up at him his mouth found hers in a long searching kiss which left no need for words.

The rest of the summer seemed to fly with Avril spending every Friday evening at Martinwold and Dean spending all his free weekends between Sylvanside and Avril. All too soon it was time for the twins to prepare for boarding school. Avril had taken them on several shopping trips to get them properly equipped but parts of the uniform had to be ordered by post. She dreaded them going away but she had agreed to go with them to see the school and she and her father planned to stay for a few days with Grandma and Grandfather Gray.

'I can't wait for you to return,' Dean said as he kissed her goodnight on the Sunday evening before they left. 'Aunt Molly was almost in tears when she said goodbye to Callum and Craig. She is really going to miss them. She has promised to write and tell them what's happening with all the animals. They have names for everything you know.'

'I know. I'm sure they'll miss the farm, not to mention your Aunt Molly's cooking. Good luck with the two farms you are going to view, Dean.'

'Thanks. I haven't much hope of getting either of them but it's all experience and Uncle Bill says they looked at several before they got lucky and were offered the tenancy of Sylvanside. I wish some of the farms on this estate would fall vacant then I might stand a better chance with the land agent, but most of the tenants seem settled. Did I tell you Doris wants to buy a café down at Gretna? Aunt Molly thinks it's a good idea for her to earn her own living and learn to be independent and even mother agrees apparently.'

Although Callum and Craig were a little tearful when it was time to say goodbye they went off happily with the other boys who would be sharing their sleeping quarters. Avril hated saying goodbye to them but she enjoyed her few days' break in Gloucestershire.

'Lint admits he doesn't know how he would have managed without you, Avril,' Grandma Gray said as soon as they were alone together. 'We are grateful to you too, my dear. We both knew how very dear your mother was and how badly he has missed her.'

'I have only done what had to be done,' Avril said simply. 'They were both wonderful to me, and very generous when I was away at university. Anyway it's better for me to keep busy.'

'Yes, it does help,' Grandma Gray agreed, 'but we don't want to see you making too many sacrifices, dear. You must consider your own happiness.'

'I do, but I promised Mum, and the boys, that I would be there for them when they come home for the holidays and I must keep my promise.' She sighed inwardly. Several times she had had the feeling that Dean was on the point of asking her to marry him. Was he deterred by her resolve to provide her brothers with the love and stability she had known herself. She would have enjoyed making his house at Martinwold into a home so they could be together, but what sort of a wife would she make if she returned to Riverview every time the boys came home for their school holidays. Everything seemed to go round in a never-ending circle with no solution.

Callum and Craig usually combined their weekly letter home and Avril was both surprised and pleased when Molly Scott told her they wrote to her about once a fortnight. She was obviously surprised and delighted herself, knowing how often they had neglected their school work in order to get to the farm.

Rosemary-Lavender was a different matter. Twice within two weeks she had written letters to Mrs Oliphant, pleading with her to ask her father to bring her home, telling her how miserable she was and how three of the girls bullied and teased her.

'It's really upsetting Mum,' Megan told Avril. 'After the first letter she tried to talk to Douglas Palmer-Farr but of course he had to discuss it with his wife. Catherine was furious. She told Mum she must not reply as it would make Rosy more unsettled.'

'That's a bit harsh,' Avril protested. 'The boys write to Aunt Molly Scott and she replies. I am glad about that. I think it reassures them we're all still here for them.'

'I'd agree with that,' Megan said. 'Mother has replied so far but it's worrying her in case Catherine is right, but she says Rosy sounds more and more unhappy with each letter. I can't help feeling concerned for young Rosy. She's always been against going away to boarding school.'

'The boys' school gets a day's holiday in October so Dad and I are going down to Gloucester for the weekend and Dad is bringing them to Grandma Gray's to join us.'

'I don't suppose Catherine will even do that for young Rosy,' Megan said glumly. 'She is always too wrapped up in the hotel and her conferences. She has made a success and she enjoys it – if only she would make a bit more time for her daughter. That's another thing – they have insisted she should be called by her full name.'

'That will not help, knowing what girls can be like,' Avril declared. 'How is Sam enjoying working at Martinwold?'

'He loves it. Of course he and Dean have always got on well in spite of the difference in their ages and Mr Turner seems to be really good to both of them. Twice he has taken them to the market with him and bought them their lunch. He explained some of the tricks to watch out for with the dealers and what to look out for if you're buying. He said it was all part of the business of farming. It's such a shame he hasn't a son of his own to carry on.'

'Yes, Dean enjoys being at Martinwold and he says Mr Turner is a much better boss than he had expected and very good at discussing things rather than dictating.'

'My parents always felt he treated his employees fairly, but he's nobody's fool. I suspect Dean is a lot more conscientious than most of the herdsmen Mr Turner has had in recent years,' Megan said dryly.

'Maybe.' Avril smiled. 'He's going to make a new downstairs cloakroom for them with an electric shower in it. That will save them having to keep the Aga cooker fuelled all summer for their hot water.'

'A shower eh? Samuel will like that.'

'The trouble is if they have no Aga they will need an electric hob or something,' Avril said wryly. 'They hadn't thought of that.'

'Men! They only have one thought at a time.' Megan grinned. 'I'll have a word with Granny C. Her new bungalow is having everything fitted into the kitchen so she'll not be needing her electric cooker. She was going to ask Samuel and Dean if they had room for her three piece suite too. She's getting a new one.'

'I'm sure they'll welcome that.' Avril smiled. 'Sam always gives up his armchair for me when I'm there.'

'I expect he thinks you deserve it. He keeps telling me what good meals you make for them on a Friday evening. He wishes you were there every night.' Megan smiled, looking for some response but Avril changed the subject.

The whole country was shocked by the tragedy which had occurred in the Welsh village of Aberfan where a huge mudslide had been washed down from a nearby slag heap and enveloped the school, killing a hundred and sixteen children, as well as twenty-eight adults. Megan shuddered as she imagined the horror and the grief of the families and she knew how upset her mother would be. Chrissie was inclined to brood over such tragedies now that she was growing older and with more time on her hands. So when she telephoned late that evening at the end of October Megan immediately assumed her distress was due to more of the news reports from Aberfan.

'Mother? Please try to calm down,' she said anxiously. 'I can hardly bear to think about the little children dying so needlessly either, but you mustn't make yourself ill. Tears cannot help them now,' she said gently.

'No, no,' Chrissie Oliphant strove to be calmer. 'I mean of course I grieve for the parents of those poor people in Wales but

I'm phoning about young Rosy. She's run away from school and they don't know where she's gone.'

'Rosemary! How can she have run away? She can't have gone far in an hour or two, Mother.'

'They didn't miss her until bedtime yesterday evening. God knows how long she's been gone, or where she can be. They should never have made her go . . .'

'Yesterday?' Megan echoed in dismay. She took a deep breath, and tried to sound reassuring for her mother's sake. 'She can't have got far, Mum. She's probably hiding in a bike shelter or a garden shed or something. They're bound to have such places at a boarding school, aren't they?'

'I don't know. Mr Palmer-Farr came down to ask whether we've heard anything, or if she'd written recently. I had a letter last week. She sounded desperately unhappy but she didn't mention running away. I haven't answered her letter yet. I wish I had now, but I feel I'm deceiving Catherine every time I write to the poor bairn.'

'Mum, it's not good for you getting this upset,' Megan said anxiously. 'Surely they must be searching for her?'

'They are, but it's such a long way away. She'll not know anybody, or the area. Mr Palmer-Farr says they've called in the police. They're widening the search. I canna bear to think about her being out on her own in the dark, in a strange place.' Chrissie began to sob and Megan heard her father take the phone from her.

'We'll let you know if there's any news,' he said. 'I think I'll have to give your mother something to help her sleep. I pray to God the bairn will be found soon. Gentry! They need their bloody heads examined. Sorry lass, I didna mean to swear at you but we're both upset. They should never have made her go away. We'll be in touch.'

Rosy was still missing the following day, and the next. Her photograph was in the papers with appeals and then there were all sorts of rumours of people believing they had seen her. The police were continuing to search in the vicinity of the school and now their own local police were questioning everyone Rosy had known, asking them to search their premises too in case she had managed to make her way home, although they didn't hold out much hope of that because it was a long distance and as far as anyone knew she had very little money. Concern grew when it became known she must have disappeared after her class were sent on a cross country run and she would be wearing only her gym skirt and shirt and possibly a navy sweater with the school monogram. The nights were chilly now. Everyone searched diligently. Joe Finkel, who had worked for Steven ever since he was a young prisoner of war, helped to search even the most unlikely places where a child could hide. They were aware that Rosy knew every nook and cranny at Bengairney. She had never been to Martinwold but she had always looked to Samuel as a sort of protective older brother and she knew he was working there, so Mr Turner's men searched too. There was no trace of her.

Megan shuddered remembering the morning they found the dead body of the tramp in the stable when they lived at Schoirhead.

'Please God don't let anything like that happen to Rosy,' she prayed fervently. Catherine and Douglas Palmer-Farr were distressed by their daughter's disappearance but the large conference which was due to be held at Langton Tower was still going ahead. For the first time in their association there was a chilly tension between the Oliphants and Catherine.

Eight days had passed since Rosy ran away from school and Chrissie Oliphant despaired of her being found alive. Every evening Samuel telephoned his parents to see if there was any news. Alexander, who had been Rosy's bosom friend throughout their eleven years, was distraught. He questioned Megan constantly and it was difficult to get him to sleep at night. Lint and Avril were equally upset. Each evening Steven telephoned Douglas Palmer-Farr, although he had promised to let them know if there was any news and not just wild rumours.

Samuel went home to Bengairney for his weekend off as usual after work on Friday. Dean and Avril discussed Rosy's disappearance and the reports which kept appearing in the newspapers.

'Thank goodness Callum and Craig have settled without any problems,' Avril said, 'but I don't think my father would have made them go if they had been as opposed to boarding school as Rosy was.'

'I can't imagine any normal loving parents who would insist on sending away their only child against her will,' Dean said grimly. 'It doesn't seem natural to me.'

'My father went to boarding school but he says he always had the stability of knowing his parents were at home and waiting to welcome him back every holiday. He says Catherine's parents were often out of the country. Her father was a geologist and her mother went with him. Catherine spent school holidays with anyone who could have her. She stayed with his parents quite often so I suppose that's how he knows her so well even though they are only half cousins. He says she never knew what it was to have a proper home life and her parents were almost strangers to her. They were killed in some sort of riot when she was eighteen.'

'Are you making excuses for her being a poor mother?' Dean asked.

'Oh no. There's no excuse for her not paying more attention to Rosy, especially when she was so upset. It makes me think how lucky I was to have a mother who loved me, but I–I think it's more important than ever that Callum and Craig should always know they have a home where they belong when they return from school, and people who love them. Dean, I *promised* I shall always be there for them. I–I know people may think it is not my responsibility. Everyone keeps telling me not to sacrifice my own happiness for their sake, but I don't think I c–could be happy if I abandoned them. It must be hard for you, or any man, to understand how I feel, but it's the way I am. I feel even more strongly now this has happened to Rosy. I–I've wanted to tell you I would understand if you feel you are wasting your life being friends with me.'

'Avril!' They had been sitting on either side of the kitchen table after finishing their meal. Dean pushed his chair back and came round, drawing her to her feet. 'Avril, my darling girl. Is that what has been troubling you?' He pressed her closer. 'Whenever I feel we are getting really close a shadow seems to come between us and you withdraw from me. I thought it was something to do with your father, or with my mother's stupid opinions. Was I wrong?'

'I don't care what your mother thinks now I know you don't share her opinions.'

'I have always known you love Callum and Craig, ever since they were born. I accept them as part of your life. They're lovely lads and I wouldn't want you to be any different. Don't you see that? I love you because you care deeply for those around you. You don't shrug off your responsibilities. My own mother doesn't know how to love and I've had enough of that. If I have to wait forever I shall still want you, and whatever package comes with you. Don't you know that?'

'N–no. I didn't think any man could be expected to share a home with two boys who bore no relation to him. They would never be a financial burden,' she added tentatively. 'My parents have seen to that, but my home will always be theirs for as long as they need me.'

'Sweetheart I think we've cleared the air of something that has been worrying you. Am I right?'

'Yes.' She smiled up at him and it was a long time before either of them spoke again. Dean was thrilled when Avril allowed him to go further than usual when he made love to her.

'You're so desirable,' he said breathlessly as he pushed aside her bra and felt her nipples harden with desire as his lips moved over her creamy skin. He knew Avril was determined never to go all the way in case she ended up like her mother but he respected her for that, even while he longed to make her wholly his.

They both knew there were still problems. Dean had no idea what his future held, or where he might need to live if he got a farm of his own to rent. How could Avril live with him if he was many miles away, and still keep her promise to be at Riverview when the boys returned? But with time and patience – and love, surely they would find a solution.

Sixteen

As a boy at Willowburn Steven had often gone round the sheds
at night with his father to check that all the animals were safe
for the night – no horses with colic, no cows with milk fever or
young beasts frolicking and getting stuck or injured.

'It's a long time to wait until morning if a beast is in pain,'
his father used to say as they made their way around with a storm
lantern. It was a habit Steven had kept up since he first had
animals of his own. He had instilled it in Dean when he was a
student at Bengairney, and more recently in Samuel. Most of the
sheds had electric lights now and things were easier, and a good
torch was better than a lantern in the old shed where there was
no electricity.

It was Samuel's weekend off but he had not felt like going out
with his friends. Rosy's disappearance had cast a deep shadow
over them all and Granny Oliphant was so upset the doctor had
prescribed sleeping pills. Steven was dozing in front of the fire
and Sam was restless.

'I'll look round the beasts tonight, Mum. Tell Dad I'm already
out there if he wakens up,' he said quietly.

'All right. He'll be glad of that.' Megan looked up from the
jumper she was knitting. 'Don't forget to look at the young calves
in the barn. We're short of room so they're in temporary pens
but one wee bull calf keeps jumping out. I'll make a cup of cocoa
for all of us when you come back in.'

'You coming out with me, Tania?'

'Not tonight, Sam. I'll finish this chapter and then I'm going
to bed.'

Sam walked slowly down the double byre looking carefully at
each cow in case there were any swellings, or other early symp-
toms of mastitis, or if any were restless and likely to come on
heat. They were not so easy to catch in the winter when they
were inside most of the day. There was a warm, pungent smell
and the cows were chewing their cud contentedly. He made his

way across to the shed where there were pens of young heifers, and then to the calf house where the younger calves were housed. It was full and the winter had barely begun.

His father took a pride in his animals and Joe Finkel was a conscientious stockman. Losses were kept to a minimum so the stock numbers tended to increase each year. The surplus heifers were sold soon after they had their first calf and his father had built up a reputation for good reliable stock so the heifers were bringing in an extra income. Sam knew his father would have liked a milking parlour and cubicle shed like they had at Martinwold so that the numbers for milking could be more flexible but Bengairney was a tenanted farm and few landlords wanted to invest in new buildings. At least their own agent made sure things were well maintained – well most of them, he thought wryly as he passed what used to be the old stable for the Clydesdale horses. He frowned thoughtfully. The agent had talked of knocking it down rather than repairing the slate roof but maybe the wooden stalls could be knocked out as Lindsay Gray was doing at Riverview? That would make way for some single, portable pens for the young calves. He turned back and opened the creaking double door.

There was no light because the stable was never used now. He flashed his torch around. It would be easier to get a proper idea in daylight. He must remember and suggest it to his father in the morning. He was turning towards the door when he heard a whimpering sound. There was a wooden stair leading to a loft over half the stable. It had been used for storing hay for the horses but it was rarely needed now. They had no horses and his father had started making some of the grass into silage instead of hay. He listened. Probably one of the cats he thought, but the whimpering came again. It sounded almost human. Sam felt the hairs rise on the back of his neck. His father would laugh if he went to fetch him and found nothing more than a couple of cats mating. He was closing the door behind him when the sound came again but it was more like a cough? Carefully he climbed the ladder and shone the torch up into the loft. The beam didn't reach the far corners but he could see there was a small heap of left over hay and an old sack or two. The sounds were plainer with a sort of shuffling. He brushed a swathe of dusty cobwebs away and climbed to the top of the ladder. Cautiously he stepped on to the floor of the loft. His heart was thudding. Something was moving beneath the thin covering of hay. The muttering came again. Sam moved forward, shining his torch. He pushed aside some of the hay with the toe of his boot and the light from the torch shone on a gym shoe and sock covered in mud. Swiftly he bent and brushed away the rest of the hay.

'Rosy! Oh my God, wee Rosy! How did you get here?' He knelt and cradled her in his arms but she didn't recognize him. She didn't seem to know where she was. She was shivering violently. Fear filled Sam.

'Rosy? It's me, Samuel,' he said urgently. He held her closer, trying to still her shivering. 'Rosy, you're safe. Look at me. It's me, Samuel . . .' His voice was rising insistently. She opened her eyes and looked up into his face, frowning. Memory seemed to return for a moment before her eyes closed again. She shuddered and clung to him. 'I won't go!' she muttered

'Hush. You're safe now, Rosy. I've got you. I'll never let anything happen to you.' He rocked her like a baby in his arms. 'They won't send you back to that school. We'll not let them.'

'Muel? Help me . . .?' she whimpered.

'I promise.' But Rosy had slumped against him. The last of her strength drained away. 'I must get you inside and warm you up. You're frozen.' But she didn't hear. It was a struggle to get her limp body over his shoulder and climb down the ladder while holding the torch but he descended carefully and breathed a huge sigh of relief when they reached the ground safely.

'You all right, Rosy?' He transferred her to his arms, cuddling her close, trying to shield her from the cold night wind as he opened the door. The only response was the incoherent muttering he had heard earlier. Her shorts and her thin shirt were damp Samuel realized as he hurried across to the house with her.

Tania thought he was joking when he called her to come and help but Megan came rushing through immediately hearing the urgency in his voice, thinking he had had an accident. She gasped, then almost sobbed with relief herself when she saw Rosy's unconscious body in his arms. Swiftly, efficiently she took control, taking Rosy from Samuel's arms while he took off his boots and coat.

'Tania, bring some warm bath towels from the airing cupboard and then run a hot bath. We must get her out of these damp clothes and warm her up. Find her one of your nightgowns.'

'There's those thick pyjamas that are too small for me. Would they be better?' Tania said, hurrying back with the towels. 'I've left the bath running.'

'Yes, put them to warm. Steven, fill up the kettle and a pan for some hot water bottles.'

'I'll carry her upstairs to the bathroom for you, Mum,' Samuel said as his mother wrapped Rosy in the thick warm towels. She was still shivering violently and she didn't seem to recognize any of them.

'I don't like this at all,' Megan said anxiously as Rosy continued her incoherent gabbling. 'I think she's hallucinating. We need the doctor.'

'I'll telephone him,' Steven said. 'Then we must let her parents know.'

'No! Not yet anyway,' Samuel said, pausing on his way to the stairs. 'She did recognize me when I found her. She clung to me and I promised I wouldn't let them send her back, then she went limp as though she'd given up struggling and it was up to me.' Steven and Megan looked at each other.

'We've no authority over her, laddie.'

'We can't make promises, Samuel.'

Sam ignored them both and his young jaw set as he climbed the stairs, his mother following behind. One of the towels fell open and as he looked down Samuel was surprised to see small buds of breasts already formed on Rosy's slight figure. He pulled the towel over her with a rush of tenderness and cradled her closer against his chest. The bathroom was warm and steamy.

'Tania and I will manage now, Sam. See to the hot water bottles will you? Put them in my bed. I can't leave her alone tonight. We'll make up the bed in Alexander's room for your father.'

'I'll do that, Mum, when I've helped you here,' Tania said. 'Why is she still shivering? Poor wee Rosy. Where can she have been all this time? I know Dad and Joe searched everywhere at least twice.'

'Maybe Rosy will be able to tell us more when she regains her senses, poor bairn. Right now she's barely with us. I think she has a temperature, in spite of her shivering.'

Doctor Burns agreed and he approved Megan's treatment so far.

'You're right, she should not be left alone tonight. I think she may get worse before the temperature peaks but I suspect this is more than a physical collapse. The child must have suffered severe mental strain. How on earth has she made such a journey alone?'

'She must have walked a fair way,' Steven said and showed him the gym shoe where the sole was worn through and the other almost as bad.

'She has some bad blisters on her feet,' Megan said, 'but they will heal if only we can get her well again.' She remembered getting blisters herself after a miserable experience but they were only surface wounds and they healed.

'Children are remarkably resilient,' Doctor Burns reassured her, 'but she should not be left until she understands she is safe. I ought to admit her to hospital but I believe—'

'Oh no, doctor, please don't do that,' Megan pleaded. 'If she were to wake up amongst strangers she might be terrified. Remember she has run away. I shall sleep beside her tonight and keep an eye on her temperature.'

'Very well. She does not appear to be too dehydrated so she must have had water, but I doubt if she has eaten for several days.'

'The poor wee bairn,' Steven muttered angrily. He had telephoned Langton Tower and Megan was glad Catherine and Douglas arrived while the doctor was still with them.

'We must take her back with us now,' Catherine said immediately, staring down at her daughter's white face and the fair curls now clean and spreading in a fan over the pillow.

'She must not be moved, Mrs Palmer-Farr,' Doctor Burns said sternly. 'The child is mentally and physically exhausted and she will need careful nursing tonight, and possibly for several nights. Mrs Caraford has plenty of experience with children. She has agreed to care for her until I give permission for her to be moved.' Catherine opened her mouth to protest.

'The doctor is right, darling,' Douglas said. He was sitting by the bed gently holding one of his daughter's limp hands in both of his. Watching him Megan had a feeling that he at least would be on Rosy's side when they decided what to do with her. Catherine on the other hand had not even touched Rosy. She seemed tense and on edge. Almost as though she sensed her mother's impatience Rosy moved restlessly in the bed and gave an unconscious little sob.

'We have a lot of people staying over the next two nights,' Catherine conceded. 'It is a large conference, and an important one for us.' Samuel was standing in the doorway and his lip curled with contempt. Megan saw the flash of anger in his blue eyes and gave a swift shake of her head. His lips closed tightly, biting back the words.

'You should let the police know Rosy has been found,' Steven said to Douglas Palmer-Farr.

'Yes, yes of course we must.'

'I expect the newspapers will want to know all about her adventures too,' his wife said.

'Newspapers?' Megan echoed. She looked at Doctor Burns in consternation. 'They don't need to know she is staying here with us, do they? We don't want to be plagued with reporters.'

'Indeed not.' He turned to Catherine and Douglas. 'If you take my advice you will tell them your daughter is recovering slowly and she is being nursed privately. When she does recover you will be wise to protect her from questions. I have seen enough reports already and I imagine many of them are exaggerated.'

'I agree, Doctor,' Douglas said firmly. 'We shall deal with the police and the newspapers. We're very grateful to you Megan for taking on this responsibility for our daughter. Your parents have been very distressed. We must tell them she is safe.'

'I telephoned them after I had spoken to you,' Steven said quietly. 'They are both very relieved to know Rosy is safe, even if it will take her some time to make a complete recovery. I think she will need very careful handling, don't you agree, Doctor?'

'Yes. Her physical condition should recover rapidly once the temperature peaks and she regains consciousness and starts eating again. Her mental condition may be another matter. She has obviously been under severe stress.' Catherine eyed him coolly and compressed her lips before turning to leave. Her husband followed reluctantly.

'I shall come back in the morning if that is convenient?' he said quietly to Megan.

'Of course it is, but don't let the newsmen follow you here.'

She breathed a huge sigh of relief when they had all gone. Tania appeared and handed her a mug of cocoa.

'I've made some for Dad, and for you big brother, Sam.' She smiled. 'You'll have to come and get it in the kitchen. I can't believe Alexander has never stirred through all the commotion. He will be really pleased to know his bosom pal is safe.'

'Yes, he has been more upset over Rosy's disappearance than he cared to admit but he never ceased asking questions and speculating about where she could be. Well Samuel, you've done a very good night's work. What made you go into the stable anyway?'

'Ah yes.' He turned to his father. 'I was wondering if we could knock out the wooden stalls – like Mr Gray is doing at Riverview. Then there would be room for some of those movable calf pens for the young calves.'

'Mmm, that may not be a bad idea,' Steven agreed. 'I shall need to ask the Land Agent's permission to remove the stalls but I think he'd agree. We'll have a proper look in the morning and do a bit of measuring up.'

Doctor Burns returned on Sunday morning. He didn't say much but Rosy's condition had not changed. She had spent a very restless night, tossing and turning, mumbling incoherently, shouting out once or twice and apparently struggling. Megan felt he was as concerned as she was herself and she was not really surprised when he came again around four o'clock.

'Ah, I came prepared to admit her to hospital but I see there has been a change for the better, Mrs Caraford. He smiled widely and bent to give Rosy a thorough examination but she barely stirred.

'She broke into a tremendous sweat and kept calling out soon after lunch time,' Megan said. 'I kept sponging her down and eventually she seemed more settled so I changed her into a clean nightgown and fresh sheets and she's been sleeping like this ever since.'

'Yes, she'll do now. You have done a good job, a very good job, Mrs Caraford.' He beamed at Megan. 'Did she recognize you?'

'I think so but she seemed utterly worn out.'

'Sleep is the best thing for her now. Don't be surprised if she wakens in the middle of the night and asks for food.' He smiled.

'I'd be pleased if she did, Doctor. I have some good chicken soup ready for her.'

Douglas Palmer-Farr arrived as the doctor was leaving.

'You'll be pleased to hear your daughter has turned the corner now and she's sleeping peacefully. You can thank Mrs Caraford for her good sense and her nursing.'

'We do thank you, Megan, more than I can say,' Douglas said sincerely when the doctor had gone.

'I should have asked you to bring some of her own clothes,' Megan said.

'I will bring them tomorrow. Did the doctor say when she could come home?'

'No he didn't. I think he would like to talk to her properly. He wants to know why she ran away and whether anything serious happened.'

'She was very unhappy. I believe there may have been some bullying. I suspect girls can be as bad as boys for that?'

'Worse, I imagine. More devious,' Megan said darkly. 'You'll not be sending her back there, will you?' she asked bluntly. Before he could answer Samuel appeared beside them in the hall.

'She can't go back. I promised her I wouldn't let you send her back there,' he said angrily. Douglas Palmer-Farr gave him a measuring look.

'It's strange that you should all care so much for my daughter, and yet she bears no relationship to any of you. I have not thanked you yet for finding her, Samuel. We're truly grateful. Another night out there and it would have been too late I suspect.'

'You still haven't said anything about school,' Samuel persisted. He had telephoned Mr Turner to see if he could remain at home on Monday until he saw whether Rosy was going to make it. Mr Turner and Dean had both agreed and they had praised him for finding her.

'The school would not have her back even if I wanted to send her there again, but I do not intend any such thing,' he said, holding up his hand as Sam opened his mouth.

'Good,' he snapped and turned away.

'Thank God for that,' Megan said fervently. Douglas Palmer-Farr chewed his lower lip and frowned.

'The school would not take her back because of the bad publicity she has caused,' he clarified dryly. 'They have written to say they are sending her clothes. However, my wife still seems convinced that Rosemary should go a girls' boarding school, even if it is in the north of England this time.'

'Oh no . . .' Megan groaned. 'Surely she has learned her lesson. Rosy could have died. Think of all those grieving parents in Aberfan. They would give their own lives to have their children safe at home.'

'We shall have to discuss it further when Rosemary-Lavender is strong enough. How is Alexander doing since he moved to the Academy? Are you satisfied with his education so far?'

'He is well and happy anyway,' Megan said flatly. 'It's early days yet but they give him plenty of homework and he does it without me needing to remind him. He seems to respect most of his teachers.'

'I see. Personally I think Rosemary would be happier too if she could go to the same school as Alexander and come home each day.'

'Then you must put your foot down Mr Palmer-Farr,' Megan said angrily. 'She is your daughter too and you could so easily have lost her. And another thing – must you keep on calling her Rosemary-Lavender all the time. In one of her letters to my mother she said she had told the other girls her name was Rosemary, or Rosy, but the teachers had her down on their register as Rosemary-Lavender so they all called her that and the other girls started to mock her from the beginning. Don't you realize how cruel children can be to each other if they think someone is different?'

'I had never thought of it,' Douglas Palmer-Farr said in genuine bewilderment. 'That is the name Catherine wanted her to have and I agreed.'

'Well if you don't mind me saying so, I think you agree with your wife far too often. Marriage and family decisions are supposed to be joint discussions.' Megan was tired after her sleepless night, and she had been worried sick about Rosy, or she would not have spoken so frankly. Samuel was listening from the kitchen and he grinned widely. He hadn't known his mother had it in her to talk to gentry like that.

Later Megan was contrite as she told Steven about her conversation with Mr Palmer-Farr.

'You did right, love,' Steven assured her, 'but it sounds as though her mother will still insist on sending the poor wee lassie to another boarding school. We all know who is boss at Langton Tower, especially since she has made a success of running the hotel. Even Joe thinks she's making the most of the publicity with the press to get free advertising for her conference facilities, telling them how busy she is and how she thought she was doing the best for young Rosy by paying for her to attend a good school.'

'I think they're mad if they send her away again after this,' Megan declared furiously.

'Well they're not likely to listen to our opinions,' Steven said grimly. 'The only person I know who might make Catherine Palmer-Farr see sense is Lint.'

'They are only half cousins,' Megan said doubtfully.

'It might be worth mentioning it to him though. We could invite him up for supper. If he talked to Rosy he would know how strongly she feels. She might even tell him some of the things she told Samuel and Tania about the bullying and nasty tricks.'

Lint often dealt with children at the hospital and he had always been close to his own sons. Rosy responded to his gentle probing more readily than any of them had expected. Afterwards he told Megan she must have been dreadfully homesick and it would get worse when the other girls started tormenting her.

'It will not be easy for her to forget some of the experiences she suffered,' he said gravely. 'I believe she would be better going to school with Alexander but I doubt if Catherine will listen to me, especially when my own boys are at boarding school.'

'But you wouldn't have kept them there if they were very unhappy, would you, Lint?'

'Definitely not. I will have a word with Catherine. When are they taking Rosy home?'

'Catherine has another conference booked for tomorrow so they have agreed she can stay until it is finished.'

'Her conferences seem to come before everything else these days, including her child,' Lint reflected grimly.

Lint couldn't remember ever feeling so frustrated and angry as he felt with his half cousin later that evening. Catherine seemed to him to have a vacuum where her common sense should be and he couldn't detect a scrap of motherly love. There was no reasoning with her.

'You're blind to the happiness and well-being of your own child,' he raged. 'All you think about these days is money and making a success with your blasted conferences. If you don't watch what you're doing you'll end up without a child and possibly without a husband – then where would you hold your bloody conferences.' Catherine stared at him. Lint never swore and she had never seen him so furious. She was hurt that he of all people should turn on her.

'It's a harsh world as you should know by now,' she said bitterly, 'My child will have to learn to stand on her own feet as I had to do.'

'Stand on her own feet? An eleven-year-old girl travels nearly the length of Britain on her own and without any money and you think she can't stand on her own feet? She told me she would rather die than go to another boarding school and believe me it's not unknown for youngsters to commit suicide.'

'Don't be ridiculous!' Catherine scoffed.

'I don't think he's being ridiculous,' Douglas said quietly, coming into the room. He had only heard the last few sentences but he had heard the raised voices and been surprised. His wife had very few relations and she was as close to Lint as anyone else he knew. At university they had both been loners and it was that which had drawn them together but he could still remember what it felt like to feel lonely and miserable and he had had some long talks with Rosy while she was at Bengairney.

'You mean to say you're taking Lindsay's part against me?' Catherine demanded indignantly.

'No, I simply think we need to do what is best for our own child's happiness. She has promised me she will work hard at school and do her homework and not go off to Bengairney during the week, if we allow her to live at home and go to the Academy with Alexander. I went up to the school today and had a talk with the Rector and a look round the school—'

'You went to the local school? You went without consulting me, or asking if I wanted to go?'

'Did you? Want to go?'

'No I—'

'Darling I've no desire to go against your wishes.' Over her head he gave Lint a little nod, indicating he should leave them now. Lint was glad to do so. Somehow he had a feeling that Douglas might – just might – take the lead for once, and consider Rosy's wishes and help her over this hurdle. He prayed that he would have the strength to stand up to Catherine's forceful personality.

Seventeen

Douglas Palmer-Farr took full responsibility for sending Rosy to the local Academy with Alexander Caraford. He promised to supervise her homework himself and help her to learn at least one foreign language. He could write French and German and speak them fluently, as well as making himself understood in four or five other languages. He began to enjoy helping Rosemary with her school work and getting to know his daughter as a young person, instead of the awkward child Catherine considered her. His recent anxiety over her disappearance had made him realize how much she meant to him and he ignored his wife's frequently pursed lips when he and Rosy shared an amusing anecdote together.

At first Rosy had refused to talk about her nightmare journey, except to say a French lorry driver had given her a lift and been kind to her. The press discovered his identity and that he had three young daughters of his own, also that he had bought her bacon rolls and a hot drink. She had scribbled a note on his pad saying, *Merci, Merci, Monsieur. Au revoir*, which he had kept and which the newspapers printed. As time passed she revealed other things. She explained to Alexander that she had only left the Frenchman's lorry because she had seen a driver in the next cab reading a newspaper and it had her photograph in it where he had folded it open. She was afraid he would recognize her. She never told anyone of the terror she had felt when she jumped down from the lorry and almost fell under the wheels of a reversing truck. It was one of the haunting memories which would still have the power to make her shudder when she was an old woman.

During the Christmas holidays she confided in Samuel, telling him she had been so hungry she had stolen a chunk of dusty bread which a woman had thrown to her hens at a small farm beside the road somewhere near Carlisle. She didn't know exactly where because she had avoided the main roads after seeing her picture in the paper. She had got lost and she thought she must have walked in the wrong direction and a lot of extra miles. She didn't know how long it had taken her.

'You must have passed near Grandma Oliphant's?' Samuel said. 'Why didn't you seek refuge with them – if not your own home, Rosy?'

'Mother had been angry with them when they told her how much I dreaded going away to school. They would have had to tell her I was there. I knew if I got to the farm where you work you would help me,' she said simply. 'You have always looked out for me, but I didn't know the way and I couldn't go any further and Bengairney is my favourite place in all the world,' she said with childlike candour. 'I was so cold and hungry.' She shuddered. 'I went to the dairy and had a big drink of milk.'

'How did you get it out of the bulk tank?'

'I drank it from one of the buckets of milk your father always keeps for the baby calves. It was horrid – thick and yellow but I was starving.'

'It would be colostrum.' The thought of drinking it, and from the bucket, made Sam shudder. 'And after that you climbed into the loft?'

'Yes.' She couldn't remember how long she had been there before he found her.

'More than one night I reckon. I might never have found you, Rosy.' Sam shivered. 'You were chilled to the bone. Why didn't you come to the house? You must have known Mother would look after you.'

'I–I don't know. I was too tired to think. I needed to escape from everybody.'

'But you could have died up there.'

'I'd rather have died than go back to that horrid school.'

'Your father says they wouldn't have you back.' Sam grinned suddenly, lightening their conversation. 'The newspapers gave them some bad press about bullying and them not missing you for a whole day. Incidentally how did you get away from the school in the first place?'

'We had to do cross country running but it was always the same route. Most of the girls were so soft,' she said scathingly. 'They were all slow, except one, and she was in the sick room with stomach cramps that day, or so she said. I was always ahead of the rest and I slipped into a wee wood and watched them go by, then I scrambled through a fence bordering the railway. I followed the lines to a station. I told the ticket inspector I had lost my ticket and my father would pay when I got off the train, but that train didn't go far. I got on a train going north but a man and woman who had been on the little train got on too. I knew I couldn't tell the same story again so I kept hiding in different toilets whenever I thought the ticket man was coming round. We all had to get off at Birmingham.'

'What did you do then?'

'It was frightening. I was so hungry and it was busy and I saw those same people watching me. I ran out of the station. It was ages before I found my way to a quiet road. I walked and walked. There was a barn in a field so I went in and fell asleep. I knew I must head north but I walked a long way. Then I got a lift in the lorry with the French driver.'

'Alexander says you're very good at French.'

'Daddy is good and he helps me, but when I leave school I want to go to a college like you so that I can be a farmer,' Rosy confided naively.

'I thought you wanted to be a vet?'

'I did.' She sighed. 'I don't think I'm good enough at science though. I love biology and we have a super teacher but Alex is much better at chemistry than I am.'

'You call him Alex now?'

'All his friends at school call him Alex.'

'Maybe you could help him with French and he could help you with chemistry?'

'I promised Mother I wouldn't come to Bengairney except at weekends and holidays.'

'You could both meet at Granny Oliphant's and do your home-work there.'

'I'll ask Dad about it, if I can persuade Alex to help me with chemistry.'

At Riverview they were all subdued as the anniversary of Ruth's death approached, although no one mentioned it. The boys were due to return to school. Avril couldn't take time off work to go with them on this occasion but Lint decided to spend a few days with his parents while he was down in their area.

Dean knew Avril had tried hard to make Christmas as normal and happy as possible for the boys, but once they were in bed on Christmas Eve she had broken down and wept in his arms. It had been an insignificant little ornament which had triggered a memory of last Christmas and her mother. It had taken Avril herself by surprise and Dean had held her tenderly, soothing her and stroking her hair as he might a child's, but the feel of her in his arms, her need of him had filled his heart with love and a desire to protect and comfort her always. It made him realize how much her young brothers depended on her for their happiness – as they had once looked to their mother. Dean knew how hard Lindsay Gray tried to make up for their mother's loss but sometimes it was Avril they needed.

Although he was happy at Martinwold and he enjoyed working with the cows and having Samuel for company there were times when Dean grew impatient with the even tempo of his life. He longed to break out, to rent a farm, to make Avril his wife, to share a home with her every day and every night; yet how could he ask her to leave Riverview and her brothers, even if he was ever lucky enough to get a tenancy? Aunt Molly understood how he felt but she kept telling him to be patient and things would sort themselves out, but Dean couldn't see how that could ever happen.

Lindsay Gray had returned from Gloucestershire the previous evening. Avril was at work at the hospital so he was at home alone when the telephone rang. Molly Scott sounded almost hysterical as she pleaded with him to come at once.

'Bill has collapsed in the byre. Doctor Anderson is out on a call . . .'

'I'll come immediately, Molly. Keep him warm and don't move him. Try to stay calm. I'm on my way.'

As soon as he arrived he went straight to the byre at Sylvanside and found Bill Scott half lying on top of the pile of hay he had dropped when pain gripped him.

'Telephone for an ambulance, Molly,' Lint ordered after a brief examination. 'I think it is angina but I'm not his GP.' He always carried a medical bag and he opened it as he knelt beside the stricken man. 'I've suspected this for a while, Bill. I'm going to give you something to ease the pain until we can get you to hospital.'

'Only indigestion . . .' Bill Scott gasped. 'Can't go – like this . . .'

'Keep still and don't try to talk,' Lint advised. 'It could have been worse. You might have collapsed in the gutter amidst the muck.' Bill responded with a ghost of a smile and relaxed a little as Lint had intended. When Molly returned to say the ambulance was on its way he advised her to be prepared to go with Bill. They will need to do some tests. You should pack him a bag.' He knew it was better for Molly to keep busy. 'Don't worry about getting home. I'll come and fetch you myself if necessary, but I will telephone Avril and tell her what has happened. She may be able to meet you at the hospital.'

Molly was eternally grateful for Avril's company when her beloved Bill was whisked out of her sight. Avril knew quite a few of the nurses and doctors by now and Molly was sure her presence helped.

'I will take you for a cup of tea while they do their examination and decide which tests to do,' Avril said, gently, 'then I shall see you back to the ward. One of the nurses will look after you. If you need me ask them to telephone me in the laboratories. You will want to stay for a while and I'm sure the doctor will explain things to you. I may be able to get away early then I can drive you home. Would you like me to telephone Dean and tell him what has happened? You will need someone to help with the milking,' she added, thinking aloud.

'Oh yes, please, Avril,' Molly Scott said, tearfully. 'I'd forgotten about the farm and everything else. Bill will be worrying and making himself worse. He will be all right, won't he Avril? They will be able to save him?'

'They will certainly do their best and he is in the right place now. I suspect he'll have to take things a bit easier. If my father's diagnosis is correct he will probably have to take medication too.'

'He came so quickly,' Molly breathed. 'I'm so grateful.'

'He said you were unable to get Dr Anderson. He was going to telephone and explain what had happened. He'll not want Dr Anderson to think he's treading on his toes. My father is not a GP.'

'He was so comforting and reassuring – to both of us.'

*   *   *

Avril got through to Dean at lunchtime. She could tell he was upset by the way he fired questions.

'They'll need help. Young Dick Forsythe is a good worker but he's only fifteen and he's never done much milking,' Dean said anxiously. 'I've been here a year now and I haven't taken any holidays. I'll ask Mr Turner if I can get a week off. It would allow me to stay at Sylvanside with Aunt Molly until we see what the doctors say. They may have to sell off the dairy herd. That would really upset Uncle Bill.'

'Apart from the work I'm sure it would be a great comfort if you can stay at Sylvanside, at least for a few days, Dean. Will the man who does the relief milking at weekends be able to manage without you for a week?'

'I reckon so. He was a student with the Oliphants so he understands what's needed but his wife doesn't want him to be a full-time dairyman because she doesn't like him getting up early, or working seven days a week. Anyway Samuel will be here and he knows the routine.'

Avril was glad to be able to reassure Mrs Scott and tell her Dean planned to stay at Sylvanside for a week until they heard the doctors' verdict.

'He says he and Dick Forsythe will do the milking. You will want to visit the hospital and you must not tire yourself out.'

'I feel as though our world has turned upside down,' Molly said forlornly, 'but Dean's a grand laddie and we're blessed with the best of neighbours with you and your father, Avril. I do appreciate that.'

Things were not as bad as Molly had feared but there was no doubt that Bill would have to take things easier. As well as cutting down on the physical work the doctor insisted he should avoid stress. Lint explained to Molly and Dean that it was a shock to a man who had worked hard all his life, to realize he was not as fit, or as young, as he had believed.

'It will be difficult for Bill to accept and he may even feel a bit depressed,' he said gently, 'so you will need to be patient, as I'm sure you are anyway.' Lint smiled down at Molly's anxious face. 'He has no cause for stress, has he? I mean things are not going too badly with the farm, are they?'

'We're all right,' Molly said. 'We've been at it a long time and we've always been careful, so he has no money worries, but farming in general isna so good for a lot of folks just now. The price of land has taken a tumble for those who need to sell.'

'But that doesn't affect you?'

'No . . . not if we can keep young Dick to help with the work. It affects the lad's family though. There's rumours that some of the creditors are pressing for a sale of the farm, and all his father does is go on drinking,' she added angrily. 'He has three fine sons and the best wife a man could wish for but the drink is like a disease with him.'

'Well you can't take on the world's problems, Molly,' Lint said gently. 'Does Bill have any hobbies?'

'Hobbies?' She chuckled. 'He's never had time for hobbies. Farming has been his life, especially his cows. If only the place had been a bit bigger we might have taken Dean into partnership now. He's young, he might have expanded a bit but it's not enough to keep two families and I ken fine he'd like to get married.' She shrugged. 'As it is we haven't enough to offer him anything like he's earning at Martinwold. Sylvanside will all be his one day of course. Neither of us have any other close family and Dean deserves a helping hand. If he decides to sell this place and use the money to get a bigger farm of his own it will be up to him but we're not ready to make any changes yet. It will break Bill's heart if he has to sell his cows and retire.'

Eighteen

The doctor warned Bill he must never go anywhere, not even to the toilet, without the wee pills to slip under his tongue in case he felt an attack coming on.

'Some day they might find a better cure,' the doctor said wryly, 'but not so many years ago you would just have died, so be thankful and do as you're told – no lifting heavy weights, nothing strenuous like a difficult calving either – and no worrying.'

Bill was determined to carry on at Sylvanside. 'It'll kill me if I give up the farm, Molly. It's my life.'

'Aye and it will kill you if you don't do as the doctor says.' Molly's face and her voice softened. 'But I know what you mean, Bill. We started off together here and we'll finish here together. Do you think young Dick Forsythe would agree to work week-ends as well? He always seems keen to earn money.'

Dick was only too willing to work. There was little happiness at home for him.

'You tell your brothers I need you more than they do, laddie,' Bill said. 'Dean has promised to come over on his weekend off and give you a Sunday free. Will that do?'

'Suits me fine, Mr Scott,' Dick grinned. 'You pay me for working but ma brothers expect me to labour for them for nothing.'

'Your father was right,' Dean told Avril a fortnight later. 'Uncle Bill does seem a bit down in spirits. I've never seen him irritable and short-tempered before. Aunt Molly was almost in tears twice when I was there at the weekend.'

'Oh dear, I do hope it doesn't wear her down.'

'I wish I had more free time to help them out, especially with the spring work coming on. They'll have a field to plough and the turnips to sow.'

'You can't be in two places at once,' Avril said, stroking his cheek as they sat in front of the fire at Martinwold one Friday evening.

'I know. I suppose if I'd stayed at Northsyke I could have helped him more. Doris might have helped but she never learned how to milk and she's not interested anyway. She gets possession of the café at Easter and she's moving down to Gretna to get things ready.'

'I hope it works out for her. Your mother will miss her help and her company.'

'You're more generous than they deserve. Do you know how much I love you, Avril? How much I long to ask you to marry me?'

'Show me,' Avril said softly. Dean couldn't resist such an invitation and he drew her into his arms, nibbling her ear lobe, teasing her with his exploring lips, but his kisses grew more demanding as desire flared between them and he knew he must stop now, if he was to stop at all. Avril felt his arousal and knew his desire matched her own. They both sighed as they drew apart.

'If only I could get a farm to rent at least I'd be a farmer instead of a labourer and I'd be my own boss. If I do get a tenancy will you marry me, Avril?'

'Oh Dean, you know I love you and I long for us to be together but – but can we wait and see? I don't want to upset Callum and Craig by talking about getting married until there's something definite and plans to be made. Please be patient with me, Dean. You know there's nothing I would like better than for us to be together, to live together and work together.' She turned to him, her dark eyes pleading.

'I know leaving Riverview and your brothers would be a problem for you, the way you feel about them.' Dean sighed heavily. 'I do understand, honestly, but I feel so frustrated sometimes.'

'I'm sure my father would do his best to cooperate and help the boys adjust to my living with you when the time comes, especially if they knew they were welcome too.'

'And they would be welcome, never doubt that, my darling. But you're right, Avril, there's no use making plans, or worrying the boys until I get a farm to rent.' Dean sighed again.

'Meanwhile, Dean Scott, I still love you very much and I realize how patient and understanding you are with me over my family.'

'I don't feel patient,' Dean said drawing her into his arms again and holding her tightly, 'but I love you even more for caring about your family. One day I hope it will be you and me and our own children.'

'So do I, oh so do I, my love,' Avril murmured before his mouth claimed hers and there was no need for words.

'What's wrong with ye, Dick?' Bill Scott asked one morning as they did the milking together. 'You look as though you've lost a pound and found a penny, lad.'

'It's ma mother, Mr Scott. She cried and cried last night but ma father still went off down to the pub as he always does,' he added bitterly. 'She wouldna say what was wrong but ma brother, Jim, came in, and he was upset, aye and angry. I know ma father owes money to a lot of folk but we didn't know he'd stopped paying the hire purchase on the tractors and the plough and on the new muck-spreader. Jim says they might have settled for reclaiming the machines and cutting their losses but two o' the big feed firms are going to force a sale o' the farm to pay them in full. It's to be sold by public auction. Soon.'

'Public auction? Are ye sure lad?'

'Jim reckons it's because nobody trusts Father not to try doing another o' his twisted deals to get out o' paying.'

'But the farm belongs to your mother—' Bill broke off uncertainly.

'Our Jim says she was foolish. She pledged the farm as security or something. That made her cry even more. She says it was so we could all keep on living there. She kept hoping Father would stop drinking and things would get better. But Jim says he's got deeper and deeper into debt.' Dick's voice caught in his throat as he added gruffly, 'Our Bob says even the cattle belong to the auction mart. They get their money back when the beasts are sold. Then they buy the next lot and ma father never gets out o' their clutches.' Bill could see the lad was near to breaking down so he patted his shoulder.

'Try not to worry son, things are not always as bad as they seem. Maybe your brothers have got the wrong story. Anyway somebody might offer an extra good price for the land.' Dick looked at him sharply, then his young shoulders slumped.

'Our Jim says land isna selling well just now and if we sell without the house and the farm steading the land will not be any use to anybody except you. Our boundary marches with Sylvanside. The river is the boundary at the bottom side and it's

England over the other side. It's like a triangle with the house and buildings at one end. He kens ye willna want to buy it after buying your own place and the land that belonged to Eskriggholm.' Dick didn't add that Jim considered Mr Scott had one foot in the grave after his heart attack. The thought made him shudder. He liked his boss and he'd learned a lot since he'd come to work at Sylvanside.

'Try not to worry, laddie. I expect your brother is worried because he and Bob have both got their businesses established at Southrigg. It would be difficult for them to get new premises, not to mention another house. They've done well.' He didn't add that they might both have saved their heritage if they had stuck in at farming and taken over from their father – not that it would have been easy. Fingal Forsythe had always been a stubborn, arrogant know-it-all, and he was ten times worse when he had the drink in him, which seemed to be most of the time these days. Even as a young man he had thought himself above manual labour. When he married Emily Sharpe he thought he had nothing to do but step in and give orders to other people. Not that it would have been so bad if he had been a good manager but he was always trying short cuts which didn't work, or thinking he was clever when he pulled off a dirty deal. Bill had never had any time for him when they were young, and neither had Sydney. Even then he had bragged that he could drink twice as much in an evening as any of his contemporaries. No, Bill thought grimly, he didn't feel the least bit sorry for Fingal, but he had a lot of sympathy for young Dick, and for his mother. Emily had been a good-looking girl in her time but she had aged fast over the last few years. She was at least five years younger than Molly but she'd looked a good fifteen years older the last time he'd seen her. He shook his head. There was nothing he could do to help.

True enough the auction of Southrigg land, all one hundred and ten acres of it, was advertised for sale in the auction mart. At the appointed time a large crowd gathered round the ring. There was a lot of noise and speculation. Bill and Sydney Scott were not the only ones who were there out of curiosity. Most farms these days were sold privately through the solicitors. Usually nobody heard the exact price which had been paid unless the buyer or the seller divulged it, and they rarely did.

The excitement and chatter died down as the auctioneer took his place and began his usual patter with blandishments about how fertile the land was and what a desirable purchase it would make. Plenty of people had sent for particulars to see exactly what was for sale but most had lost interest when they realized the house and buildings were not included. Forsythe was not a popular man at the best of times so there would be no neighbourly bidding to push the price up. The auctioneer asked for an opening bid of fifteen thousand pounds to start him off. There was silence. He began once more praising the fertility of the land, all in a ring fence.

'It's not a ring it's a bloody long strip,' one farmer muttered.

'Aye and the low meadow floods when the river is high,' someone else remarked. The auctioneer lowered the bid. At twelve thousand he waited, scanning the crowd around the ring. His eye fell on Bill and Sydney, standing together. He raised his eyebrow at Bill, silently urging him to bid. Bill's eyes widened and he shook his head emphatically.

'Ye'd better not catch his eye again,' Sydney whispered, 'He'll be taking it for a bid.'

'He knows I'm not interested. He telephoned last week to quiz me.'

'Eight thousand to start then?' the auctioneer persisted, searching the faces. He was frowning now. He hadn't expected it to be such a struggle. True, the land had not been well farmed for the past ten years but it was good fertile loam and it could all be ploughed except the strip of meadow beside the river. His mouth tightened. 'Seven thousand then . . .' There was silence. He scowled. That was as low as he dared to go. Even if he sold at seven it wouldn't clear all Forsythe's debts. The solicitors acting for two of the big feed firms were intransigent. If they didn't get their money from the sale of the land they had insisted the farm would have to be sold as a whole, including the two houses and the buildings. He waited as long as he could then announced the land was withdrawn. There was a communal expelling of breath. There would be plenty of interested buyers when it was sold as a farm with a house to live in, and buildings for the stock. Bill felt the tightness in his chest. If he'd had half the money and been a younger, fitter man, he might have bid for the land

and borrowed from the bank. He found his pills and slipped one in his mouth.

'The auctioneer is coming this way,' Sydney whispered, nudging him in the ribs. 'You all right, Bill? I reckon he wants a word.' He was right. They had both known Archibald Story since they were boys. He was past retirement age now but he was still a slippery customer and he still controlled the firm. He began with his usual complimentary greeting, telling Bill how well he was looking.

'I'm disappointed you didn't put in a bid, Bill. The land adjoins Sylvanside. You would have had the best farm in the area.'

'I'd have bid if I'd had that kind of money going begging,' Bill said dryly, 'or if I had been fifteen years younger.'

'What about you Sydney? Your son must be ready to farm on his own by now surely?'

'Maybe he is but we haven't got that kind o' money to hand over,' Sydney said flatly. The older man pulled at his lower lip.

'Forsythe has made a bad job of things,' he admitted. 'I knew his wife's family well. Her father died when she was in her teens and her grandfather left her the farm. It hasn't brought her the happiness he hoped. Forsythe wouldn't have married her if she hadn't had the farm. She'd have had a happier life without it and that wastrel of a husband.'

'Aye, she didn't deserve the dance he's led her,' Bill agreed. 'And they have three fine sons.'

'Yes, Emily had hoped there would be enough money left after paying off the debts for her and her younger son to emigrate to Australia. She has a cousin out there and she had made up her mind to leave Forsythe. I don't know what the family will do now.'

'I didn't know young Dick was planning to go to Australia?' Bill said.

'Oh he doesn't know anything about it, but her cousin promised to help them find a house and work for the boy, and maybe get him a start in farming if Emily took him over there. The older boys knew what she was planning. You sure you don't want to put in a bid, Bill? I reckon the bank would lend you some of the money.'

'It's no good playing on my sympathy,' Bill said. 'It won't work. I feel sorry for Emily Forsythe but Southrigg is out of my reach.

I'm too old to be taking on bank loans.' The auctioneer knew when he was beat. He nodded.

'The whole farm will have to be auctioned then.' He turned on his heel and left.

'He must be getting an old man now,' Sydney reflected, watching him walk away, 'but he's as wily as ever. Forsythe was a fool to get into the auction company's clutches. Several farmers who had been standing by came up to chat, mainly out of curiosity.

'Did he persuade ye to buy it then, Bill?' one man asked directly.

'Afraid not.' Bill smiled wryly.

'Forsythe doesna deserve rescuing. He's drunk already and it's not three o'clock yet.'

'He needs treatment,' another man said. 'He can't resist the bottle. I've heard he hides it all over the place, and he's been betting on the horses recently, but that's no way to clear his debts.' So the gossip went on with the stories getting even more exaggerated as Bill and Sydney walked away to their car.

'I don't suppose Dean will be over tomorrow. He's working this weekend, isn't he?' Bill mused aloud.

'You'll know his routine better than I do,' Sydney replied with a smile. 'Were you thinking of telling him about the auction?'

'Aye, I'll give him a ring tonight, unless you want to tell him how it went?'

'No, I'll leave it to you. He's only been back at the house once since he went to Martinwold and he didn't get much of a welcome.'

'Grizel doesn't know how lucky she is. He's a grand lad.'

'Ye were always keener on the stock than I was,' Sydney reflected. 'Dean should have been your lad. He's just like you were when you were courting Molly and desperate to get a place of your own. I'm happiest with my dogs and a flock of sheep.'

'Aye, and escaping to the hill for a bit o' peace,' Bill chuckled.

Bill Scott telephoned Dean that evening to tell him about the fiasco over Southrigg.

'Remember this is Friday so Avril will be there,' Molly reminded him in a loud whisper. 'Don't take up too much of his time.'

'I'd forgotten Avril would be there,' Bill said after he had put the phone down. He was frowning.

'I realized that. It's no use Bill, I know you think Southrigg would have been a grand investment and made this place big enough for Dean to join us as a partner but—'

'Well it would. I thought Sydney might have considered it when the auctioneer asked him if Dean wasna ready for a place of his own yet,' Bill said dejectedly.

'I know it's an opportunity which will probably never come again,' Molly said patiently, 'but it's not for us at our time o' life. You have to stop thinking about it, Bill. Anyway it's one thing to buy a farm at the value of a sitting tenant but it's another thing for Sydney to buy land with vacant possession, especially when there's no house with it. Besides now that he's bought the café and a house at Gretna for Doris he wouldn't be able to afford it.'

'I suppose you're right.' Bill sighed heavily. 'But if he'd given Dean his share out o' Norhsyke he might have been able to borrow the rest from the bank.'

'I doubt if the bank would have loaned Dean that much when he's not in a farm at all,' Molly said reasonably. 'Besides life is hard enough without the lad starting out with a huge loan from the bank, and where could he have lived if he gets married?'

'I know all that, Molly, but—'

'But nothing. There's nothing you can do and remember the doctor said you shouldn't get stressed and that means no fretting over things you can't do anything about.' Bill nodded silently. His mind had been going over and over the day's events since he parted company with Sydney and he had needed to take another of the doctor's wee pills. It amazed him that such a wee bit of a thing could bring him such relief.

'I can't help thinking if Sydney had anybody else but Grizel for a wife he would have had a bid . . .'

'Listen, Bill, I feel heart sorry for Emily Forsythe and her lads but I'm more worried about you and your health. I don't want to be a widow. D'ye hear me?'

'Aye, I hear ye, lass.'

'Yes, but d'ye heed me? Put it out of your mind. I'll make a drink of cocoa and we'll have an early night.'

Dean, with Steven's encouragement, had looked at almost all the farms which came up for rent, even though they knew they often went to the sons of existing tenants. He received a letter in the post

on Saturday morning informing him that he had not been successful
in gaining the tenancy of the last farm they had been to see. It was
on an estate on the other side of Dumfries so he had not mentioned
it to Avril. He doubted if she would have wanted to live so far
from her young brothers. He had told Mr Turner that he had applied
for the tenancy when he had taken a day off and he had promised
to let his boss know what transpired, so he went up to the farm
office to give Mr Turner the news.

'Well, Dean, I'd be a hypocrite if I said I was sorry,' Mr Turner
remarked, 'but that's because I'm selfish and I want to keep you
here. Are you very disheartened?'

'I don't know,' Dean admitted. 'I was on the shortlist so I
thought I might have a chance, but it wasn't set up for dairying.'

'I didn't think it was the right place for you, Dean. You're a
fine herdsman and you'd only feel frustrated if you didn't get any
satisfaction from your work.'

'I suppose so.'

'I was down at the auction mart yesterday. Did you hear about
the sale that never was?'

'Southrigg you mean? Yes, Uncle Bill telephoned last night to
tell me about it. Mrs Forsythe is a nice woman and the two oldest
sons are making a good job of their own businesses but the auctioneer
reckons the creditors will press for the whole lot to be sold.'

'Life is hard for some people,' Murdo Turner reflected, 'not that
I've any sympathy for Forsythe himself. It's only what he deserves.'

Neither of them had yet heard of the events which had taken
place after the sale the previous night, arousing even more gossip
and still wilder speculations.

Nineteen

Since Bill's heart attack Lint had made a habit of collecting the Scotts' newspapers from the village shop on Saturday mornings, along with his own, and walking up to Sylvanside with them. He usually stayed for a cup of coffee and a chat with Bill. Molly welcomed his visits. She knew her husband enjoyed a man to man talk and Lint was genuinely interested in what was happening on the farm. Sometimes the two of them would walk over the fields to see a group of heifers or a cow which was due to calve, or one which had been ailing.

'Did you always want to be a doctor, Lint? I'm sure you and your sons have inherited some of your grandfather's farming genes,' Molly teased. She knew Lint also kept an eye on her husband's health and she was glad.

So on Saturday morning, while they waited for Molly to make the coffee, Bill told Lint about the abortive attempt to auction the Southrigg land.

'So what happens now?' Lint asked.

'The creditors will insist the farm will have to be sold with house and buildings, according to the auctioneer.'

'But that will mean the Forsythe sons moving out, won't it?'

'Aye, it could put the two lads out of business if they have to look for new premises as well as houses. You'll remember Jim? He helped you make the big doorway to your buildings. He's the eldest. His wife is expecting a baby and he's built a nice wee house out of one of the barns.'

'Surely it's not usual for there to be no bids at all?

'The auctioneer was constrained by the Forsythe's debts. He couldn't take bids below a certain figure but even when he went down to seven thousand he didn't get a bid. According to salesmen's gossip Forsythe is owing most of that for feed and fertilizer. Young Dick was really upset when he arrived this morning. He didn't look as though he'd slept much. He said there'd been a terrible row last night. His mother was crying because they'd have nowhere to live. Jim and Bob wanted to discuss things so they hid the car keys to prevent their father going off to the pub. Forsythe lost his driving licence a while ago but apparently he drives down the back farm track and leaves the car at the bottom. He's nearly at the village then and he walks to the pub. Dick said he knocked Bob out of his way and drove off on the tractor. He hadn't come home when Dick left for work this morning, but he often stayed out all night when he was very drunk.'

'It's not much of an example for a man to set his sons,' Lint reflected. 'Does he not realize the damage he must be doing to himself? Can't he be persuaded to get help when he's so addicted to alcohol?'

'Doctor Anderson has tried to talk to him more than once,' Bill said, 'but he's not the kind o' man to listen to reason.'

Lint was taking his leave of Molly and Bill when Bob Forsythe drove into the yard with a screech of tyres. He looked distraught and his face was white except for a large bruise under one eye.

'Whatever's the matter, lad?' Bill Scott asked kindly.

'I've come to get Dick. There – there's been an accident . . .'

'What sort of accident?' Lint asked swiftly. 'Can I help?'

'Nobody can help.' Bob was almost sobbing. 'We didna know until we went to look for the tractor.'

'Your father? Dick said he hadna come home when he left the house at six o' clock this morning.' Bill said.

'He often slept under a hedge or in the barn and we'd had a row so we weren't surprised he didna come into the house, but the beasts hadna been fed and we needed the tractor. Jim went down the back road to see if he'd left it there. He found the tractor with father trapped underneath it. He must have misjudged the curve in the track and rolled it over the banking. We – we barely recognized him,' Bob added in a hoarse whisper.

'Dear God,' Molly breathed. 'Whatever next? As though your poor mother hasna had enough.'

'What's happening then, lad? Do you need Dick to help? He's a bit young . . . Maybe I can help?'

'He'll have to know . . . I wanted to save Mother telling him. Doctor Anderson said Father would be killed instantly. He sent for the police and the fire engine. They lifted the tractor. The police have taken his b–body away.' Bob hid his face in his hands. 'I wish we hadna got so angry with him . . .'

'So you've come to take Dick home?' Molly asked gently.

'Aye. Mother is in an awful state.'

'Well if there's nothing Dick can do to help why don't you let me give him his dinner and then I'll break the news to him,' Molly said. 'Once he hears what's happened he'll not feel like eating and he's done a good morning's work. He'd be better with some good food inside him.'

'Mrs Scott is right, Bob,' Lint said sympathetically. 'Unless there's something useful he could do he would be better here.'

'I'll drive him round later. Maybe I can offer a wee bit o' comfort to your mother, Bob? Unless she has somebody with her? I don't want to intrude,' Molly suggested diffidently.

'You're a good woman, Mrs Scott. Our Dick keeps telling us that. Ma doesna have anybody. She hasna been to the village, or anywhere else, for more than a year now. She's lost all her friends through ma father,' he added bitterly, 'and now she'll lose her home. The tractor is wrecked and it wasna insured.' He rubbed his temple in a gesture of despair. 'Jim paid the insurance on the two houses and the buildings. He was afraid Father might set them on fire some night when he was drunk.'

'It's a bad business,' Bill Scott said awkwardly, 'but he's dead now . . .'

'I ken and we shouldna speak ill o' the dead!' Bob muttered. 'That's what mother keeps saying, but God knows she's had plenty o' cause to speak ill o' him, even if he was ma father.'

'Aye, we understand, lad,' Bill said sympathetically and patted his shoulder. 'You get back to your mother now and tell her we'll bring Dick home in a wee while.'

Avril was speaking on the telephone when Lint arrived home. He guessed it was Dean from the conversation.

'I have some news for him,' he said in a low voice. 'Tell me when you're finished?' A wee while later Avril came into the kitchen.

'You can speak to Dean now, Dad. He was phoning to tell me he didn't get the tenancy of the farm he went to see.'

'Come and listen, but it's not good news.'

'It's not his Uncle?' she asked sharply, anxiously.

'No, it's Mr Forsythe.' He told Dean about the accident and Mr Forsythe's death.

'Does this mean Dick will not be able to help Uncle Bill?'

'He had been at work this morning. I don't know what will happen tomorrow but as far as I can tell there's nothing he can do to help at home so it would be better for his sake to stick to his work routine. It will not help his mother to have him hanging around the house. I'll let you know what's happening though. I'm sure I could give Bill a bit of help with the afternoon work this weekend. I can't milk the cows but I can feed calves and clean the byre and take the cows back out to their pasture if they're sleeping out at night.'

'I'm sure Uncle Bill would be grateful,' Dean said, 'and so would I. I shall not be free until next weekend.'

Avril noticed her father was preoccupied for the rest of Saturday and again on Sunday morning. He seemed to be mulling something over in his mind but she couldn't imagine what would make him look so serious.

'I'd like to discuss something with you, Avril, if you will come through to the room?' Lint said after lunch on Sunday. Avril looked at him sharply.

'You're not worried about Bill Scott are you, Dad? I thought he seemed to be coping quite well now that he's accepted the doctor's advice.'

'He is, and Mrs Forsythe agrees that it is better for Dick to be working at Sylvanside so Bill will have help, except for the day of the funeral. They can't arrange that until there's been an investigation.'

'I'll join you as soon as I've tidied up the kitchen.' She felt a twinge of anxiety. It was not often her father spoke so formally, or looked so solemn.

Lint drew in a deep breath and looked shrewdly at Avril as she seated herself opposite him.

'I get the impression you and Dean are disappointed when he keeps getting on the short lists but not quite managing to get a farm to rent?' he said.

'I'm disappointed for Dean's sake,' Avril admitted, 'but deep down I hoped he wouldn't get a farm so far away. I hate the thought of being away from Riverview when the boys come home, but I know I can't expect Dean to wait forever. Now the future is a blank again.'

'You really love Dean, don't you, Avril?' Lint asked gently.

'Yes, but I love my brothers too and I've promised to marry Dean if he gets a farm to rent.'

'I've known for some time that Dean loves you, and you've always been the best of friends, but I get the impression he feels he's not good enough for you while he is working as a labourer?'

'You're right, but if Martinwold had been nearer I think I would have persuaded him that didn't matter. Living in a tied house bothers him far more than it would bother me so long as we were together.'

'Pride I suppose.'

'Yes, and he knows I want to keep my promise to Callum and Craig and be here for them when they come home. Don't say I must not make sacrifices for the boys, Dad. It would be a greater sacrifice to be without them. They're my family and I need them as much as they need me. And I promised them – and Mum.'

'I understand how torn in two you feel, my dear, but I don't want you, or Dean, to lose your chance of happiness. So, I've been thinking about the land which the Forsythes are trying to sell. Bill Scott says he would have tried to buy it if he had been younger. He says there would be plenty of scope for him and Dean to farm in partnership if he had twice the acres.'

'We both know neither Dean nor his uncle can afford to buy the land,' Avril said flatly.

'No they can't, but Bill Scott reckons land is the best long-term investment there is because there'll never be any more of it. He says land, labour and capital are the three limiting factors to expansion in farming. He already has some of the land and the stock and Dean has the labour, and one day Bill reckons he will get a share of Northsyke if his parents retire.

'They have no plans to retire. Anyway Dean doesn't believe in waiting to step into dead men's shoes – that's his expression, not mine.'

'I respect him for wanting to make his own way in the world but we can all benefit from a little help sometimes and I think you may be the one who can give exactly the right help to enable Bill Scott and Dean to farm together and for Dean to give his uncle the support he is beginning to need now that he has angina. Think about it. You and Dean want to get married. You want to stay nearby. Dean wants to farm, and to help the Scotts now they're getting older. Am I right?'

'Yes, but how can I wave a magic wand?'

'It's not magic. You have to thank your grandfather's foresight and your mother's desire to provide for you.' Lint sighed heavily.

'I don't understand, Dad, but I don't like to see you looking so sad.' He gave her a wan smile.

'Let me explain. Remember I told you how hurt your mother was when she returned to the vicarage and old friends shunned her?'

'Yes, I do remember.'

'I should have told you they were not all like that. One of your grandfather's parishioners was a lawyer and he remained a good friend too. When he knew your mother intended to bring you up alone he advised your grandfather to take out a twenty-five year term assurance on Ruth's life. Remember she had no mother and no siblings or even close relatives. An insurance would provide money to pay for your education if anything happened to your mother. Your grandfather arranged it and paid it until Ruth started working as a teacher. She kept paying it. The premiums are low because young people are not expected to die and if they live for the stated term no money is paid out.' He sighed again. 'Life is a gamble. I know you would rather have your mother alive and well than any amount of money, Avril.'

'Oh I would, I would . . .'

'I know my dear. However, you are still under twenty-five so the insurance has to be paid out. My solicitor has had some difficulties with the insurance company and the money has only recently been cleared. You will be receiving fifteen thousand pounds. You could still study for your doctorate without any help from anyone if you wanted.'

'I don't want to study any more. I–I don't want the money either. It must go to the boys.'

'We took out a similar insurance on both our lives for each of the boys. No amount of money can replace a parent's loving care, especially a mother's. I am the trustee for all of you. Their money will be held in trust until they are eighteen, when it will be used for their education.'

'I see . . .' Avril sank on to a chair and hid her face in her hands, weeping silently. Lint came and put a comforting arm around her shoulders.

'I know exactly how you feel, dear child. All the money in the world can't make up for the death of someone we love.'

'No, nothing can.' Avril sobbed. 'But you know that . . .'

'I just wanted you to understand how your mother had planned for you. Also if anything should happen to me – God forbid – the twins will be well provided for. I don't ever want them to be a burden to you.'

'They would never be a burden. Ever since they were born I've been glad to have a family who really belonged to me.'

'I know my dear, but it is your future and your happiness we must consider now. There is no reason why you shouldn't have the money and use some of it to buy the land at Southrigg.'

'Me buy the land?' Avril echoed.

'Yes, with the money from the insurance if it is what you and Dean and the Scotts want.'

'I didn't know . . .' Avril whispered brokenly. 'I never considered . . .'

'I have no doubt Bill and Molly would welcome Dean sharing the responsibility, especially if it means they can continue to live at Sylvanside for the rest of their lives. So it is up to you and Dean.'

'But you said there was no house included in the sale.'

'No. That may prove a problem and a bigger price than Dean is willing to pay, but everything comes at a price. Do you think he would consider making his home here, with us?'

'Dean live with us?' Avril's eyes widened. 'Surely you wouldn't want that, Dad? This is your home. I can't let you sacrifice your peace and privacy for us.'

'As I said, my dear, everything comes at a price. Do I want to live in a large empty house on my own, waiting for my sons to come home to bring a little laughter? Or do I want to go on sharing it with you, and with the man who can bring you happiness, knowing my sons will still have a familiar place to call home, with people they love. Time changes everything, Avril, and I am not thinking only of the next few years but of the lifetime which I hope lies ahead of you and Dean. When the boys are a few years older and more independent I have plans for changes to my own life.'

'You would marry again?' Avril asked, her voice low and sad.

'No, never that. Your mother was the only woman I wanted to marry and there will never be another Ruth. You, too, have paid a price, my dear. I know you would rather have had your mother than all the money in the world.'

'Oh I would, nothing can replace Mum.'

'I understand, but you must look forward to your future with Dean now, Avril. Your mother would have wanted that so I think we need to have a serious talk with the Scotts and Dean together. The sooner the better if we are to offer for the Southrigg land, but they may see things differently and we must accept their point of view,' he warned.

Dean was puzzled when he received a telephone call from Aunt Molly on Monday asking him if he would come over for supper straight after milking on Tuesday evening.

'There's something we need to discuss with you lad and it can't wait. And Dean . . .'

'Yes, Aunt Molly? You sound tense. Uncle Bill has not had a bad report from the doctor, has he?'

'No, nothing like that. It's just – I know how proud and independent you can be. Bill was just like you. His pride nearly came between us when he was struggling to get a farm to rent. Don't let pride stand in the way of your happiness, laddie. It makes a lonely bedfellow. See you tomorrow.' Before Dean could ask her what she meant she had put the phone down. He puzzled over her words all the next day.

Lint had given the Scotts a hint that it might be possible to buy the adjoining land if a satisfactory agreement could be reached for farming it, but he didn't go into detail. As far as they were concerned it was an ideal solution. They would pay him a fair rent, but would Dean consider Avril even more beyond his reach if her father owned half the land. Lint had his doubts about Dean's acceptance too but it was more from the point of view of sharing his home. It didn't occur to him that it might be an entirely different angle which would make Dean blind with rage.

Twenty

Lint outlined his idea for buying the Southrigg land as he had discussed it with Avril but in his enthusiasm for the idea he failed to make it clear that it would be Avril, and not himself, who would pay for, and own the land. There was no doubt that Bill Scott considered the purchase of a hundred and ten acres of fertile land as a good investment for anyone with the money to spare, especially considering the circumstances which made Southrigg a real bargain.

'I would welcome the chance to rent it from Lint, even at my age, but I really need you as a partner Dean to make the best use of it and bring the land back to fertility. It would please Molly and me greatly if we could go into partnership together.'

'It would indeed,' Molly beamed. 'We could make a decent living for all of us with twice the acres.'

'There's nothing I would have liked better than to rent the land from Mr Gray,' Dean nodded, 'but there's a problem . . .'

'Oh? What might that be?' Bill asked with a frown.

'Avril and I were planning to get married if I got a farm to rent. There is no house included with the Southrigg land. If the creditors force a sale of the whole property, including the house and buildings, there will be a plenty of interested buyers then. The price will shoot up.'

They all looked towards Lint. His demeanour had been unusually grave throughout the discussion and it was even more so now as he turned to look Dean in the eye.

'There's always a price to pay Dean, and you may consider my suggestion is too high a price for you to consider. I shall understand and respect your decision. By far the highest price I have ever paid has been losing the wife I loved. It is because we have lost Ruth that I am offering you a home with us at Riverview. If necessary we could divide the house, certainly we would rearrange the rooms to give you and Avril privacy – but at the end of the day you would be part of a family when the boys return home for holidays. All I ask is that you give it your careful consideration and remember that time can be shorter than we think.'

Dean smiled. He felt buoyed with anticipation and excitement. He would consider anything which made it possible for him to become a full working partner with his uncle and have enough prospects to ask Avril to be his wife.

'I have always known Avril's family mean everything to her,' he said, 'and since Mrs Gray's death I have acknowledged that she comes as a package with two young brothers attached.' He grinned at Avril. 'I don't think that is too high a price to pay for marrying the girl I love, but –' and his own expression grew serious – 'it is a high price for you to pay, sir, to share your home with us, and possibly –' he glanced at Avril – 'more children, crying babies?' Lint's face relaxed a little.

'I hope there will be children eventually, Dean. I have no doubt there may be times when we all wish things were different, especially when we are tired from lack of sleep, whether due to patients needing my attention or calving cows needing yours, or teething babies needing Avril's. These things can be overcome with tolerance and patience. As I explained to Avril, I believe it would be preferable to sitting in Riverview on my own with only memories for company and waiting for my sons to come home to bring a little cheer. When the boys are old enough to be more independent I have plans of my own which I intend to carry out before I am too old. I have developed an interest in tropical diseases and I plan to spend some of my vacation in London studying and learning more about them with a view to spending time in Africa eventually. So you see I shall not be under your feet for ever and time has a way of passing by more swiftly than we realize.'

'Well!' Molly exclaimed. 'Africa? Helping the little children there?'

'You never told me that's what you planned to do, Dad,' Avril said, turning to look at him in astonishment.

'You have seen me reading the books. I thought you might guess, my dear. So you see I shall be happier when that time comes if I know you are not alone, and I should feel reassured to know the boys have a base they regard as home when they need one, although I am hoping they will join me sometimes when they are old enough.'

'So the next step then is to see Mrs Forsythe and put in your offer for the Southrigg land, Lint?' Bill prompted. 'It would be better done before the creditors force her to sell the whole place. I wouldn't expect they'll do anything until after the funeral but it wouldn't do to delay. Once we know whether you have got the land, Dean will need to give Mr Turner a decent period of notice. We would need to have a proper lease drawn up to make it legal and fair to you and to us,' he added.

'Yes, you're right, Bill. I should be failing in my duty as a parent and a trustee if I failed to protect Avril's interests. The land will be in Avril's name since she will be paying for it. You and Dean will have to decide whether you pay her a rent or make her a partner. So long as it is fair and legal I am agreeable as her trustee. We—' His attention was fixed on Bill Scott so he didn't hear Dean's gasp, or see the colour drain from his face.

'No!' Dean interrupted, more loudly and stridently than he realized. Lint looked at him in surprise. Dean's face was taut with anger and his blue eyes blazed as he stared at Avril. 'Why didn't you tell me?' he demanded through gritted teeth. 'Why did you keep it a secret that you have so much money? Were you afraid I might want to marry you for your fortune?' His mouth clamped shut but there was hurt as well as anger in his eyes.

'I didn't keep it a secret, Dean,' Avril whispered desperately. 'You don't understand . . .'

'Oh I understand all right. You're as bad as my mother – hoarding money in the bank. Keeping control, not wanting anyone else to know what you've got to . . . to—'

'Dean!' Molly Scott spoke sternly. 'That's a terrible thing to say. I'm sure there's an explanation?' Lint looked at them gravely.

'Maybe I didn't explain very well. You two should talk and Avril can explain—'

'There's nothing to talk about,' Dean said bitterly. 'Avril has deceived me and—'

'There's always a reason to talk things over,' Molly said determinedly. 'You take Avril home right now and clear the air between you. And for the love of God, Dean, don't let that Scott pride stand in the way of happiness. Lint, I will make a cup of cocoa and give them time to straighten things out.'

'Remember we can't afford to delay,' Bill Scott called to Dean's retreating figure, 'and you're a fool if you think Avril is anything like your mother.' His uncle's displeasure did nothing to cool Dean's anger and hurt.

They left together in a silence which continued until Dean drew the car to a halt at Riverview.

'Are you coming in?' Avril asked uncertainly. She had never seen Dean so angry. She felt hurt and bewildered by his outburst.

'Can you explain why you kept your wealth a secret?' Dean asked scathingly.

'It was not a secret,' Avril insisted, resenting his scorn. Her mouth firmed. 'Are you coming in or not?' He followed her inside.

'I can't believe tonight's revelations about the woman I thought I knew and loved. I must be a blind fool, or a stupid one – or both.'

'You are both,' Avril snapped, 'if you believe I would deceive you.'

'What else would you call it? God knows it's bad enough being a labourer and you with your education and career.' Avril wanted to tell him nothing mattered to her without the man she knew and loved, but she was hurt that he thought she would deliberately deceive him, and he had accused her of being like his mother. Was that how he really thought of her?

'I thought you were the best friend I have. Now I wonder. Maybe you're the one who is like your mother? You have always said she didn't know what she wanted, that nothing ever made her happy. Perhaps you've changed your mind now there's a chance for us to marry. Does marriage scare you when it gets closer?' Avril spoke in anger but she was surprised to see colour stain Dean's neck and face. When he remained silent she stared in disbelief. Even as he opened his mouth to explain she turned on her heel and rushed out of the kitchen and up the stairs.

'Close the door behind you.' Her voice was choked with tears but she had no intention of letting Dean see how much he had hurt her. He was tempted to follow and take her in his arms. Then he remembered why they were quarrelling. How had Avril managed to make him feel guilty? She was the one who had been secretive and deceitful.

Twenty-One

Samuel was in bed and asleep by the time Dean returned to Martinwold. He stripped off his clothes and climbed into his own bed but sleep eluded him. His head was crammed with thoughts and none of them made sense. When he did sleep he had a nightmare. Avril had fallen down a cliff and was clinging to a ledge by her fingertips and he couldn't reach her. Any second she would fall hundreds of feet. He was helpless to . . .

'Dean! Dean are ye not getting up this morning?' Samuel shouted from the bottom of the stairs. There was laughter in his voice as well as urgency. 'I've got the cows into the parlour and the first units are on.'

It was almost a relief to waken up but Dean's head spun as he leapt out of bed. He never overslept.

'I'm coming!' he called.

When he walked into the milking parlour Samuel grinned at him, but the grin turned to a frown. 'You look rough!' he remarked. 'What's wrong? Are you ill? Do you want me to—'

'I'm fine,' Dean snapped, then 'Sorry, Sam. Don't mind me. I had a bad night, that's all.'

'It looks like it! You don't look as though you've been to bed. Were you very late home?'

'No. Let's get on with the milking, we're late enough.'

'Right.' Samuel accepted the change of subject but he knew something was upsetting Dean. He was always so even-tempered. 'You haven't forgotten you promised to take me in for my driving test after dinner, have you?' he asked, anxiously. Dean groaned. He had forgotten.

'I'll be ready. What time have we to be there? Do you want a run around the town beforehand?'

'If we've time it might help steady my nerves,' Sam admitted.

'Nerves? I didn't think you had any,' Dean quipped, doing his best to summon a smile.

When the morning's work was finished Samuel suggested they should go into town, have a drive around and then grab something to eat to save them making dinner at home. Dean nodded. He hadn't the energy to argue. He didn't think he had ever been so unhappy in his life, not even when his mother was at her worst. Samuel passed his driving test. He was over the moon. He telephoned Bengairney to pass on the news to his parents.

'Oh Sam, I'm so glad. Congratulations, son,' Megan said. 'Your father is up in the top meadow fencing with Joe. I'll tell him when he comes in. It makes me feel old to think I've got a son old enough to drive.' She chuckled. 'Tell you what, we'll have a wee celebration. You and Dean come over for your supper tonight and I'll make something a bit special.'

Dean didn't feel in the least like celebrating but he had no excuse to refuse Megan's invitation. He forgot he was supposed to have phoned his Uncle Bill. He was lost in his own thoughts and miserable company they were.

After Dean and Avril had left Sylvanside the previous evening both Bill and Lint talked on assuming everything would be resolved between Avril and Dean. They had known each other too long and too well to let a little misunderstanding come between them – or so the two men believed. Molly was not so sure and she voiced her doubts aloud.

'I don't think it is such a "little" misunderstanding in Dean's eyes. He has more than his share of the Scott pride,' she said in troubled tones. 'We thought it was you who would be buying the land, Lint, didn't we Bill?'

'We–ell that's true. It never occurred to me that young Avril had the money to buy it, or that she would want to. That's why I suggested we must draw up a lease.'

'I'm sorry,' Lint said. 'I didn't intend to mislead anyone.' He explained how Avril would soon receive the money from the insurance company because her mother had died before she attained her twenty-fifth birthday. 'She doesn't feel she has any right to it. She says I have kept her all these years and paid for her education, but Avril and Ruth brought me the greatest happiness a man can dream of and if the money can smooth her path in life then I shall rejoice for both her and Dean.'

'It doesn't seem to be smoothing it right now if it's caused a quarrel between them,' Molly said unhappily. 'I pray they can sort things out. I love them both as if they'd been my own bairns and I've thought for a long time they will make a wonderful match.'

'They've been the best o' friends since school days. They'll soon patch things up,' Bill said comfortably. 'Meanwhile would you like me to call on Mrs Forsythe tomorrow, Lint? I could ask her not to be rushed into doing anything until she's had time to consider a possible offer. I'll not mention your name until you're ready to call on her yourself of course. I reckon it would ease her mind and give her and the lads the strength to stand up to the big boys.'

'That's a good idea, Bill,' Lint said. 'If I knew the family I would have gone over myself to offer my condolences but I think it would be better to discuss business after the funeral. 'What do you think to an offer of nine thousand for a private sale, if we pay the solicitors' legal fees?'

'I reckon that would be a generous offer in the circumstances,' Bill nodded. 'There'll be no auction fees so she might settle for eight or eight and a half?'

'No, we'll offer the nine thousand and make it clear to her sons that it is a final offer and non-negotiable.'

'Spoken like a real businessman,' Bill Scott nodded approvingly.

Bill waited impatiently for Dean to telephone at lunchtime the following day.

'They might even have fixed a wedding date,' he said with a grin at Molly. But Dean did not phone and there was no reply when Bill tried to contact him. He grew irritable.

'Now Bill, it's no good getting worked up,' Molly soothed. 'You know the doctor said it was bad for you. Why don't you go over and have a talk with Mrs Forsythe anyway.' Molly breathed a sigh of relief when he got shaved and changed and set off for Southrigg.

There was no call from Dean in the evening, and no reply to

Bill's telephone call either. He telephoned Riverview. Avril
answered almost immediately. She had been hoping it would be
Dean. Bill heard her disappointment. His heart sank. So they
hadn't sorted out their quarrel yet. Dean and his bloody pride
he thought irritably, forgetting he had once been just as stubborn. He asked if he could speak to her father.

'I'll take it in my office,' Lint said and Avril wondered dully
what they had to talk about that was so private. She alternated
between hurt that Dean believed she would deliberately deceive
him and regret that she had not made him listen to her
explanation.

After he had discussed his visit to the Forsythe's with Lint
Bill decided to telephone Northsyke and speak to Sydney. He
was beginning to share some of Molly's fears that Dean might
allow his pride to stand in the way of his happiness. The brothers
discussed the advantages and disadvantages of buying Southrigg
but Syd had always known when his younger brother was
worried.

'It's the bloody Scott pride,' Bill burst out. 'Dean thinks Avril
has been hiding the fact that she has money to buy the land, but
she wasna deceiving him. She didn't tell him because she only
found out herself when her father told her about the insurance
and Lint is only concerned about Avril's happiness. It doesn't
worry him that it will be her money buying the land, so why
should Dean get on his high horse and gallop all over his own
happiness and the lassie's as well?'

'Well you of all men should know about that, Bill,' Sydney
reminded him. 'Remember how you felt when Molly's folks
offered to help you buy stock for Sylvanside. You nearly had a
heart attack then.' Sydney's tone grew serious. 'I hope you're not
going to let this business bring on another?'

'You're as bad as Molly, telling me to keep calm and not to
worry, but this is Dean's future we're talking about, as well as
ours, and it's a golden opportunity all round.'

'All right, all right, calm down, Bill. I've been thinking for a
while that we ought to pass on Dean's share of this place so he
knows where he stands when he does get a place of his own,'
Sydney said. 'I've thought about it more since we bought the
café for Doris and there's a house with it for when we can retire.

I'd like to make sure Dean get's his fair share if anything should happen to me. It might help his pride if he can put some of his money towards buying the land, or into buying the extra stock you'll need.'

'Can you afford to pay him his share?' Bill asked, anxious now in case he had worried Sydney.

'We have enough left in the bank to give him some of what he'd get. I'll talk to Grizel about it tomorrow.'

Sydney had expected his wife to be reasonable over Dean's share of the money now that Doris was happily settled. Grizel herself had been pleased when he had agreed to buy the house conveniently next to the café and with a fine big garden. He mentioned his plans as he was finishing his breakfast the following morning. Grizel stared at him then opened her mouth to protest. He silenced her with a kiss, taking her by surprise. He grinned like a schoolboy.

'Think about it Zel. I'd like to see them both settled and happy. We'll talk about it when I come in for ma dinner.' He went off whistling happily, with Gyp and Ben, his constant shadows, at his heels. He was happy. It would be grand to have Dean living so near and he would feel easier about his brother if Bill had Dean to take some of the responsibility.

The warmth and laughter at Bengairney had always made Dean feel both welcome and happy but for once his mind was preoccupied with Avril. He wished he'd gone to Riverview to talk to her instead, though his pride rebelled at the fact that she had so much money, and he couldn't believe how badly she had deceived him, or how hurt and disillusioned he felt. If she could deceive him now how would it be if they were married?

'You're not eating much, Dean,' Megan remarked, 'and you look deadly tired. Are you keeping well? I hope living with Samuel is not getting you down?'

'No, no, I'm glad of his company and his help,' Dean assured her.

'He was glad of me this morning,' Sam grinned. 'He overslept and he looked as though he'd spent the night on the tiles.'

'I never knew you to oversleep, Dean, all the time you were

here as a student,' Steven said, looking at him shrewdly, 'and you don't look that great now.'

Alexander had been pestering Sam to go outside with him. He wanted to show his elder brother the twin heifer calves which were to be his if he looked after them. Tania had gone to her room. She was doing well at school and she was conscientious about homework.

'Well, Dean? Something bothering you about work?' Steven asked when the kitchen had emptied and only Megan remained. Dean frowned. He hadn't intended to discuss his affairs, or his mixed-up feelings, and yet he found himself pouring out the events of the previous evening.

'I didn't go to the auction,' Steven said, 'but I heard they didn't get a bid. Of course the land is pretty well useless to anyone without the house and steading, the way it's situated.'

'It's between Sylvanside and the river so it would be ideal for Uncle Bill. When Mr Gray mentioned buying it Uncle Bill thought he could rent the land from him and we could go into partnership.'

'I didn't know Lint was interested in buying land,' Steven whistled. 'So what's the problem?' he asked, puzzled.

'It turned out it is Avril who would be buying the land!' he said bitterly. 'She never mentioned she had that kind of money. Why would she keep it a secret? Did she think I might marry her for her money?' he asked angrily.

'Avril would be buying the land?' Megan asked. 'Are you sure, Dean?'

'That's what her father said.' He flushed and bit his lip. 'I–I accused her of being as secretive over money as my mother, of – of hoarding it and not telling anybody. Avril isn't a bit like my mother really. I don't know why I said that. But it was a shock. I feel at a big enough disadvantage as it is. I haven't even got a house to offer her.'

'What you're really saying, Dean,' Megan said carefully, 'is that you don't like the idea of your wife owning half the land which you and your uncle would be farming?'

'Yes! Yes, damn it,' Dean said. 'A man expects to provide for his wife, not the other way round. What really hurt is that Avril kept her money a secret. Why did she do that? She has always told me they didn't have any money to spare before her mother married Mr Gray, and she didn't care what sort of work I had, or that I lived in a tied house. She even said she wouldn't mind living with me at Martinwold, except that it is too far from her brothers when they come home for holidays.'

'Dean,' Megan said sternly, 'your views may be admirable but they are a bit old-fashioned these days. Things have changed since the war. Women don't expect their husbands to provide everything for them on a silver platter. Most women—'

'My mother did.'

'Mmm, well there are always exceptions and your mother is a different generation to Avril. Most women want to help their husbands if they can. It seems to me it is your pride that is hurt. I think you'll be very foolish if you allow it to stand in the way of happiness.' Dean looked at her. He wasn't looking for sympathy, but he had thought Steven and Megan would understand how he felt, but there was neither sympathy nor understanding in Megan's level green gaze as she looked back at him.

'As I understand it, Dean,' Steven said slowly, 'your uncle and aunt have always made it plain they intend to leave their farm to you some day. Am I right?'

'Yes, but I've no intention of waiting to step into dead men's shoes. I have to make my own way in life,' Dean insisted.

'Maybe, but your uncle really needs you to share the responsibility for the farm since his heart attack?'

'Yes.'

'And he's willing to take you into partnership right away if he can rent the extra land?'

'Yes. When my father retires I shall get my share from Northsyke but that could be years yet.'

'Precisely, and you expect Avril to accept that and be grateful?' Steven's tone was harsher than he had intended but for the first time he felt the pull of kinship for Avril; she was his niece after all, even though he had never really acknowledged that fact, even to himself.

'I don't expect Avril to be grateful,' Dean protested. 'I love her. I want to share everything with her as my wife.'

'And yet you're too proud to take anything from her in return. If she buys the Southrigg land there's nothing to stop you and your uncle paying a rent to her, as you would have done to her father.'

'I suppose so, but that's not the point.' Dean frowned. 'Why didn't she tell me she had the money, or that she intended buying the land?'

'I doubt if she even thought about it,' Steven said. 'It sounds as though your uncle and Lint decided between them. They probably believe that buying the land would give you the opportunity you crave, to farm your own place, and it would allow you to get married. Land should be a good investment for Avril's money. They were trying to do what's best for both of you but right now your pride is preventing you from seeing that.' Steven's tone was sharp with frustration.

'I didn't know Avril had any money either,' Megan said quietly, trying to dispel the tension. 'Ruth always had to work to support herself and Avril.'

'I can hazard a guess where the money has come from and if I'm right Avril will not have had time to get used to having it,' Steven said.

'Where do you think it has come from then?' Megan asked curiously.

'Do you remember how suspicious I was when Ruth first came to stay with my mother? I thought she was looking for charity or at least free accommodation?'

'Yes, I remember you being afraid Ruth might take advantage.' Megan nodded. 'Especially after your mother told us Fred was Avril's father. You didn't believe it at first.'

'No I didn't, or at least I needed to be convinced. Ruth sensed how I felt. She resented my suspicions and you know how fiercely independent she could be. One day I suppose I'd niggled her; she turned round and told me I needn't worry that she would ever burden my mother, or anyone else, with her child. She said if anything happened to her she had taken out some kind of insurance which would ensure there would be money to pay for Avril's keep and her education. She called it a term insurance I think. I can only guess that Ruth died before the term was reached so the insurance company would have to pay out to Avril.'

'Goodness, do you think Ruth had some sort of premonition?' Megan asked.

'No, I don't think it was anything like that, but her own mother died with cancer when Ruth was still a child, didn't she?'

'Yes, I think so. Her father and a great aunt brought her up.'

'Apparently one of her father's parishioners advised him to take out the insurance on Ruth's behalf. She told me she paid it herself when she qualified as a teacher. Ruth was a single parent. I suppose the man thought money would make an orphan child more acceptable to some people.'

'Yes,' Megan shuddered. 'Thank God Ruth lived to see Avril grow up and get her degree.'

'She hasn't seen her sons grow up though,' Steven reflected.

'No, but at least they have a father and I'm pretty sure Lint will provide well for them.'

Dean had sat in silence, listening.

'Mr Gray said last night that there was always a price to pay,' he said, quietly, sheepishly. 'I didn't realize what he meant then.'

'No, Avril paid a high price in losing her mother. I'm sure she would rather have had Ruth alive and well rather than the money,' Megan reflected.

'If only she had explained . . . We were supposed to sort things out last night but we were both angry and upset. We said things we didn't mean. We've never quarrelled before.'

'Well it's a bit late to go over there tonight,' Steven said, 'but you could always phone and arrange to meet tomorrow.'

'Yes, you do that, Dean,' Megan urged. 'Let not the sun go down upon thy wrath – and all that.'

'You're right, I will phone, but I'll phone from home. It may take a while –' he gave a faint smile – 'if she'll still talk to me that is.'

'I reckon she will,' Megan said with a smile. 'True love never runs smoothly, and I'm sure Avril has loved you for a long time, Dean, even before she realized it was love.'

'Oh my goodness!' Dean clapped a hand to his forehead. 'I was supposed to phone Uncle Bill by noon today. I completely forgot. We'd better get home. I'll shout Samuel. Thanks for a lovely meal and – and everything else.'

'That's all right, Dean. We shall be glad if we've helped you sort things out a bit,' Steven said. 'Wisdom only comes with old age.'

'Swallow that pride, Dean, even if it is a bit indigestible,' Megan called after him with a laugh.

Easier said than done, Dean thought later while he waited for Avril to come to the phone. He had never heard her sound so cool and distant when she eventually greeted him.

Twenty-Two

Avril had waited all evening hoping Dean would come to see her. They had never had a serious quarrel in all the years they had known each other. She had not slept well after he left and it had been an exceptionally busy day at work. She felt drained and despondent. She was getting ready for bed when her father shouted her down to the telephone. She was tense and her tone was chilly.

'Avril I need to see you,' Dean said quickly, urgently, half afraid she might cut him off. 'Can I come over tomorrow evening? I can't tell you how sorry I am I said such hurtful things to you.'

'I suppose we both did a bit of that,' Avril admitted, her tone possibly one degree less frosty, but still wary. Dean went on to explain about Sam passing his driving test and the celebration meal at Bengairney this evening.

'I see. Your Uncle Bill has been trying to telephone you all day. He has phoned my father twice. He was worried about you.' There was reproach in her voice. 'It's not good for him to get upset.'

'I know. I was so busy thinking about us – you and me – that I forgot about phoning him. It's getting a bit late now.'

'It is, but I think he'll sleep more easily if he knows you're all right. I'll say good night and let you get on with it.'

'But I can see you tomorrow evening?' Dean persisted.

'I shall be here,' Avril said. Normally she would have asked him to join them for their evening meal Dean thought and his heart sank. What if Avril could not forgive the things he'd said to her? He shuddered. What good would pride be to him then, without her? What good would anything be without her to share his life?

He dialled the number for Sylvanside. Aunt Molly answered.

'Oh Dean! I'm glad you've telephoned. Are you all right, laddie?'

'Yes, I'm fine.' He explained why he had been away at lunchtime and then most of the evening. Then he added honestly. 'To tell the truth I was still mulling things over in my head and I forgot I was supposed to phone Uncle Bill by midday.'

'Well he's just gone up to bed but I know he'll want to speak to you. Can you hang on?'

Dean had never known his uncle be so repetitive, or talk so long on the telephone before. He kept reiterating what a good arrangement it would be if they could rent the Southrigg land and go into partnership. He didn't mention his conversation with Sydney. He didn't want to raise Dean's hopes in case Grizel proved to be as awkward as she had been in the past.

'There'll never be a better opportunity, Dean. What does it matter whether we pay the rent to Lint or pay it to Avril?'

'I know, I know, Uncle Bill, but you don't understand. Avril and I quarrelled over it. We've never quarrelled before and we need to sort things out between us before I reach any sort of decision about the future.'

'You'll need to make up your minds so you can give Mr Turner plenty of notice.'

'I shall,' Dean said wearily. 'It could take weeks to settle the Southrigg land even if Mrs Forsythe agrees to a private sale.'

'Oh I reckon she'll be relieved to get it over,' Bill Scott said with enthusiasm, 'and the sooner the better. The creditors are biting at her heels by the sound of it.' It was late by the time Dean managed to pacify his uncle with a promise to call at Sylvanside tomorrow evening. He felt exhausted as he crawled upstairs to bed. He set his alarm clock to make sure he did not oversleep again.

The day seemed to drag and by evening Dean knew he had never felt such a bundle of nerves.

'If you're not going to eat your pudding, I'll have it,' Samuel said with a grin. Dean passed it to him.

'I'm not hungry. You can do the washing up to repay me for my pudding.' He summoned a smile in response to Sam's indignant look. 'I'll do it tomorrow night,' he added peaceably. 'I'm heading off now.'

'You're all dressed up. Are you taking Avril somewhere special? Give her my love.'

'I will.' Dean made his escape.

Lint and Avril were just finishing their dinner when Dean arrived.

'Come and have a cup of coffee, Dean. You're earlier than we expected. You should have come for dinner,' Lint said. Avril flushed.

She had not invited him. Lint frowned, sensing the strained atmosphere. 'I think I'll take mine into my office,' he said. 'It seems to me that you two still have a few problems to sort out.' He poured his coffee and left them.

'I'll leave the dishes to soak in the sink,' Avril said. 'Shall we go for a walk up the hill before it's dark?'

'All right,' Dean said readily. He would feel better outside. He tugged at his collar and tie as though they were choking him. 'We always did go up there to discuss our problems, didn't we?'

'Yes.' Avril sighed. 'I'm sorry for the things I said about you being like your mother, Dean, but I still don't understand why you're so angry.'

'I'm not angry now. I think I understand a bit better how you come to have so much money of your own,' Dean said carefully. 'I hadn't realized it was at the expense of losing your mother – some kind of insurance I believe?'

'Yes. If my mother had lived until I was twenty-five there would have been nothing to pay out,' Avril said flatly. 'But I still don't understand why you flew into such a temper?'

'I know, and I'm sorry. Pride I suppose,' Dean said sheepishly. 'I still feel I shouldn't be asking you to marry me unless I can afford to keep you and give you a reasonable standard of living so it's difficult to accept that you're so much better off than I am. I think it was the shock of discovering you had kept the money a secret. Why did you do that Avril? Don't you trust me? I have always thought we didn't have any secrets from each other.'

'I didn't keep it a secret. I didn't know about it until recently and it doesn't feel like my money,' Avril said dully. 'It shouldn't be mine. If it had to be paid at all it should have gone to my father. He has paid the insurance premiums all the years since he married Mum, he has kept me in food and clothes and given me everything I needed, he paid for my education at university. The money should belong to him. But all the money in the world can't compensate for losing Mum.'

'No, I can understand that,' Dean said quietly. 'I'm truly sorry for the things I said. I didn't mean to hurt you, Avril, but I know I did. It was the shock. You're as different from my mother as any person could be.'

'And how do you feel now? Do you still resent me having

money to buy the extra land, even though it means your uncle and you can go into partnership, and that in turn means we could be married?'

'I admit I still feel at a disadvantage. You have looks and intelligence, a good education and a career – and now wealth. I can't think why you want to marry me when you could take your pick of any man who took your fancy.'

'Because no one else has ever taken my fancy,' Avril said simply. She stopped and looked up at him. 'None of the things you mention matter to me. You are the man I love.'

'Oh God, Avril, I don't deserve you!' Dean said, drawing her into his arms and holding her tightly. 'The last two nights have been hell, wondering if I had destroyed the most precious thing in the world – your love and respect.'

'I hope we never quarrel like that again, Dean,' Avril said with a shudder and curried even closer inside his jacket, wrapping her arms around him, feeling his strength and warmth. Dean put a finger under her chin and lifted her face to his. His kiss was tender and loving but Avril's urgent response was like a match to a tinder box. Passion flared between them and it was some time before they drew apart, with Dean breathing hard as he strove to control his desire.

Much later they walked back down the hill together, hand in hand, stopping every now and then to smile at each other and exchange another kiss.

'We must get married soon,' Dean said urgently. 'I don't think I can wait much longer to make you wholly mine, Avril.'

'I know.' She looked up at him with a tremulous smile. 'I feel the same. Will you mind very much sharing a home with my father?' she asked anxiously.

'I wouldn't mind sharing my home with a gorilla so long as it meant we could be together, always.'

'A gorilla?' Avril chuckled. 'I don't think my father is quite that bad.'

'Of course not.' Dean grinned. 'He's always made me welcome. I think he realized a long time ago how I felt about you.'

'Yes, he understands how we both feel, but he's truly grateful that we are both willing to keep a place in our home and in our hearts for my brothers for as long as they need us. I know not many men would be willing to do that, Dean. It means more to me than if you had been the wealthiest man in Scotland. It makes me love you all the more.'

They stopped again to seal their love with another lingering kiss and it was dark by the time they returned to the house.

Lindsay heard them come in and he came out of his office to meet them, one eyebrow raised quizzically.

'I don't think I need to ask,' he smiled. 'You both look transformed, and very happy again. I am relieved about that or I would have blamed myself for trying to organize your lives.'

'Oh no!' Dean said. 'It was my silly pride which got in the way. I'm still finding it hard to accept but I know now that I don't want to spend the rest of my life without Avril. In fact we would both like to be married as soon as we can arrange it.'

'One step at a time,' Lint warned, but he was smiling. 'The first thing we need to do is see Mrs Forsythe and put in a firm offer for her land. If she accepts it – and your uncle seems sure she will, Dean, then you can go ahead and make plans for your wedding.'

'I'd rather not have a wedding, Dad,' Avril said, her dark eyes pleading for understanding as she looked from one to the other. 'It wouldn't be the same without Mum. I would like to be married quietly, but in Church.'

'You would make a beautiful bride, my dear,' Lint murmured, 'but I shall leave all the arrangements to the two of you. Whatever makes you happy will make me happy too. Right now I think you should go up to Sylvanside and let Molly and Bill know you have sorted things out. I have to say, Dean, I think your uncle will be more disappointed than anyone if we can't do a deal over the Southrigg land. He has set his heart on the two of you going into partnership. It seems to have given him renewed vigour.'

'It will certainly be a challenge,' Dean said ruefully. 'Forsythe had neglected the farm for years. There will be drains to sort and fences to mend and I doubt if he has limed any of the fields since I left school. I'm sure Mrs Forsythe and her sons will realize that though. Once we get it back into good order and reseed some of the oldest pastures I think it will be more productive than a lot of the Sylvanside land.'

'You know better than I do about such things, and I know your uncle will be relieved to hear you're ready for a challenge.'

'Oh I am, I shall relish it. We'll go up there now.'

'I'd better wash the dishes first,' Avril said. 'It may be late before we return.'

'Off you go,' Lint smiled. 'The dishes are all washed and put away.'

'Oh Dad, I didn't leave them for you, really I didn't,' Avril protested.

'If you weren't here, my dear, I would need to cook my own dinner as well as wash dishes. Now you see, Dean, why I don't want to lose her.' He smiled at them both. 'Actually I think you can get a machine for washing dishes. Perhaps I should buy you one for a wedding present. It would save your time, Avril, especially when the boys are home too. I don't want them to be a burden or come between you.'

'You've given us enough already,' Avril said and reached up to kiss his cheek. He had more lines these days and his hair had grown quite silvery. She was not the only one who missed her mother.

'I don't think you need worry about the boys.' Dean smiled. 'I often wished I'd had a brother. The twins have such zest for life I reckon I shall enjoy their company as much as Avril does.'

As Dean and his uncle discussed the future with new enthusiasm that evening neither of them dreamt of the events which had occurred at Northsyke earlier in the day. No one had bothered to inform them.

Sydney had given a lot of thought to his conversation with Bill. He had always known Dean was proud and independent so he could understand him being disconcerted to discover Avril had enough money to buy the Southrigg land. Well there was nothing he could do about that but he could hand over Dean's share of Northsyke, or at least as much of it as he could raise without affecting the farm. He had set Doris up with a business of her own and even Grizel seemed pleased to know they would own a house when they eventually retired.

He had forgotten just how strenuous it could be handling bullocks which were big enough for slaughter but he had always taken a pride in presenting his stock at its best. They had only one more bullock to clip but he had an insulin injection every morning and he knew he ought not to go on much longer without food. He always carried a special little tin of sugar cubes and he stopped to eat two or three, hoping that would boost his blood sugar enough to let him finish the last of the bullocks before he and the two men stopped for dinner.

'Right,' he said with satisfaction as he stepped back to admire the fine-looking animals in their newly bedded pen, 'we'll get our dinners now.'

'They're looking well, boss,' Bobby said with a grin. 'They should fetch a good price eh, Jim?'

'Aye, aye, that they will,' the old man agreed.

'I havena looked round the sheep yet,' Sydney said, bending down to pat each of his patient collies. 'I'll take the dogs and do that straight after dinner then I shall be back in time to help load the bullocks into the lorry. The driver said he'd be here about half past one so you two could tidy up the barn until then.' The two men strode off to their cottages, chatting amiably. Old Jim had been born at Northsyke and lived in the same cottage all his life, first with his parents and then with his wife. He had known Sydney since the day he was born.

'Did ye see the boss eat yon sugar cubes?' he asked Bobby. 'I dinna like to see him needing that. I remember when he was a young man and first starting wi' yon disease. We thought we'd lost him more'n once.'

'Aye well it was hard work this morning, but I've never seen him take a turn as bad as the ones ye talk about, not in the five years I've been here,' Bobby said. 'Ye shouldna worry so much about him, Jim.'

Sydney was well satisfied with his morning's labour and he was ready for his dinner. He looked up in surprise when Grizel thumped his plate down in front of him, followed by a huge dish of spotted dick and custard, which he had never liked even before he became diabetic. She stood back, hands on hips, glaring down at him.

'Aren't you going to eat your dinner with me, Grizel? I thought we might discuss how—'

'Discuss! There's nothing to discuss. Dean went away and left us. If he gets any money it will be over my dead body.' Sydney frowned. He had genuinely believed she would be reasonable now they had bought the café for Doris, with her own little flat above it, as well as a decent house nearby for when they wanted to retire. Usually he enjoyed stewed rump steak with carrots and onions so he was already tucking in, but he groaned inwardly when he saw Grizel's pursed-up mouth and gimlet glare.

'You have to be reasonable. Doris is independent now with her own business and we've bought a house for ourselves; it is Dean's turn for help and he needs it now,' he said, laying down his knife and fork and holding Grizel's gaze with a determination she recognized. Sydney didn't usually bother to argue or quarrel with her but when he made up his mind she knew he had a will of iron.

'He doesna deserve it! He'll only go and get married to – to that girl. I'll not have her benefiting after me scrimping and saving.' It was on the tip of Sydney's tongue to tell her Avril had enough money of her own to buy the Southrigg land, but then it would be just like Grizel to say they had enough in that case.

'You should be thankful he has chosen a decent, capable lassie. Anyway I've decided to give him the money we have in our private account. That will not affect the business and we shall still have our income from the farm and the stock to sell when we retire.'

'I forbid it!' Grizel shouted hysterically and banged her fist on the table.

'Dean worked hard and he got no wages. We owe him the money.' Sydney got to his feet now, pale with anger and frustration. He stared down at his wife's face, tight with resentment. 'He deserves the money and I shall see that he gets it – even if that means selling the bloody house!' He strode out of the door, his food forgotten.

The two dogs stood up and wagged their tails at sight of their master but for once Sydney barely noticed his beloved collies. They followed him meekly as he strode towards the track leading to the higher fields and the sheep. As soon as he opened the gate into the bottom field they circled him, wagging their tails with joy. Although Gyp was getting old she still loved to work the sheep. They ran ahead of Sydney then paused, looking back, awaiting his commands. Sydney sighed. If only humans were as loyal as dogs, he thought, the world would be a better place. They crossed the first field together but at the gate of the second, steeper field Sydney whistled them to round up the flock and bring the sheep nearer. They obeyed instantly. The sheep were coming in steadily when Gyp stopped on the top of a knoll and gave three sharp barks. Sydney looked up, scanning the field. He whistled a command to bring Gyp and her sheep towards him but she stood firm and gave one quick bark. Sydney knew then that something was wrong. There was one ewe which had rolled on to her back twice already in the past few weeks. She was a good ewe and Sydney didn't want to lose her but it meant certain death if one got stuck on her back for very long and couldn't get on to her feet. He realized from the way Gyp was standing guard that she was either lying dead or in urgent need of his help. He quickened his pace but the ground was fairly steep and his legs were beginning to feel weak and a bit unsteady by the time he reached Gyp. The ewe was lying so still with her four thin legs pointing to the sky that he thought she was dead for a second or so. Gyp went nearer and gave a little whine. She quivered. There was still a spark of life. Sydney tried to pull her over on to her side but she was a heavy ewe. He walked round to her other side but she was in a hollow so there was no slope to make it easier. He had to get her on to her side somehow so that she could get up. Once they were on their feet the sheep usually recovered almost instantly. Sydney lowered himself and, using all his weight and strength he gave a tremendous heave, and then another. The ewe rolled over on the second push. Seconds later she sprang to her feet and trotted off to join the rest of the flock. Gyp wagged her tail and Ben came to join them.

'Good girl,' Sydney said, patting the collie's velvety head. Ben came closer and Sydney moved to pat him too but his legs were wobbly and he staggered. He was sweating. He didn't feel so good. His dinner – he remembered then that he had left most of it. Sugar, he must have sugar. Even as he fumbled in his pockets for the little tin he remembered he had used some earlier and he hadn't filled it up yet. The two dogs gazed up at him, anxious now, sensing their master's panic as he searched for the tin. He managed to pull it from his pocket but his fingers all felt three times their normal size. He couldn't open it.

'Damn Grizel and her bloody mean . . .' The tin opened. The remaining sugar cubes bounced out and rolled in the grass. 'Oh

God,' Sydney muttered in desperation. He sank to his knees, scrabbling for them. His hands wouldn't do what he wanted. He was shaking uncontrollably now. 'Home, Ben, home . . .' He didn't know whether he had uttered the command aloud. Somehow it didn't seem to matter . . . Vaguely he knew he should find the sugar lumps, but it was too late now and he was weary . . . so weary . . . He looked up at the sky. How peaceful it was up there with the clouds floating gently by . . . His jerking limbs alarmed the dogs. They watched anxiously, waiting . . . A scream rent the air. Ben ran away, frightened by the unearthly sound which had come from his master. But he could not leave. He crept on his belly back towards Gyp. She was whining softly, rubbing her nose against Sydney. Blood was beginning to trickle from his mouth where he had bitten his tongue. She gave a soft growl at Ben and stared down the glen towards the farmyard. The young dog hesitated, circling them uncertainly then he shot away, head down.

Twenty-Three

Old Jim was wheeling a barrow load of empty sacks out of the barn when he saw Ben streaking across the low field on his own. He called the dog to his side and fondled his ears. 'What's the matter then, boy?' he asked softly. The dog looked up at him with trusting brown eyes then turned his head towards the fields. He gave a little bark and moved a few paces away as though asking Jim to follow.

'Hey, Bobby,' Jim called. 'I reckon something's amiss wi' the boss, or wi' the sheep.'

'Och, Jim, I keep telling ye not to worry so. The boss is a grown man and he's younger than you. He can look after himself.' But Ben was pushing his cold nose against Jim's hand and edging away, then repeating the manoeuvre. Jim knew he had to follow the dog. He had felt uneasy about Sydney all morning.

'I have to go and look for Sydney,' Jim insisted.

'Ye're just trying to get out o' cleaning the barn,' Bobby mocked.

'Maybe, but I reckon Ben is trying to tell me something is wrong.'

'Take the tractor then if you must go. It'll be a lot quicker than your old bandy legs can take you.' Bobby grinned to take the sting out of his words.

'Maybe ye're right for once, young Bobby.' Jim hurried towards the tractor as fast as he could. Ben jumped up beside him but when they reached the fields the collie jumped off and pushed at the first field gate. Jim opened it and drove through while Ben darted ahead like an arrow. Pausing now and then to make sure the tractor was following. He led Jim to the next gate, then up to the knoll where Gyp stood guard over her master, barking now and then to alert anyone who might help. She wagged her tail furiously when she recognized Jim, but he stared in dismay at the sight of blood trickling from Sydney's mouth and him lying there unconscious. He bent closer but he didn't know what to do or how to help. He would have to get the mistress. He shuffled away as fast as he could and climbed on the tractor, commanding the two dogs to stay with Sydney. Bobby was looking out for him.

'The cattle lorry is coming up the track. Where's the boss? We'll need him to load the bullocks.'

'Never heed 'em,' Jim snapped, then explained quickly. 'Run tae the hoose and tell the mistress. She should ken what to do. I'll hook on the trailer. We'll need it to lift him home.'

Grizel stared at Bobby's frightened face.

'Unconscious? B–blood trickling f–from his mouth?' she repeated. 'I'll telephone the doctor.'

'Shall we bring him home on the trailer?' Bobby asked.

'Yes! No! I don't know. Wait there while I speak to the doctor.' She remembered she had raged at Sydney and he hadn't eaten his dinner. If he died it would be her fault. What good would the money be then . . .? 'Yes? Hello, Doctor, yes it is Northsyke.' Swiftly she explained then hurried back to Bobby, waiting at the door. 'You're to bring him from the field. The doctor is on his way. Wait while I bring a cushion for his head. And a blanket. Oh God, do be careful.'

'Aye, mistress,' He hurried back to the yard where Jim had hooked up the trailer but he was wondering whether he and the old man would manage to lift the boss. The lorry driver was waiting by the bullock shed. Bobby explained what had happened.

'I'll come with you,' the man volunteered. 'Sydney is a decent man. I hope he's going to be all right.'

It was the following morning before Grizel telephoned Bill from the hospital. She had refused to leave until she was convinced Sydney would recover.

'Have you phoned Dean?'

'No, I haven't got his number here.'

'I'll phone him.'

It was midday before Bill managed to contact Dean when he was in for his dinner. 'Your mother sounded more shaken than I've ever heard her,' he said, 'but she says Sydney is going to be all right. Maybe she's getting older and more easily upset, like the rest of us.'

'I don't know whether to go to the hospital to visit Dad this evening, or whether I ought to go over to Northsyke to see the animals and how the men are managing,' Dean said, frowning at the telephone receiver. 'Jim is too old for heavy work but at least he knows what needs to be done if Bobby will follow his instructions.'

'You visit your father, Dean, and let us know how he is and I'll go over to Northsyke and check on things there. I know Sydney was planning to send some fat bullocks away yesterday.'

Dean was relieved to find his father looking better than he had expected that evening.

'You gave everybody a fright,' he said. 'How are you now?'

'I'm fine except for a sore tongue. I must have bitten it. Thank God old Jim had the sense to realize there was something wrong when Ben returned to the yard alone. Doris was sitting by the bed. She looked happier and less sullen than Dean had ever seen her.

'I have things to do at the café before I open in the morning,' she said. 'I would have stayed longer, Dad, but now you have Dean for company I'll get away.' She turned to smile at Dean. 'I've been trying to persuade Dad to retire from Northsyke now that he's got both of us off his hands. Don't you think it would be worth considering, little brother?'

'I think it might,' Dean agreed slowly, 'so long as it's what father wants.' He looked at Sydney considering. 'If the garden at the house is as big as you say maybe there would be room for a few kennels? You could still breed and train your collies. It would keep you occupied and in touch with the other sheepdog handlers.'

'I never thought of that,' Sydney said, 'but you're right, lad. It might be the best thing all round. I think I gave your mother a nasty shock. She was trying to persuade me to give up the tenancy of the farm when she visited this afternoon and she agrees we should pay you your share of the money. Has she been getting at the pair of you to persuade me?'

'No,' they said in unison, shaking their heads.

'Must be wise minds think alike, Dad,' Doris said. 'I'll go now but I'll come and see you tomorrow evening if you're still in.'

'I'm hoping to get home tomorrow,' Sydney declared. 'I wonder if they got the bullocks away after me getting them clipped and ready.'

'Yes, they did,' Dean informed him. 'Uncle Bill went over to Northsyke this afternoon and he phoned just before I left to say everything is fine. He said the lorry driver had helped to get you home from the field, then he and Bobby and Jim loaded the bullocks between them.'

'Ah good. That's one thing less to worry about then,' Sydney said with satisfaction. 'You did the clipping when you were at home, Dean. It was harder work than I remembered. Maybe I will think about retiring and having more time for my dogs. I know plenty of hill men who would be glad to let me run the collies over their land if I help them gather in their flocks at clipping time.'

Mrs Forsythe and her two older sons were greatly relieved when Bill Scott kept his promise and brought Lindsay Gray to Southrigg, but she still negotiated for five hundred pounds more than he had offered. They reached an amicable settlement when Jim and Bob offered to renew the boundary fence which would mark the edge of the original yard as their own territory. They also agreed to use only the short drive from the main road and leave the back track by the river for farm vehicles.

'All we need to do now,' Lint said with satisfaction, 'is to contact our respective solicitors and wait for them to complete the searches and draw up the new boundaries. I shall see that you have the ten per cent deposit to fix the deal as soon as our solicitor approves of the conditions we have agreed. Please let me know if your own man should have any quibbles.'

'I thank you from the bottom of my heart,' Mrs Forsythe said with feeling. 'I thank you too, Bill.' She turned to look at him and flushed slightly. 'Richard has really enjoyed working for you at Sylvanside. He says he has learned a lot and now I shall be taking him away when he is getting useful to you. Once our affairs are settled, I am planning to emigrate to Australia. I think there will be more opportunities for him out there and it is better for him to get away from all the gossip. People can be cruel.'

'I understand,' Bill said kindly. 'Dick's a grand young laddie and a good worker. If he needs a reference out there just let me know. I'd be pleased to recommend him.'

It seemed to Avril that everything moved with the speed of lightning once an agreement had been made to buy the land. Dean was anxious to give Mr Turner a decent period of notice so that he could find another dairyman to take his place but Murdo Turner reassured him.

'As a matter of fact I think it's a relief dairyman I shall need. Young Finn has been asking for extra overtime since his wife had the baby and stopped working. He was always a good fellow with cows when he was a student with John Oliphant and Chrissie, but he didn't want to be a full-time herdsman. His wife didn't like him working seven days a week and getting up early.'

'Has he changed his mind then?' Dean asked in surprise.

'Since you've showed him how to handle things in the milking parlour he thinks it's a lot easier than the byre.' Turner's eyes twinkled. 'Then again his wife didn't want him tied down but now she has a young baby they're missing her wage so I expect she'll be glad of the extra money he'll earn as dairyman. Samuel will be with us for a few more months until he goes to college and he seems to know what he's doing.'

'He does,' Dean said nodding. 'He's a grand stockman and he's used to the milking parlour now.'

'Yes, that's what I thought so I'll give Finn a trial period when you leave, Dean. I don't need to tell you I'm sorry to lose you but I've always known you would move onward and upwards one of these days and I wish you well.'

'Thank you,' Dean said, flushing with pleasure.

'You could finish at the end of May if you want but I'd be obliged if you would agree to come back and do the relief milking with Samuel every fortnight until I can employ someone to take Finn's place as a general worker and relief dairyman. Do you get possession of the Southrigg land at the end of May?'

'We do if the solicitors get on with the legal formalities, and I think they will because the creditors are pushing for their money. The end of May would suit me very well indeed,' Dean said with satisfaction.

'I thought it might.' Murdo Turner nodded. 'But you'll come back to do the relief milking until I get fixed up?'

'I'll be happy to do that,' Dean agreed, his spirits soaring.

'And am I right in thinking there's wedding bells in the air? Don't forget I shall expect an invitation. Avril is a grand lassie.'

'We—ell . . .' Dean hesitated and bit his lower lip. 'We are planning to get married but Avril feels she can't face a wedding with all the trappings without her mother. So long as we can get married I don't care what sort of wedding we have but I'm sorry about the invitation, Mr Turner. We're planning to be married quietly in Church and then we're going away for ten days together before we settle down to work.'

'Ah, I understand, Dean.' Mr Turner clapped him on the shoulder. 'A wedding is a wedding though so I'll be giving you a present to wish you well. How would you like the heifer stirk out of the Jade family? She's just about ready for the bull so you would be able to choose which one you want to mate her with.'

'I can't . . . I don't expect . . . She's far too valuable,' Dean stammered, his eyes wide with surprise.

'I know you don't expect things, laddie,' Mr Turner said warmly, 'but you've earned it. I think you'll do well and I'd like you to have that wee heifer. I hope she will breed well for you.'

'Dean I think you should keep it to yourself that Avril has enough money to buy Southrigg,' Bill advised. 'If Grizel hears about it I guarantee she'll try to cut the money your father is intending to give you.'

'I've already told my father,' Dean said.

'Aye, but he learned a long time ago that some things are best kept to himself. It was a private sale so nobody will be sure who the purchaser is yet and Lint handled the negotiations on Avril's behalf.' He chuckled. 'I've heard all sorts of rumours. One man thought I'd bought it, then somebody told me you were the buyer. One man said it was Mr Turner. I listen and keep quiet.' Bill's eyes twinkled.

'Then I'll do the same,' Dean agreed, 'at least for now, but when father told me how much he was giving me I suggested I should pay half of it with Avril. Both she and her father think we should use my money for the extra stock and another tractor.'

'So long as Avril agrees I'd say that's a good idea,' Bill nodded. 'The quicker we get the cow numbers up the sooner the milk cheque will increase and you'll need a decent income when you have a wife to keep. Have you got the arrangements made for the marriage service?'

'Yes. The banns were read out in church but we haven't broadcast the day or the time of the actual service.' He flushed, then confessed, 'Mother has been a bit subdued since Father's last turn. I don't want to risk her turning up and causing any more trouble.'

'I think you're wise, but I suspect Grizel has learned her lesson.'

'I hope you and Aunt Molly don't mind not being there. We're only having Avril's father and Mrs Caraford, and Samuel will be my witness. Avril is very tense. I think she will be relieved when it's over.'

'Aye, the lassie coped well – too well some might say – when her mother died. Since the twins went to boarding school she's had more time to grieve and Molly thinks it's affecting her now. A couple of weeks on your own will do you both a lot of good.'

'I'm certainly looking forward to it.' Dean grinned. 'There'll be plenty of work waiting when we come back. Some of the Southrigg fields will need ploughing and reseeding to get them back to good grazing pasture for next year.'

'Ye're right there,' Bill nodded, taking time to draw on his pipe. 'It will be a challenge but I reckon we shall both enjoy it.'

Twenty-Four

Megan persuaded Avril to go with her to choose a dress for her wedding and Tania pleaded to go with them.

'It may be a quiet ceremony but it doesn't mean you shouldn't look your best on your wedding day, Avril dear, for Dean's sake. I know it is what your mother would have wanted,' she added.

'I suppose so,' Avril murmured uncertainly.

'I know the owner of a wee shop where they sell some lovely clothes. We were not bosom friends but we both lodged in the girls' hostel when we attended Dumfries Academy. She was always good at art and sewing and now she has her own business.'

Avril enjoyed the expedition more than she had expected, but she had never tried on so many outfits in her life. Left to her own devices she would have settled for a royal blue suit with a matching hat but Megan said it was more suitable for a going away outfit. In the end she bought it anyway because she really liked it and it fitted perfectly. Both Tania and Megan told her she looked beautiful in a cream silk dress.

'This is perfect for the occasion you describe,' the shop owner said with a nod of satisfaction. 'The simplicity of the style gives you an air of elegance and it would take you anywhere, but the lace bolero with its tiny covered buttons and long tapering sleeves transforms it into a dress for a very special occasion.'

'What about a matching hat?' Megan asked, looking round the various creations.

'With such lovely hair she does not need a large hat,' the woman said. 'If you can give me two hours I could create exactly the right sort of frivolous little hat to match the dress and suit a young bride.' She brought out a large box of cream silk flowers and opened a drawer containing pieces of lace veiling in various shades. She matched them with the dress. 'I have in mind, something small but elegant. Can you trust me to create just the right thing for you?' she asked, smiling at Avril. 'Will you be wearing your hair up or down?'

'Oh up, I think . . .'

The woman took hold of Avril's thick fair hair and held it in a knot on top of her head while looking at her from all angles in the large mirror. 'Yes . . .' She held a cream rose with three smaller rosebuds to one side of Avril's head. 'It will be a pleasure to make exactly what we need to complete the outfit.'

'In that case we'll go and have some lunch,' Megan said. 'My treat today, Avril,' she insisted as they left the shop.

'I do wish you'd been having bridesmaids, Avril,' Tania sighed. 'I would have loved to be one in that pale blue dress they had on the model. It was exactly my size too.' Megan gave her daughter a thoughtful look as they found a table in one of the hotels. Tania was fifteen now and beginning to take more pride in herself. Alexander and Rosy often teased her.

When they returned to the shop Megan asked if Tania could try on the blue dress.

'She has just had her fifteenth birthday,' she explained 'but she didn't know what she wanted. If the dress doesn't look too old on her I might consider buying it.'

'When you see it closer,' the owner said, 'the material is woven with sprigs of forget-me-nots in a slightly darker shade of blue with tiny pale green leaves. It is the material which makes it exclusive and therefore more expensive. The style is simple and together I think it is eminently suitable for a young girl —' she smiled at Tania — 'on the threshold of womanhood,' she added tactfully. 'The wide sash can be worn around the waist or over the shoulders as a wrap.' She eyed Tania carefully, 'It might be a little short. You are slim, but you are as tall as your mother.'

'But the Mary Quant styles are short,' Tania protested when her mother looked dubious.

'This is a time when almost anything goes from mini to maxi and the midi in between in the fashion world,' the woman said. 'Certainly you are slender enough to wear short skirts. I confess I cringe when I see some of your age group in what they consider the latest fashion.'

'There's no harm in trying it on I suppose,' Megan sighed, 'if you don't mind taking it off the model?'

So Tania ended up with a belated birthday present which delighted her, while Avril felt her own confidence increase as she viewed herself in the complete outfit, including a cream patent purse and matching shoes. There was no doubt the woman had great skill in fashioning exactly the right headwear to suit both the dress and her customer. Avril was pleased she didn't need to scrimp for this occasion. She gave a silent little thank you for her mother's thoughtfulness in making all this possible but she had to blink hard to keep back the tears. Almost as though she was reading her thoughts Megan said, 'Your mother would have approved and she would be so proud of you, Avril. She wore a deep pink dress and jacket for her own wedding I remember.'

Avril dropped Megan and Tania off at Bengairney but she refused to come in for tea.

'I want to get home and try on my new clothes again,' she said, feeling more light-hearted than she had felt for a long time. Megan saw the new radiance in her face and was pleased she had insisted on the shopping trip.

'Tania, I want you to keep your new dress for a special occasion,' she said as they entered the kitchen.

'Oh Mum!' Tania protested. 'When do I go to any special occasions? I do wish Avril was having a proper wedding.'

'I can understand how she feels. She still misses Ruth terribly, although she doesn't make a fuss, and Dean's mother would have been more hindrance than help. But what do you think about us making a surprise party as a welcome home? We could invite their friends and make a buffet supper.'

'Oh Mum that's a super idea! I'm sure Avril and Dean would enjoy it. I'll help you do some baking.'

'I might hold you to that, young lady,' Megan said with a smile.

Hannah Caraford telephoned to tell Megan the wedding ceremony had gone off without a hitch.

'Avril looked beautiful,' she said with a break in her voice. 'Ruth would have been so proud. I am glad you advised her over the dress, Megan. As soon as the ceremony was over and Dean turned to kiss his bride all her tension seemed to evaporate. She looked radiant. Indeed they both looked truly happy.'

Avril had felt a secret dread that Dean's mother might show up at the church at the last minute with some reason why the wedding should not go ahead but as they drove south all her fears evaporated.

'I have a surprise for you, Mrs Scott.' Dean grinned. 'I knew I wouldn't be able to wait until we'd driven all the way to Cornwall before I can make you mine. The Turners were in the Lake District the last time they went on holiday so I asked if he recommended any of the hotels. He promised to get a couple of addresses for me but you'll never guess what he's done.'

'He's not told Samuel or anyone where we're staying?' Avril asked in horror.

'No, at least I hope not. He has booked us in and paid for two nights' dinner bed and breakfast. He said I should regard it as an extra bonus and make the most of it.' Avril saw the colour rise in Dean's cheeks and she guessed Mr Turner had said more than that.

'That's really kind of him. He must have thought a lot of you, Dean. I must confess I'm glad we're not driving all the way to Cornwall today.'

'So am I. Can you follow these directions?'

'It looks very grand,' Avril said in awe ten minutes later, as Dean drew the car to a halt in front of a smart hotel overlooking the lake.

'You deserve the best,' Dean said softly but his colour rose again as he recalled his boss's comments about the first night of their married life being a night to remember. He hoped Avril would not be too nervous to enjoy it.

'I can tell Mr Turner, or the men, have been teasing you,' Avril said. 'Are you going to tell me what they said?'

'It was nothing bad – only that a special girl deserved a special place.'

'I'm not that special. I think I'm beginning to feel nervous.' Dean turned towards her and drew her into his arms.

'You mustn't be nervous, not with me. You're my darling wife now.' His mouth claimed hers in a lingering kiss. They forgot they were in a public place until someone gave a gentle toot on a car horn. Avril blushed, but her dark eyes were shining with happiness.

Dean knew how tense she had been as their wedding drew nearer. Since it was such a quiet ceremony he had assumed it must be their honeymoon which bothered her. He had longed for the time when he could make her truly his but now that time had come he hoped he would be patient and gentle with her, above all he didn't want to hurt or frighten her.

'Ah, Mr and Mrs Scott,' the grey-haired receptionist repeated. She looked up at them with a beaming smile. 'The honeymoon suite on the third floor.' She beckoned to a young man. 'Joseph, please show Mr and Mrs Scott to suite number one please.'

'Gosh, this is so spacious!' Avril gasped with pleasure. 'It has everything.' She bounced on the huge bed like a delighted child, then investigated the small fridge which was stocked with drinks. 'The view of the lake is spectacular – and look at all this . . .' On a table in front of the windows were two glasses and a bottle of champagne in a cooler, as well as a bowl of fresh fruit and a beautiful arrangement of pink roses. Dean smiled at her delight.

'Mr Turner sure has done us proud, hasn't he?'

'He certainly has . . . Where does that door lead?' She crossed the room to investigate. 'Oh Dean, come and look at this. I've never seen such a huge bath in my life.' She turned and flung herself into Dean's arms. 'It's big enough for both of us to get in together.' Dean's eyes widened. Avril looked up at him, her brown eyes dancing with mischief. 'You're not shy, are you, Dean. You must know how much I've longed for this – for us to be together. I mean really together. Now we needn't worry any more about getting babies or anything else . . . I love you so much Dean and you have been so patient.'

'Ah, Avril, sweetheart . . .' Dean said gruffly, as Avril removed his tie and began to open the buttons of his shirt. Desire flared in him as he pressed her close.

'Shall we try the bed first?' he whispered and lifted her in his arms, 'and then the bath.'

'Yes please . . .' Avril said softly before his mouth found hers in a kiss which left them both breathless. Dean couldn't believe how happy it made him to discover Avril's desire was as great as his own, or the way she responded to his caresses, taking his breath away as her hands explored his body with increasing fervour.

'You said you were nervous sweetheart?' he whispered, his breath coming faster.

'Not with you, Dean, never with you my darling . . . Please, oh please love me, Dean.'

Some time later they soaped each other, revelling in the feel of each other's firm young limbs as they relaxed in the scented water in the huge bath. Dean nibbled her ear lobe, murmuring endearments. 'You've made me the happiest man on earth.'

'And I'm the happiest woman,' Avril laughed softly.

The following morning they ordered breakfast in their room but when they went downstairs ready to explore the paths beside the lake Avril was convinced everyone must know they were newly married when she looked at Dean and saw his blue eyes shining with love. She was unaware that her own face was radiant with happiness.

'I think we should send Mr Turner a postcard,' she said, stopping outside the small post office to examine the selection on a stand. She looked up at Dean with a mischievous smile. 'We'll simply say "Everything is absolutely perfect," and he can interpret that how he likes, don't you think?'

'All right.' Dean grinned back at her. 'I know exactly how he'll interpret it – and who wouldn't when I have the most wonderful girl in the world.'

They spent a blissful ten days at the secluded cottage in Cornwall, walking, swimming, making love. Dean insisted on taking her out to dinner several times to one of the hotels down in the little town and they walked back hand in hand in the moonlight. All too soon it was time to leave for home.

'I promised Granny and Granddad Gray that we would spend a night with them,' Avril said a little anxiously. 'Will you mind, Dean.'

'Of course I don't mind, sweetheart. At least not so long as they don't put me in a separate room,' he said with a grin. 'Seriously, I thought they were a lovely old couple when they came up to stay with your parents.'

'They are wonderful and I know they will be pleased we're married. I'm so happy. I'm sure the whole world must know.' Dean glanced sideways and smiled.

'You're taking my concentration away from my driving,' he teased, patting her knee. 'You make me want to stop the car and make passionate love to you.'

'Mmm, you'll have to wait until tonight, we're nearly there.'

★   ★   ★

Back at Bengairney Megan asked Hannah what she thought to
her idea of a welcome home party.

'We—ell, yes, it would give everyone a chance to wish them
happiness. Yes, I think it's a good idea. Let me know if you would
like me to do some cooking, Megan.'

'All right, if you're settled into the bungalow? Have you got
used to the new cooker?'

'I miss my Aga but everything else is splendid.'

'I am pleased you have no regrets. It was a good idea of Mr
Paterson's. Do you think we should invite him to the party?'

'I think he would be pleased. He's known Avril since she was
a little girl and he always had a tender spot for her and Ruth.'

'All right. Don't mention it yet until I've spoken to Lint to
see whether he agrees. I'll telephone him tonight. There's not a
lot of time to let everyone know and to prepare things.'

Lint agreed it was an excellent idea. 'I did wonder if Avril and
Dean might feel a little flat when they return. They were so wrapped
up in each other I think they forgot the rest of the world.'

'I expect you're feeling a bit flat and unsettled yourself, Lint. Will
you mind sharing your home with a young married couple?'

'No. I've always liked Dean. I think we get on well and this
house is far too big for me to rattle around on my own. We're
doing a little rearranging of the rooms.'

'I'm glad the twins are not going to be unsettled with more
changes.'

'The twins! I wonder if I could get them home for the party.
It would be a surprise for Avril and they would enjoy the excitement.'

'That would be lovely if you can arrange it. I suppose we must
include Dean's parents when his aunt and uncle will be here.
Can I leave that to you?'

'Yes, I'll speak to them.'

Megan made several phone calls that evening.

'Dean got on well with Mr Turner,' Steven said. 'He's given
them a pedigree heifer for a wedding present, as well as a set of
crystal glasses. Mrs Turner insisted they were more like a wedding
gift. I'll invite them if you like.'

The following morning Megan discussed the party with her
mother.

'Will you be inviting the Palmer-Farrs?' Chrissie asked.

'I don't know,' Megan said. 'Catherine has been rather cool since the episode with Rosy. I think she was angry because Rosy sought refuge with us.'

'She's been cool with everybody, even her husband,' Chrissie said grimly. 'He is enjoying having Rosy at home again. He helps both her and Alexander with their French homework. She's a different child now. Catherine should be grateful she's safe and well. Just think of all those poor parents in Wales who will never see their children grow up.'

'Yes, Mum, it is terribly sad but you mustn't think about it. It is good for Alexander having Rosy for competition. He's working harder at school,' Megan said. 'I'll think about inviting Catherine and Douglas. They are the only relations of Lint's who live near enough to come. I'll leave it until tomorrow evening before I contact them so don't mention it if you see Catherine. Dean and Avril were going to spend a night with Lint's parents on their way home so that will please Mrs Gray. There's always been a bond between her and Avril.'

It had not occurred to Megan that Alexander would discuss the party with Rosy on the school bus, or that it would be the first thing Rosy would tell her parents when she got home from school. Catherine stared at her.

'You mean to say all their friends and relations will be crowded into Bengairney? And Lindsay has never even mentioned he's holding a welcome home reception!'

'There's no need to be so indignant,' Douglas said reasonably. 'I don't suppose Lint will be organizing it if it's to be a surprise for Avril and Dean.' Catherine was not listening. As soon as she thought Lint would be home from the hospital that evening she telephoned him. He had had a busy day in theatre and he was tired and hungry. He scowled at the receiver as he listened to Catherine ranting on.

'You must know I could give them a far better party here. You might have thought of asking me to do it. It would be an opportunity to show the locals what a success we have made of restoring Langton Tower,' she raged. Lint sighed and hung on to his temper with an effort. Sometimes he thought the only thing in Catherine's mind was proving what a success she'd made.

'It is Megan's idea, Catherine. I am not even paying for the food. She is doing the catering, but I expect Chrissie Oliphant and Mrs Caraford will be helping her. I am only supplying the drinks.' Catherine was silent for a moment, thinking. It hadn't occurred to her that Megan would be providing everything for free.

'Well we could do it all so much better here,' she said stubbornly. 'I have the kitchens and staff and we have the space.'

'Bengairney has plenty of space. Megan said she would lay out a buffet in the kitchen. Avril wouldn't want anything too grand.'

'I can do informal too,' Catherine said sharply. 'And I am a relative.' Suddenly it seemed important she should do this. Ever since the awful fiasco with Rosemary-Lavender running away from school Catherine had had the feeling people were cool with her, even Chrissie and John Oliphant who had proved to be such treasures. She had a niggling feeling they all thought she was a failure as a mother, even though she had made such a success of the hotel and conference centre. Even her husband and daughter seemed to shut her out. 'We haven't given Avril a wedding present yet. This could be our gift to her,' she went on.

'Catherine you must take it up with Megan and sort it out between you,' Lint said wearily. 'I'm having nothing to do with it but I can tell you now that if you make a big fuss Dean and Avril may well refuse to attend. If they had wanted a wedding with all the trappings I would willingly have paid for one. I don't think you realize how badly Avril still misses her mother, especially at times like this.'

'There's no need to get angry,' Catherine said. 'I thought I was making a generous offer.' And seizing an opportunity to show off your premises, Lint thought cynically.

'I'm not angry, I'm very tired and my meal is ready. You and Megan sort things between you and let me know what you have arranged. Good night.'

Catherine was not very happy about telephoning Megan. Secretly she felt a little jealous of the way she made everyone feel welcome without apparent effort. Even her own daughter would spend all her time at Bengairney if she had not made a promise to stay at home during the week and work hard at school. She had to admit too that Rosemary-Lavender was a happier child now than the thin, pale waif who had returned from boarding school.

Megan was taken aback by Catherine's phone call and even more so by her suggestion that they should hold the party at Langton Tower.

'But it is only friends and family we're inviting,' Megan protested. 'I intended to telephone you tomorrow night to invite all three of you.'

'Oh yes? Alexander has already invited Rosemary-Lavender.' Megan felt a flash of irritation. Why must Catherine persist in calling her daughter by both names?

'Rosy knows she's always welcome whatever we're having. I don't know what to say about the party. I'm certain Avril would not want anything too formal. We should be lost in your huge conference room.' She couldn't think of any other excuse for refusing.

'We shall not use the conference room. I'll hold it in the dining room and people can mingle in the hall and lounge. Have you invited the Turners from Martinwold?' So that's who Catherine is aiming to impress, Megan thought waspishly.

'We hope they will come,' Megan said carefully.

'And the Wright-Mantons?'

'Definitely not. Mr Turner doesn't get on with his son-in-law. We would not be attending either if they were invited.'

'All right, no need to be like that. You're as bad as Lint. He almost bit my head off. I shall give them the party as a wedding present then, but he said he'd pay for the drinks.'

'Don't you want me to provide any of the food then?'

'No. My caterers will see to all that.'

'Very well. I have baked a fruit cake so I shall concentrate on decorating that. We'll bring it with us on the Sunday evening.' Megan's tone didn't allow for argument over that and Catherine accepted the offer graciously.

'I wish we weren't going there for the party,' Chrissie Oliphant said when Megan told her. 'I've never had a meal there for all we have helped with all the renovations to Langton Tower.'

'You must come, Mum,' Megan insisted. 'My greatest worry now is that Catherine will make everything too formal and Avril will hate it. I wish I'd never suggested a party.'

'Don't feel like that, lassie,' Chrissie Oliphant comforted, as though Megan was still a schoolgirl. 'Of course I shall come, and your father too. After all most of the folks are ordinary, everyday people and Lint has always treated us as equals even though he is far above the likes o' us.'

'I'm sure Lint doesn't feel he's any different to anyone else. He grieves just the same as we do.'

'You're right. We must all make sure it is a happy and informal atmosphere for Avril and Dean's sake. I am looking forward to meeting Dean's uncle and aunt. They sound really nice people.'

'Yes they are, and you're right, Mum. It is up to us to be ourselves and to laugh and be happy, whatever stylish airs Catherine puts on.'

Twenty-Five

Avril could scarcely believe it when her young brothers ran out to greet her, almost before Dean had stopped the car. They hugged both Dean and herself, bubbling over with laughter and excitement.

'Dad told us you and Dean have got married,' Callum said gleefully.

'And he says Dean is going to live here for ever and ever and we can see both of you whenever we want,' Craig added, but with the faintest question in his dark eyes.

'That's right. We shall both be here whenever you come home,' Avril assured him with a big hug and a kiss. 'But this is a lovely surprise. How did you get here?'

'We travelled on the train. Mr Travers, our housemaster, drove us to the station and made sure we got on the right train. He spoke to one of the men in uniform and told him where we had to get off.'

'But we knew where to get off,' Callum said. 'Daddy was waiting for us on the platform.'

'Well, it's a lovely surprise.' Avril chuckled. 'But aren't you going to let us inside? We're dying for a cup of tea, aren't we Dean?'

'We are.' He grinned down at Craig who was now tugging him by the hand.

'We've come so that we can go to your surprise party,' he informed him. Dean raised his eyebrows questioningly at Avril. Her eyes widened and she shrugged to let him know she knew nothing either. Lint greeted them in the hall.

'I should have known these two couldn't keep a secret,' he said ruefully, bending to kiss Avril's cheek, and then shake hands with Dean.

'You didn't say it was a secret, Daddy, only a surprise,' Craig said innocently.

'Something smells good,' Dean said, sniffing the air.

'Yes, we want you to eat plenty of tea because there's to be a buffet supper and I've no idea what time we shall get it.'

'Where is this surprise party then?' Avril asked.

'Ahem . . . It was to be at Bengairney – Megan wanted to give a small welcome home party for your close friends and family to offer their good wishes, but I'm afraid Catherine intervened when she heard about it via Alexander via Rosy. She insists on having it at Langton Tower. She is providing the food as a sort of wedding gift to you both.' Dean noticed Avril's father was looking uncomfortable, clearly unsure of their reaction.

'We shall enjoy it wherever it is, don't you agree, Avril?' he said cheerfully. 'I don't think anything could make me happier than I am already.'

'Mmm, me too,' Avril said, 'but I'd rather have gone to Bengairney. The company will be good wherever it is though and it's a kind thought. So that's why you two rascals are home?'

'Of course. And we've got you a present.'

'Come and see the tea we've made for you!'

'We?' Avril asked with a grin as she moved into the kitchen.

'Well hello you two.' Aunt Molly came forward to hug them both and congratulate them, her eyes bright with happy tears, while Bessie smiled and shook hands with them, offering her own good wishes.

'Can we start now?' Craig asked. 'It's years since I've had a pancake for tea,' he added with an exaggerated sigh.

'Years is it old man?' his father teased. 'And what about you, Callum?'

'I'd like one of Aunt Molly's potato scones, please, or maybe three?'

'I've brought plenty. Help yourselves boys.'

'There's loads of presents to open in the sitting room,' Craig said gulping down a mouth full of pancake and raspberry jam.'

'Are there?' Avril looked at her father, her eyebrows raised in surprise.

'That's right.' He smiled. 'A lot of them from people I had never met. You are a very popular pair you know and everyone wants to wish you happiness.'

Tea was a boisterous happy affair but when they were finished

Dean decided he would change his clothes and walk up to Sylvanside to see what his uncle was doing.

'He'll be pleased to see you, laddie. He's really looking forward to you working together.' When they were alone in the kitchen Molly turned to Avril with a smile. 'I'm pleased to see you both looking so happy, lassie. I'm afraid we couldn't have a welcome home party without inviting Dean's parents,' she added, looking anxious.

'Of course not,' Avril agreed instantly. 'I don't think anyone could spoil my happiness anyway.'

'I think Grizel will be all sweetness now anyway. Bill was talking to a farmer at the market this week and his wife and her friend had been to Doris's café while Grizel was there. She hardly knows them but she couldn't wait to boast. "My son and his wife have bought all the land at Southrigg",' Molly mimicked with her eyebrows raised almost to the ceiling. Avril couldn't help but laugh. 'Doris is not coming tonight. She reckons she's too busy but nothing will keep Grizel away when the party is to be at Langton Tower. I expect she'll be boasting about that next.' Molly's face sobered and she looked anxious. 'I hope it will not be too posh. I've been thinking I ought to have bought a new outfit instead of my navy blue dress with the white lace collar.'

'You'll be lovely,' Avril said, hugging her impulsively. 'We shall not care what anyone is wearing. Oh, Aunt Molly, I can't tell you how happy I am.'

'Then that's all that matters. I could see the minute you both walked in that getting married was the best thing that has ever happened for both of you and I never knew a young couple more deserving.'

An hour later Lint shouted Avril to the phone. 'Tania would like a word,' he whispered.

'Oh, Avril, I'm so glad you're back,' Tania said breathlessly. 'Did you have a lovely time?'

'We did, but what's all this about a party.'

'That's why I'm phoning. Uncle Lint said it would be better to warn you both. You don't really mind, do you?'

'Of course not. The boys announced the surprise before we got in the door. Did you know they are home? They are looking forward to seeing Alexander and Rosy but they don't think they should get dressed up.'

'That's what I wanted to ask you. You will wear your new cream dress won't you?' Tania pleaded, sounding very young and uncertain. 'I do so want to wear my new dress but Alexander and Rosy keep saying I shall be the only one who is all dressed up.'

'Of course you will not be the only one, Tania. You'll look lovely and I shall have to wear my new dress to keep up with you,' Avril teased.

'Oh good. Mum wanted to have the party here but Mrs Palmer-Farr insisted she should do it. Mum has made a super cake for you and Dean to cut. I do hope it will be a lovely evening for you both?'

'I'm sure it will, Tania, and please tell your mother it was a very kind thought and it doesn't matter where it is held because we shall be among friends and we are both so happy.'

'I'll tell her that. She has been worried in case you didn't want a party at all. We'll see you tonight.'

Avril went up to her bedroom, the room which she would now be sharing with Dean. She felt her cheeks flush as she looked at the large double bed. A tender smile curved her mouth and her eyes held a dreamy look as she remembered how gentle and considerate Dean had been the first time in spite of his obvious desire. She had soon discovered she had the power to thrill him as much as he thrilled her and in the days which followed they had shared an ecstasy beyond their wildest dreams.

She turned her gaze from the bed. Her eyes widened. There was a door in the opposite wall. It had never been there before. She sniffed. Was that the smell of paint? She crossed the carpet and tried the handle of the door. It opened inward and she gasped. The small bedroom which had been next to hers had been converted into a bathroom with a walk-in shower, a toilet and a wash hand basin set into a unit, stretching the length of the wall where the original door had been. The walls were tiled in a pearly oyster shade which gave an appearance of both light and warmth. It was unbelievable. Avril turned and ran downstairs.

'Dad? Dad,' she called excitedly.

'Here I am. Molly and Bessie have both gone home to get

ready for the party. I thought we should invite Bessie since she has been coming here so long.'

'Oh yes, of course she should be invited, she's almost part of the family by now, but the new bathroom? I can't believe it. It's beautiful but I had no idea . . .'

'That's my surprise for both of you.' Lint smiled at her obvious pleasure. Avril had always had such an expressive face and her dark eyes were alight with affection and gratitude.

'But however did you get the changes done in such a short time?'

'I did a deal with the Forsythe brothers. They came one day while you were out and measured up and decided what would be possible. They made the doorway through and built up the original one as soon as you left. They had everything ordered and ready to be fitted in. I think they have made a good job but of course they know all the best tradesmen for any work they can't do themselves.'

'It's wonderful, but I never thought of you doing anything like that for us.'

'Dear Avril, you deserve it and I know how convenient an adjoining bathroom can be, especially when the boys are home. I want Dean to feel comfortable and at ease. This is his home too and every newly married couple needs privacy. If you think of any other changes either of you would like to make you must tell me. These things are always open to discussion remember.'

'Oh, Dad,' Avril said tremulously. She hugged him tightly. 'You've always been far too generous to me.'

'It's always been my pleasure, my dear. Now I think we had better get changed ready for this party.'

Catherine Palmer-Farr might be lacking in motherly instincts but there was no doubt she had a flair for organization and for knowing what suited her varying clients. There were none of her usual elegant flower arrangements. Instead the large hall and, what she called her second dining room, were decorated with huge bunches of coloured balloons and swathes of coloured gauze with beautifully tied ribbon bows. She had brought out the old candelabra, which had been in Douglas's family for generations, and these were filled with coloured candles. She had not lit them.

Catherine was convinced all children were vandals and would set the place alight. She still thought of the Caraford family as a wild bunch, forgetting that both Tania and Samuel were now sensible young adults. She blamed Alexander's influence for Rosemary-Lavender's continuing love of animals and the farm. Lindsay was bringing his two sons but at least they should be learning to be well-mannered young gentlemen, she thought with resentment. They were both at boarding school, as her own daughter ought to be. It was not enough for Catherine that Rosy was excelling in her school work, and in the school hockey team, and most importantly she was happy. Her mother still thought she needed to become a young lady. She had been surprised though when Rosemary-Lavender had requested a new dress for the party. Catherine had insisted on buying a longer length than Rosy had in mind after seeing Tania in her new blue minidress. She was not the neatest of sewers but she had learned how to hem during her few weeks at boarding school and she had no compunction about cutting three inches off the bottom of her new dress and hemming it up. Sneaking the iron to her bedroom had been more of a problem but the hem was duly pressed and Rosy secretly hoped Samuel would notice how grown up she was these days. Her mother had talked of having some dancing later and she hoped he would ask her to dance. Alexander was her very best friend but he was six months younger than her and recently she had grown several inches taller than him – a fact which annoyed him.

Everyone was already assembled by the time Avril and Dean arrived. Avril felt overwhelmed by the cheers, the good wishes, hugs and kisses, but the clasp of Dean's hand was warm and reassuring. One of the last people to greet them was Grizel Scott.

'Welcome to the Scott family, Avril,' she said and kissed Avril's cheek. She nodded at Dean. 'You're getting a better start in farming than we had, make sure you do a good job.' Beside her Avril felt Dean expel an exasperated breath as his mother moved away.

'I don't know how my mother managed to greet you as though she was the best of friends after the trouble she has caused,' he said, indignantly.

'Don't worry on my account, Dean.' Avril smiled up at him. 'We may never be the best of friends but at least we shall not be sworn enemies. How could we be when she has given me her son?'

'Ah, sweetheart, I've just spent a heavenly week —' he lowered his voice to a whisper — 'with a lover more passionate than I ever dreamed of . . .' He grinned when Avril blushed as he had known she would, but then his eyes grew tender and serious as he added, 'But only you could be so charitable about my mother, my darling girl.' He drew her into his arms, stealing a kiss before he led her on to the dance floor to start the dancing and begin the rest of their lives together.